Can't Help
Falling
in Love

Can't Help Falling in Love

A Novel

SOPHIE SULLIVAN

ST. MARTIN'S GRIFFIN
NEW YORK

To my readers, who made it possible for me to keep going
at something I love. And to my family, for the same.

First published in the United States by St. Martin's Griffin, an imprint of St. Martin's Publishing Group

www.stmartins.com

Designed by Gabriel Guma

All emojis designed by OpenMoji—the open-source emoji and icon project. License: CC BY-SA 4.0

The Library of Congress Cataloging-in-Publication Data is available upon request.

ISBN 978-1-250-91060-8 (trade paperback)
ISBN 978-1-250-91061-5 (ebook)

Our books may be purchased in bulk for promotional, educational, or business use. Please contact your local bookseller or the Macmillan Corporate and Premium Sales Department at 1-800-221-7945, extension 5442, or by email at MacmillanSpecialMarkets@macmillan.com.

First Edition: 2024

10 9 8 7 6 5 4 3 2 1

Sometimes circumstance blinds us at first
from seeing people for who they really are.

—DAN LEVY

One

If there were an award for the absolute worst at waitressing, Alexandria Danby would, hands down, be the recipient. She may have medaled in track through high school and university—but currently, the only thing she'd earn a trophy for was mixing up the most orders.

People used to call her Alexandria the Great. These days, serving people food and drinks while cleaning up after them made her feel more like Alexandria the Absolute Worst.

A tiny orange drop of butternut squash soup splashed against her left thumb, burning the pad, causing a wince but not distracting her from her target. *Customer. They're customers, not targets.* The sandwich was easy; it just sat all nice and flat on the plate. It was the damn liquid stuff sharing the space that wrecked things. As a onetime star runner who'd won a full scholarship because of her impressive athleticism, she should be able to walk twenty feet from the outdoor pass-through bar to the goddamn table without a hiccup. But she was quickly learning that agility and speed didn't translate to every activity. Particularly not ones that involved a lot of multitasking.

Two of the three grandmotherly-type women waiting on her arrival watched with encouraging expressions on their collective faces, one of them nodding with a too-wide smile. The third mostly looked `curious about whether Lexi could deliver the food without incident. Two plates? No problem. It was the third with the soup that made her feel like she was jumping hurdles with her ankles tied. The way to make some real money would be running a side hustle, placing bets on how many things she'd forget in one shift. Whatever that number was, a quick glance toward the hot guy at the table in the corner of the glassed-in patio, still waiting to be greeted, added one to the total. When he lifted his gaze from the Sandra Brown book he held—great taste—he gave her a smile that bolstered her spirit. *Dig deep.* That's what her coach used to say before competitions. *If you've dug down as far as you can go, keep digging. You want it, you work for it.* Lexi hadn't thought of her university track coach in years.

Just a few more steps. It was a gorgeously sunny Saturday for the last week of September. Little beams of light danced in the spots where the sun came through the glass roof, hitting the fall-colored glass candleholders. Sometimes the Pacific Northwest had bluer skies in fall than some of the summer weeks. As much as Lexi enjoyed the vitamin D, the brightness was currently creating a beacon-like blind spot in her path, the little beams bouncing, making it impossible not to blink. Her left arm wobbled just a little, her left pinkie finger cramping. Since when was salad heavy? She needed to start working out again. *Almost there.* She set all three items down with a little too much relief, her breath whooshing out of her lungs right as a splash of butternut squash soup slopped over the edge of the bowl.

One of the women gave a small squeal. The soup didn't even touch her but Lexi flashed a repentant smile, quickly wiped it up, and stepped back. Whatever. She'd made it to the table, remembered everything they ordered, and only had one customer waiting. She was taking the win.

The cozy warmth of the patio heaters combined with the direct sun overhead had sweat pooling at the base of her spine. To hell with working out; this job counted as cardio. Lexi pushed the wayward brown tresses escaping her top bun behind her ear, her customer service smile making her cheeks hurt.

"Is there anything else I can get you?" *Make the customer happy.*

If she didn't start making some better tips, this job was pointless. No one took a second job for fun. The paycheck, in addition to the one from her full-time job, was clearing the last of her—though not technically *hers*—debt. She was so close she'd decided the tips could be used for tuition. Her bestie, Maisie, was friends with some of the waitresses who'd told her they pulled in hundreds of dollars in tips each week.

A block up from Pike Place Market, a major tourist attraction in Seattle, Fairway Bistro was a popular spot. Lexi had taken the job just over a month ago. Easy. Simple. How hard could serving some drinks and food be? Famous last words.

She didn't earn anything near hundreds a week, but she'd had enough to pay the deposit for one of the final three courses she needed to complete her degree. Problem was, the rest of her tuition was due in a couple weeks, and so far, she'd only saved up a few hundred from all of her shifts combined.

"Could I have that refill on my coffee, please?" one woman said.

Lexi covered her wince with a grin. She hoped. *The coffee she asked for ten minutes ago and you promised to bring right over.* Then someone else had wanted extra napkins and another customer had been leaving. These ladies were three of the most patient customers Lexi had had lately. She should be tipping them.

She nodded. "Of course. Sorry about that. Coming right up."

When she turned, the hot guy was still reading his book. She could kiss him just for not yelling out the standard *Hey you* because she hadn't taken his order yet.

Huffing out a breath, shoulders back, she moved to his table, pulled her pad of paper and a pen from her apron. Proactive waitressing, a new sport. His hair, a dark shade similar to her own, looked like he'd run his hands through it more than once.

"Hi. What can I get for you?" Absentmindedly, she rubbed the spot where the soup had burned her finger.

He looked up and Lexi felt heat of another kind zip over her skin. This one more pleasant. With that hair, his strong, square jaw and easy smile, dressed in a carob-colored, expensive-looking sweater over a collared shirt that brought out gold flecks in his dark-brown eyes, he could grace the pages of L.L.Bean's fall catalog.

His lips twitched before he said, "Maybe not the soup."

Her breath froze in her lungs for a brief second before she laughed. Ouch. Apparently, her lack of skill was obvious. Excellent.

"Funny guy. I could get them to put it in an extra-large bowl," she joked.

Fortunately, she only had the two other tables on the patio, the section her manager had relegated her to. She understood preventive damage control. The inside of the restaurant was packed and other serving staff often bragged about the money they brought in on the lunch shift.

"You're doing great," he said, his voice low and husky but, more endearingly, *genuine*. It was a lie but she damn sure appreciated the words. She actually *was* getting better, other than when taking orders, serving, keeping her station clean, and socializing all needed to happen at the same time.

"Not true. But thank you."

He grinned. "I'll have a BLT with fries and a Coke, please."

She nodded, even as she wrote it down. She wasn't forgetting anything this time. When she reached the door, she glanced back, certain she'd felt his gaze on her, but he'd already returned to his book. Most people had their phones out before their butts hit the seat.

Coffee, Coke, sandwich, and fries. She was back on track. Inside, weaving through tables and rushing wait staff, Lexi went to the coffee machine and grabbed a carafe, then thought better of it and just filled a fresh cup before asking the bartender for the soda. While he poured that, she entered the order. Part of her struggle was the stupid system they used to order everything. It seemed more complicated than necessary.

The manager, Brett, moved around the popular downtown Seattle restaurant like a suited ninja, bussing tables for the employees who had too many customers to keep up. Five weeks in and he still couldn't trust Lexi completely with more than five tables. If they weren't so short-staffed, she didn't know if she'd have gotten the job at all. That and Brett's crush on her bestie were the only things keeping her employed.

On her way back outside, a bus girl, a sweet teen who made Lexi feel ancient, pushed the door open for her.

"Thanks," she said, breathing easier with just a couple of beverages in her hands, even if one was hot coffee.

"No problem."

Her brain ran through a list of reminders. She needed to set up the umbrellas before Brett asked. People could still burn despite the cool temperature outside and she didn't want that on her conscience.

Positive thoughts. You've got this. No burning customers with soup, coffee, or sunshine. She noticed the dirty dishes on a side table that she hadn't managed to clean yet as she brought the coffee over.

"Everything tasting okay so far?" she asked as she set the beverage down safely.

Her smile was genuine. The socializing part was actually pretty fun most of the time. When she wasn't overwhelmed. At twenty-five, she felt like her days of juggling a busy life were forever ago. This job reminded her that it took some getting used to. One of the women, the skeptic, raised a brow, reminding her of Bitsy, the elderly woman who owned the boutique clothing store for mature women where Lexi worked full-time. Her gaze followed Lexi's placement of the coffee.

"It's great, dear," one of the other women said with enough kindness that Lexi thought she might actually get a decent tip.

"Excellent. I'll come by in a few to top up the other drinks," Lexi promised.

She'd clear and wipe down the dirty table after dropping off the cutie's soda. She just needed a plan before she hit the ground running—which, surprisingly to her, waitressing at a busy restaurant didn't always allow for.

"Here's your soda. Anyone joining you for lunch today?"

She cringed inwardly. The answer seemed pretty clear since he'd already ordered and was happily reading his book. Normally she was better at small talk, but this guy's gaze scrambled her brain.

"Much to my mother's dismay and my delight, no," he said, his left cheek showing a hint of a dimple.

Lexi smiled. Disappointed mom. She could relate. "Uh-oh. Let me guess, Mom wants grandbabies?"

He laughed. "Got it in one. Are you fairly new here?"

She nodded. "I am. I've been here just over a month but I work full-time at a clothing store so I can't cover that many shifts. I'm Lexi, by the way."

She should have started with that. Training 101. She was supposed to say, *Hi. I'm Lexi. I'll be your server. What can I get for you?* Close enough.

"Nice to meet you, Lexi. I'm Will."

Nerves of a different kind fumbled around like drunk, uncoordinated butterflies in her stomach. She didn't have time for sober or drunk butterflies, but it was a nice reminder of what they felt like.

"Nice to meet you too, Will."

Looking at his soda, he asked, "Mind if I get a straw?"

Duh. "Of course. Be right back."

Hurrying back into the restaurant, she took a few breaths, the scent of burgers and deep-fried goodness making her stomach growl.

Pots and pans clattered. Plates and glasses clinked. There were four other waitresses working, a couple of them picking up orders at the indoor pass-through bar while Brett did plate garnishes and quality checks.

Grabbing a straw, Lexi gave herself a minute to tell the butterflies to calm the hell down. Brett walked behind the bar to help the bartender fill some orders. He was a quiet sort. It unnerved her; he was probably one of those people who took it all in, said very little, but had itemized thoughts and opinions on everything.

He gave her a small smile. "Can you set up the umbrellas before you come back?"

Cursing on the inside, she nodded. "Of course."

Taking the straw out to the patio, she saw the three women laughing over their meals. Happy customers.

Will's mouth was tipped up as he stared at the book. He saw her approach and his smile grew as he set the book down.

Lexi waved the straw. "Here you go."

"Thanks," he said.

Lexi extended her hand, the straw in her fingers, her gaze stuck on his, noticing how deeply brown his eyes were. They were captivating in a way that could suck a person in, make them want to see if they changed when he laughed or when he got turned— Something blocked her hand right before her fingers hit the cool glass. She felt it tipping before she broke eye contact to see that she was accidentally pushing the drink over. She dropped the straw and, hurrying to right the glass, knocked it more. Yup, Coke splashed over the rim, dotting the book edge and the table.

"I'm so sorry," Lexi said.

Will moved quickly, setting the book on his lap, grabbing his cutlery and undoing the napkin it was wrapped in. He sopped up the mess while she pulled a couple of extra napkins from her apron.

"No harm." His voice was deep and calm.

"Your book," she said. Frustration mounted in her chest like a sports car revving in neutral. *Just one day without spilling something on someone.*

"It's fine. Just a splash of Coke. If I get desperate for caffeine later, I can lick the cover."

Lexi snort-laughed, then slapped a hand over her mouth. She closed her eyes so she wouldn't roll them at herself. Had she thought she could handle the socializing part? Clearly, she wasn't winning trophies for that either.

"Are you going to stand there with your eyes closed?" Amusement tinged his tone.

"I'm considering trying to back up and leave without opening them."

His laugh was unguarded and fun. Damn it. She bet the corners of his eyes crinkled.

She opened one eye, dropped her hand so she could pick up the wet napkins. "It'd be easier if you just close yours while I go. Then we can pretend this never happened."

Forced to open both eyes, she reassured herself that not much had spilled. He picked up the straw, removed the damp paper wrapper, stuck it in his glass, and put his lips on it. Her stomach fluttered, not unlike the way the wrapper did when he dropped it to the table. Smiling around the straw, he took a large sip. His brows drew together.

"This might be diet."

Lexi groaned, took the glass when he passed it. "I'm sorry."

"Don't be. Now I don't have to feel guilty for having more."

If only all of her customers were so sweet, adorable, and forgiving. "Be right back." Maybe she'd go home with hardly any tips today, but it wasn't so bad after all. If she could just stop putting so much pressure on herself, just take a breath now and again, things would smooth themselves out.

For the first time since her life had fallen apart three years ago, she was heading in the right direction. She'd get better at this with practice. Things might have come easily to her throughout high school and university, but it didn't make her a failure that this had a learning curve. *Dig deep.* It was time to remember how good she'd been at that.

Time to prove to herself she could be again. Alexandria the Comeback Kid. She was so close. Maybe then she'd be able to get a do-over.

She'd had big plans for herself. Everyone had cheered her on, believed in her. Friends, family, people she couldn't remember the names of. Most Likely to Succeed. That was her, destined for a life worthy of her name.

Those yearbook declarations didn't take into account the snowball of bad luck that had yanked the synthetic rubber track out from under her feet when she was just three classes shy of finishing college. The avalanche that followed had kept her buried. Until now. She was going to get out from under it. One table at a time.

Two

Lexi couldn't fight the little bounce in her step as she dropped off Will's soda—the right one this time. Without spilling it. She cleared her tables, put the umbrellas up, and received a decent tip from the three ladies. Progress.

Brett's lips moved but he didn't quite smile. "Can you cover for Tiff Monday morning?" he asked as he refilled the ice.

"I can't," she said, with real regret. There was a Monday-morning seniors group that preordered their meals and tipped great. She'd just have to carry food without dropping it. "I still have my full-time job. I'm sorry."

"I'll ask someone else," Brett said, gesturing to the pass-through bar when the bell rang. "That's your table-two order."

Because she didn't want to walk away with him seeming disappointed, she took a tiny leap and shared an idea she'd been turning over. "I was thinking that if you wanted to capitalize on having the senior crowd on Mondays, you could run a couple of specials geared toward them, maybe even do a buy one meal get half off if you bring someone new on a Monday morning." Regulars were great, but turnover and volume were better.

Brett's lips pursed in a considering way. Two years younger than her, he had a degree and ran a staff of twenty so she wasn't sure he'd take her suggestion.

The kitchen bell chimed again, reminding her of her order. Brett arched his brows, saying nothing about her idea and everything about what she should focus on without speaking at all.

She was thinking about missed opportunities as she brought Will his sandwich. The side of fries smelled delicious. She needed something to eat. Will set his book to the side as she approached. His soda was empty again. He could really put them away. *Or maybe he wants you to keep coming back to his table.*

Running a hand through his thick, dark hair, he gave her the kind of grin that stuck in a person's head for longer than it should. The kind she'd probably see later when she closed her eyes.

His brows lifted. "This looks great. Thank you," he said, putting a napkin across his lap.

"You're welcome. The food here is really good. Something I appreciate since I'm not great at cooking. Breakfast foods are my sweet spot. Trust me, if I was cooking for you, you wouldn't be saying thank you." Her cheeks warmed immediately as she set the plate down. Why had she said that? Why would she be cooking for him?

Will didn't seem bothered by it. He picked up a fry, lips quirking. "Not one of those people who think the way to someone's heart is through their stomach?"

Lexi set a few extra napkins on his table, picked up his glass. "Sure. That could work. As long as it's not my food they're serving up."

Will laughed, the sound more enjoyable than the smell of fries. That was saying something since she was getting hungrier by the second.

"I'll be right back."

Two guys walked onto the patio, seated themselves at a table for six. Six people ordering food at once was a lot. Though they could just be table jerks—a specific type of customer that sat at much larger tables than they needed.

"Be right with you," she told them. Hurrying to the bar, she ordered Will's refill then grabbed her pad and pen off the tray. She shoved them in her apron pocket—basically the waitress version of a fanny pack. She envied the waitresses who, despite wearing the apron and having notepads and pens, didn't need to write stuff down. Her memory had become as sedentary as the rest of her life.

Leaving the tray, she took Will's soda to him, asked how everything was.

His gaze sparkled with amusement she didn't understand. "Delicious. Thanks."

"No problem."

She hurried away, her heartbeat racing at the thought of those guys being joined by four other people. *You can do this. You've done it before. Step by step. Take their orders, deal with the rest as it comes.*

"Hi, guys. I'm Lexi. How are you today?" She pulled her pad out of her pocket.

The darker-haired guy slid his sunglasses to the top of his head. "Better now," he said, winking at her.

It took effort to keep her eye roll internal. She didn't mind a little flirting, but cliché, cheesy lines weren't her favorite.

"We're good. How are you?" the red-haired guy asked.

"Can't complain." Not at the moment, anyway. With a wide smile, she gestured to the rest of the table. "Are you expecting others?"

The dark-haired guy shook his head. "Nope. Just us. We'll have two of whatever is on tap and on sale."

So, just table jerks. Relief whipped through her. Two-top table? She could handle that. Once she got them settled, she could even handle another. It was just the all-at-once that stressed her out, flustered her, made her feel like she was running in four directions simultane-ously with no view of the finish line.

"Sounds good. Be right back."

They picked up the menus and started talking about a concert they'd seen. Lexi glanced at Will. He was already looking her way. Their gazes locked and he sent her a soft smile. Her shiver had nothing to do with the temperature.

"You good?" She mouthed the words more than said them.

He nodded. Lexi was hyperfocused as she returned to the bar, ordered the drafts. More customers had shown up. The music could barely be heard over the chatter. Other waitresses served large tables of four or more. *Not a competition.* Brett saw her at the bar, handed one of the busboys a bin, saying something to him before coming to fill her order.

"The other sections are getting slammed. Next table needs to be yours," Brett said, pouring the beer.

"No problem," she said, pleased she sounded confident. "I've only got the two tables. I'm ready."

He nodded, set the beer on her tray. "You're getting better at this, Lexi. Don't let yourself get flustered."

"Thanks." He really was a nice guy. He'd given her plenty of chances to get this right. Channeling the girl she'd once been, the one who'd tackled every obstacle like a hurdle in track, she straightened her shoulders. She had this.

The two guys ordered a plate of nachos and a basket of wings, which made things even easier. They kept their flirting to a minimum and Will looked perfectly content munching on his fries, reading his book. When the wings-and-nachos order came up, she took it out to the table, noticing their beers were low.

"Awesome. Thanks, cutie. We'll take a couple more beers. Too bad you can't join us," the dark-haired wannabe Casanova said with another wink.

"Can we get some side plates, too?" the other guy asked.

"Of course. Be right back."

Why did some people think that because she was serving them food, they were free to call her what they wanted, say whatever came to mind? She needed tips, not dates. Even if she could juggle something else in a schedule packed with two jobs, school, and her mom, she wouldn't be interested in either of these guys. Her gaze wandered to Will and her belly fluttered.

"Thanks, honey," Redheaded Guy said, pulling her attention back to them.

Smile. A little flirting goes a long way when it comes to tips.

Back at the bar, Brett poured her drinks, smiling widely at a waitress who'd just shown up for her shift.

"Reese is here," Brett said like she couldn't see with her own two eyes. "You can take your break. You get a fifteen. She'll watch your tables. Take these out first." He nudged the beer forward.

For the first time, Lexi wanted to argue with him. She didn't want a break. She didn't need it. But since she wasn't the boss, she didn't have much choice. Eventually, when she got her degree, she'd be in a better position. *She* could be the boss. And take a break when she damn well felt like it. She put her apron on her tray before picking up the pints. Brett moved it and her tray behind the bar. How could she get better if they pulled her away from the stove just as it heated up? He'd just given her a pep talk!

Say something. Tell him you're ready to prove yourself. Instead, she took the beer, headed for the patio. She wanted to finish her own tables today, earn her own tips.

"Can we get those plates, sweetheart?" Dark Hair asked as she dropped off the beer.

Irritation mounted. Maybe Brett wouldn't think she needed a break if she remembered the things she was supposed to. "Right. Sorry. Be right back." She needed a shirt that said that.

Stopping by Will's table, she asked if he wanted more soda. His lips twisted in thought. It was an adorable enough gesture to cut through some of her mad.

"One more. Why not? It's a beautiful day and I just got to the good part of the book," he said, passing her his glass.

"The whole book is excellent. One of my favorites by her," she said, aware of how his voice slid over her, smooth and rich, erasing her annoyance. Their fingertips touched around the glass, giving her an odd dual sensation—icy glass under her palm, heat from his fingertips brushing hers.

A jumble of female voices sounded behind her. More customers. She should just take their orders. Show Brett and herself that she'd be fine. *Greet them, ask if they'd like a drink, let Reese know, and take your break.*

"If I burn, I'm blaming you, Lena," an oddly familiar voice teased.

"You won't burn. If anything, you'll have a rosy glow for your photo shoot this afternoon," another equally familiar voice said around a laugh.

Why did she recognize their voices? Lexi's hand wobbled, making the ice clink against the glass. How was it that a voice could transport a person back in time? She knew those voices. Knew those women. From another time when she'd been a hell of a lot more than she was right now.

Turning her head as slowly as possible, she chanced a look before whipping her face back toward Will. *No. No. No. Why now? Why not six months from now when I've got my shit together? Why not never? Or when my life hasn't imploded?*

"You okay?" Will's dark brows moved closer together, his forehead wrinkling.

It took her a second to acknowledge him over the buzzing in her ears. Memories rushed back, flitting through her head like an old-time film reel.

"I haven't eaten here. It better be worth the points," that voice said. Jacqueline O'Dell. Her nickname in high school was, predictably, Jackie O. Most likely to grace the cover of a magazine. Once upon a time, they'd been friends, both of them heading into life full of optimism and power. Lexi hadn't seen her in years.

"I've heard it's great," Becca said. Rebecca Kramer, most likely to throw themed parties, had been another girl in their circle.

One more quick glance showed that they still suited the role of It Girls perfectly. Jackie with her long, silky brown hair. She waved her hand at the two other women, the sun catching on the iceberg-sized diamond weighing down her ring finger. Their laughter and words ran over one another's with the kind of levity Lexi couldn't remember feeling.

Lexi's stomach pitched. She nearly lost her grip on the glass. Will stood, stepped toward her. Lexi's head spun.

"I don't think anyone works out here," said the unknown woman with straight jet-black hair, gorgeously lined dark eyes, and a bright-pink top, looking around. Her gaze caught Lexi's. "Do you work here?"

The other women looked over. Lexi wished she'd dressed better today instead of throwing on her black jeans and a plain white T-shirt. She'd felt cute when she left the house. Fashion wasn't exactly high on her radar these days.

It took Jackie less than a nanosecond to recognize her, which should have felt good. Lexi had been someone once or *felt* like a someone. In hindsight, it was easy to feel accomplished in the tiny realm of senior year when you hadn't taken a step into adulthood and reality yet. As Jackie squealed and came closer, Becca followed suit, and Will slid back down in his chair.

"No, she doesn't *work* here! Oh my God. Alexandria. What are you doing here?" Jackie's arms closed around her neck, nearly strangling her with enthusiasm. Will reached out and took the glass back from Lexi's open, frozen arms.

"Wow, you look great," Becca said, picking up where Jackie left off when she finally released Lexi's neck.

They stood in front of her and before Lexi could speak, they gestured to her, looking back at their gorgeous friend.

"This is Alexandria the Great. Seriously. She set every track record we had in school. She beat most of the guys' scores in several events. Full ride to college, baby." Jackie's energy reminded Lexi of the nights they'd studied together, the parties they'd attended after meets. The fun they'd had when they didn't know how hard the world could really be.

An older couple seated themselves on the patio. The nacho-and-beer guys looked over, one of them waving at her.

"That's Lena," Becca said, pointing to their now seated friend. "Lena, Lexi." Becca's voice was bright with an enthusiasm that matched her gaze when she turned back to Lexi. "What have you been up to? It's been forever."

Everything spun as if she'd polished off all the beer she'd served today. Lexi sank into the chair behind her, more out of necessity than anything else. Will's brows rose. Their gazes locked, his widening. He gave a subtle shrug, then looked up at Becca.

The smile he gave the woman should have shocked Lexi back to life. It was nothing short of vibrant. Like he was enjoying himself. "We're having lunch," Will said.

Like they'd just noticed him, Jackie and Becca gave Will a once-over.

Jackie made a little humming sound in the back of her throat. "No shock you locked down a hottie." She poked Lexi's shoulder with a polished pink nail. "Hi. I'm Jackie. Those are my friends Becca and Lena." Each woman waved with their introduction and Will simply nodded in response.

Lexi curled her own fingers into a fist. Those three women might look like they hadn't aged since high school, but they were only a few years shy of thirty. They could do better in terms of conversation. At least she kept her own thoughts on Will's smile and eyes in her head.

Lexi still hadn't uttered a word. What could she say? *Nice to see you? What can I get you to drink?*

Jackie stuck the back of her hand in Lexi's face. "You're not the only one." She waggled her hand. "I said yes. And if you think this is gorgeous, you should see my man."

"Nice to meet you, Lexi," Lena called over, still in her seat. "Ladies, I hate to break up the reunion but one of us has a law firm to return to."

Becca grinned; her pixie-cut blond hair suited her cherub face. She hooked a thumb toward Lena. "Someone just made partner."

"Congratulations," Lexi said weakly. She followed it with two thumbs-up because she was just that cool at the moment.

"Okay. We have to catch up but Lena's right. We need to order lunch." Jackie looked around the patio. "If we ever get a waitress. Jeez. Becca, you said this place was good."

Becca shrugged. "My followers recommended it highly." She looked around, then settled on Lexi. "Sorry. That sounded pretentious. My *followers*." She laughed at herself. Maybe it was easier to do that when life wasn't kicking your ass.

"She's an internet sensation, if you didn't know. She just got a major book deal," Jackie said, beaming like a proud parent.

Engaged. Book deal. Lawyer. The nacho guys called Lexi's name. They must have heard it from all the commotion. Jackie looked over at them and waved.

When she turned to Will, she winked and leaned in. "This one hasn't changed at all. Miss Popular."

"Looks like it," Will said, eyeing Lexi.

"We're sorry. We'll let you get back to your lu—" Jackie stopped, looking at Will's table with only one plate and the one glass.

Lexi's heart leapt like a car battery jumped with cables. "We shared.

We share everything," she said, her voice way too loud. She gestured to the table, then picked up a fry and shoved it in her mouth. Hungry as she'd been, it tasted like sawdust.

Will ran a hand over his own mouth, and Lexi had a feeling he was fighting a smile.

The two women *ooh*ed but stopped when Lena cleared her throat.

"Let's exchange numbers before we go," Jackie said as they went to their table.

One of the nacho guys stood up—the dark-haired one—heading for Lexi. Reese chose that moment to come out to the patio, tray in hand, smile wide. Nacho Guy asked her for the plates Lexi hadn't brought. Reese nodded and headed for the older couple, not knowing the three women had arrived first. Didn't matter. She moved with an ease and fluidity Lexi could only relate to if there were a track under her feet. How long had it been since she'd run? And why the hell was she worrying about that now?

Reese glanced at Will, started to speak, then did a double take at Lexi sitting there across from him.

"Uh, Lexi?"

Becca looked over from their table. "Oh my God. You really haven't changed at all!" She shook her head, looking at Lena, then Will. "She knew everyone back then, too."

"We'll take another Coke," Lexi said, thrusting her glass out to Reese, who came to their table.

Brows disappearing into her bangs, Reese accepted the glass. She leaned in, close to Lexi's ear. "We're not really supposed to take our breaks with customers."

Lexi nodded. "Extenuating circumstances," she whispered back.

The waitress straightened and looked back and forth between her and Will. "Would you like a drink as well?"

Will smiled, laying his forearms on the table. He'd nudged his plate forward. "Oh, no thank you. Lexi and I like to share everything."

Understandably, the waitress only looked more confused. She drew out the word "Okay . . ."

Taking Will's plate and the glass, she headed back into the restaurant. She'd probably tell her boss and he'd have another reason to question hiring her.

Left as alone as they could be with the patio filled up and Lexi's past a couple of tables over, she leaned in.

"I'm so sorry," she whispered.

Will was obviously a genius because he put his elbow on the table, bending his arm so it acted as a shield of sorts but made it look like they were just completely into each other.

"For which part?"

Lexi's nose scrunched up. There was a lot to choose from. "I just need a minute. I don't want them to know I work here." She tilted her head to the side ever so slightly.

Will's eyes crinkled around the corners when he was amused. *Noted.*

"I cracked that code, thanks."

Reese returned like some sort of speed-waitressing champion, leaving side plates and happy customers in her wake. She took all of the orders and left baskets of house-made tortilla chips to tide people over. She wasn't even sweating.

Stopping at Will's table, she dropped off the soda. "Two straws," she said, one pierced brow arched.

Will laughed out loud and handed her a credit card Lexi hadn't even seen him pull out. "Perfect. Thank you."

"No problem."

Oh, but there was. So many problems. Lexi didn't know what to say as she sat there trying to figure out how to undo this moment. Reese returned what seemed like seconds later with the credit card receipt.

"Brett's on his way," she said urgently.

"Shit. Shit. Shit."

"We don't like Brett?" Will asked conspiratorially, signing the receipt, then returning his card to his brown leather wallet. Lexi noticed the faint monogram: WMG. She wondered if it was his initials or the brand.

Way to be focused. Because that's what really matters right now. "Brett's my boss."

"Uh-oh," Will muttered.

That was the understatement of the century. Lexi stood abruptly. Will followed suit. Reese stepped back. Jackie looked over, her drink partway to her lips just as Brett stepped outside.

"Oh no, you're leaving?" Jackie set her drink down and dug around in a purse that probably cost more than Lexi's entire collection of jewelry.

"You're leaving?" Brett's irritation was crystal clear.

Jackie stood, and headed over with a card in hand. "You call me. I'm having an engagement party tonight. You have to be there. No excuses. If I don't see you, I'm coming to find you. It's been way too long. See you tonight." She smiled up at Will, pointed at him. "You too."

Lexi spun around, her heart a jackhammer in her chest.

Time for a new nickname. She was officially Alexandria the Cursed.

Three

Will knew, on some level, that it was wrong to be enjoying himself so much. After slipping on his lightweight coat, he grabbed his book, tucked it under his arm, and put one hand gently on Lexi's shoulder. The woman, tall and lanky with a gorgeous mass of wavy hair piled like the Leaning Tower of Pisa on her head, was what his youngest sister would call a hot mess. He'd never understood the term before. Or realized it didn't tell the whole story. She might be having a bad day but that smile, the steely determination to keep going—those things were extremely captivating.

He knew only the bare minimum. Her name was Lexi, she went scary pale when she was nervous, she didn't want to talk to the women at the other table, and waitressing wasn't one of her special skills.

Even with that little bit of intel, he had a feeling that she was not the type of woman who wanted to be rescued. Which would be a good thing in normal circumstances because Will was not that guy. As he repeatedly told his mother, hoping she'd take the hint, he was no one's prince. But he'd been in enough boardroom standoffs to know how to make a strategic exit.

As Brett closed the distance between them, Will squeezed Lexi's shoulder.

He leaned down, spoke low so only Lexi could hear him. "If you trust me for five minutes, I'll get you out of here smoothly."

She turned her head, bringing their faces incredibly close. He noted the little freckles across the bridge of her nose. Her brows furrowed. "Better than the alternative." She glanced back at the women, gave a big smile and small wave.

Brett looked closer to twenty than Will's own age of thirty. He wore his department store suit well enough. Will knew the type— decent guy looking for his shot to head up the ladder. If such a thing existed at a small, one-off, albeit popular restaurant.

Will turned to face the manager, reaching out a hand as he angled himself between the guy and Lexi. Brett stopped in surprise, shook Will's hand, giving him the opportunity to clap the guy on the shoulder, lean in, and firm up Lexi's excuse. "Hey, Brett. I'm Will. A friend of Lexi's. She's got a family emergency. I'm going to take her home. Can you meet me at the front door with her bag or whatever she brought to work?"

No one else could hear them but he saw Lexi, from the corner of his eye, watching them with worry.

Brett, the no-nonsense manager Will expected him to be, nodded quickly. "Absolutely. Of course." He looked over at Lexi. "Take care of yourself."

Lexi's nose scrunched up adorably. Will nodded to the women watching them closely, thanked the waitress, and took Lexi by the arm. They went out the glass patio door that ought to be locked if they didn't want people eating and running off. They'd walked around the side of the building that led to the front entrance before she stopped.

"Oh my God. I can't believe I just walked out on a shift because I was too much of a wimp to tell my former high school friends I'm a waitress. What am I doing?" She looked up at Will with regret and disappointment that made his heart muscles clench. The front door of the restaurant opened. Brett saw them immediately and passed Lexi a jean jacket and a huge cloth shoulder bag.

"I'll find someone to cover the rest of your shift, Lexi. Good luck with everything."

Will nodded, taking her things. "Thanks, man. We'll keep you updated."

The best offense was generalization. Fill in none of the blanks but make the opposition feel useful. Like they'd helped arrive at the necessary conclusion.

Brett hesitated a moment, then went back inside. Will turned, looking down at Lexi as he passed her the bag and jacket.

"Thank you. I don't even know what to say." She shrugged. "I'm so sorry."

"Why don't we take a short walk? Help you clear your head while you decide what to do next."

She pulled on the worn jacket that was too thin to combat the cool weather, settled the strap of her large purse across her body, making the T-shirt scrunch between her breasts. Will immediately lifted his gaze, focused on her face. When she shoved both hands into her hair, most of the tower toppled. She pulled out some invisible pins and the loose waves bounced around her face, making her look even more lovely.

"Everything happened so fast. I was just thinking maybe I didn't completely suck at the whole waitressing gig and things would turn around." She made a dismissive sound, lowered her hands.

"You don't suck," he said. He had two sisters and a mother. He knew to keep his commentary brief. She probably just wanted to vent.

An amused smile hovered on her lips. "Thanks for lying."

The honesty surprised a laugh out of him. They stepped around a couple arguing on the sidewalk, heading in the direction of the market. They could stroll along the water, then he'd walk her to her car and likely never see her again. The thought made his gut cramp.

"I'm not lying. Entirely. That was the best pastrami sandwich I've had." He didn't even know he liked pastrami.

Lexi stopped abruptly and turned to face him. "You ordered a BLT."

Will fought the laugh but felt his lips quirk. "I did."

Lexi groaned, tipping her head back. When she straightened and looked at him again, she frowned. "Why didn't you tell me I gave you the wrong order?"

He shrugged as they started walking again. "I figured it was the universe's way of telling me to break out of my routine."

Lexi's laughter floated like musical notes on the late-September breeze. "Or its way of telling you to pick another restaurant."

"No way. Becca's followers are right. The food is good, you're charming, and the other waitresses are great," he said.

She laughed again, as he'd hoped. "Nice. I can't even argue. I'm probably going to lose my job now. What did you say to Brett?"

"That you had a family emergency. I'm sure they'll give you another chance."

She made another dismissive noise. His phone buzzed in his pocket. He had a meeting this afternoon and was probably cutting it close. They turned right on Pine Street, which headed toward Pike Place Market. The steep road had them slowing their pace.

"Thank you. I think Brett's given me as many chances as he's willing to, though. It's for the best. I took the job for the tips but it's a lot harder than I expected."

He couldn't comment on the serving aspect of it as he'd never done it but it didn't *look* all that easy. "I gave you a great tip," he assured her.

"You're a nice guy, Will. Thank you for helping me escape my self-made drama."

They walked in silence for a few minutes, long enough for him to realize the quiet didn't feel awkward with her. He needed to go but he wanted to make sure she was okay. He assured himself he was just being a good guy. He wasn't already far too invested in this intriguing woman. He wasn't caught up in the way she seemed vulnerable with a steel spine, funny but self-deprecating, smart but slightly unsure. Who was he kidding? Those dualities pulled him in even as all that hair, that long, lithe body, and her expressive face squeezed his lungs.

"So, track star?"

Hands in her pockets, staring straight ahead, she nodded. She had a strong profile, an elegant, almost stubborn jaw he couldn't seem to stop looking at. The women he dated were somewhat superficial, focused more on shopping, decorating, and the next sponsored event than they were worried about earning tips or looking bad in front of some old friends. Of course, most of the women he went out with, until he'd told his mother to knock it off, were from her social circle. Daughters of friends. He'd prefer to be a workaholic than have his mother try any more matchmaking. Lexi . . . fascinated him. Not just her looks or the contrasts but how she stared at the water like it held the answers in its gentle waves.

"Once upon a time," she finally answered. "Sometimes it seems like that was someone else's life and I just have really amazing memories of it."

"Memories always make things seem better than they were. We tend to idealize them."

She stopped walking as the street flattened out. "You must have somewhere better to be. Thank you for today. I'd say you're off the hook for Good Samaritan duties for the rest of the month, at least."

He smiled, not sure what the unsettled feeling in his chest meant. "Will you go tonight?"

Lexi tilted her head. The smell of fish and ocean wafted over them. "Go where?"

"To Jackie's party. She was quite adamant about you going."

Another snort-laugh. It was ridiculous and adorable at the same time. The last several women his mother had set him up with were like façades. He could sense more to them but they refused to show it. They were all polite laughter at his jokes, exaggerated air kisses, and telling stories of who they knew. Alexandria, as far as he could tell, was just absolutely herself, no matter the situation. God, that was refreshing as fuck.

Appearances mattered a lot to the Grand family. It was why Home Needs wanted to partner with them so badly. The Grand name and reputation were crystal clear, family-oriented, and stable. Will didn't mind any of those things but he hated phoniness. Maybe that's what was missing from his life: something *real*. Lexi was disheveled from the last few minutes and still, she was the kind of beautiful that etched into a man's brain and distracted him.

"Hard pass. The last thing I need is to go to some swanky party where I'll stick out like cheap tequila at a fine-wine soiree. It's hard enough knowing everyone else made it out alive and I'm just treading water."

The sadness that tinged her tone tore at him. It shouldn't. It was none of his business. He had his own issues. His own life. It was jam-packed with meetings, mergers, social engagements, and making sure they moved through each quarter successfully and in good financial standing. On top of that, his parents were going all out for the company's fiftieth anniversary celebration, and the Grand siblings were making sure it went off without a hitch while explaining to their mother that who they brought to the party shouldn't matter.

He imagined bringing Lexi to that party. It made him smile despite the fact that he hated attending those types of events. She stood here thinking she wasn't worthy of going to a party just because some women seemed to have it all. Will ought to bring her to one of their company functions or charity events just to show her that any shine could be dulled if you polished it enough. If you dug a little deeper. Just because someone looked like they had their act together didn't mean they were perfect or their life was. As far as he was concerned, and from what little he knew, this woman had once been proud of herself. For good reason. She'd been great at several things and life had obviously thrown her a few cheap shots—but that didn't mean she was any less than anyone else. She hadn't given up. She was busting her ass at more than one job trying to turn things around.

That kind of gumption with the right backing and a little luck led to great things. If it didn't, his grandfather wouldn't have been able to create their company, Grand Babies. His grandfather hadn't had anything when he started. He'd worked hard, night and day, scraped by and saved until he was able to open a tiny store that sold high-quality baby products. Success wasn't a straight path.

For the third time that day, the sandwich and the impromptu patio exit being the first two, Will did something without thinking it all the way through.

"You need to go to that party. You seem more like a fighter than a quitter to me. No matter what you wish you were doing, you should be proud of who you are right this minute."

She regarded him skeptically for a moment, her brown eyes full of an emotion he couldn't name. "You don't even know me."

Will checked his watch, saw the load of messages he'd missed along with the time. When he looked up, she'd crossed her arms over her chest. Closing up, protecting herself from more of life's punches.

"I have a Zoom meeting scheduled. I need your number so I can pick you up for the party tonight."

"Excuse me?" She squared her shoulders.

"I was invited too, remember? It's rude to pull a no-show. Besides, where's the harm? Do you have a boyfriend? Husband? Girlfriend? Wife?" *Please say no.*

She tilted her head again, a small smile playing on her lips. "Way to cover your bases. No. I don't, but let me answer your question. Where's the harm in going to a party I don't want to go to, surrounding myself with people from high school who did incredible things with their lives, and going on a date with a guy I barely know? Where to begin." She tapped her index finger to her chin.

He chuckled and held out a hand, waited for her to slip her phone into it. "I'll put my number in your phone. Life's all about risks. You seem like you could use a night out. Going will show you that beneath the shiny clothes and phony smiles, everyone is fighting the same fight, just trying to figure it out. And I didn't say *date*." Though he wanted to. But he'd take seeing her again in whatever form she was comfortable with. "Just two new friends hanging out at a party they were both invited to."

Her left brow rose, her lips twitching. "And pretending to be a couple."

Will leaned in just a touch. She smelled like french fries and vanilla. A strange yet enticing combination. "Jackie did say she'd come looking for you if you didn't show. Plus, you'll be saving me from another family dinner where my mother assures me my biological clock is going to explode if I don't lock someone down soon."

Her burst of laughter echoed in the wind. He didn't want to be drawn to her but he couldn't deny he was.

"You should probably tell your mom that's not how it works. But you *did* rescue me."

He nodded and passed back her phone, hoping she wouldn't look at it until later. "And I ate pastrami for you."

She fought a smile. "That's true. Fine. I'll text you. But we aren't staying long."

"You're the boss. Say the word and we'll go."

Lexi grinned. She gave him her number. "Safe word will be *pastrami*."

Four

Lexi was craving a pastrami sandwich by the time she got home. Since she was in charge of the shopping and hadn't had a chance to hit the store this week, that craving would go unsatisfied. She did, however, take a few minutes to center herself after parting ways with her gorgeous rescuer. She even placed an online order for groceries to be picked up tomorrow. Multitasking, the greatest workout of all.

Letting herself into the house, she listened for sounds that her mother was awake. Gwen Danby spent a lot of time sleeping. It was just one item on the long list of things that worried Lexi about her mom.

Her childhood home, a two-story basement entry, could be described on one of those reality fixer-upper shows as "full of potential." A person just needed a boatload of money and some skill to return it to its formerly charming, not-run-down state.

Lexi tossed her bag on the entryway table, hung her faded jean jacket, and took the stairs up. The second floor was mostly open, with the living area straight ahead, the dining area to the left and an archway through there to the kitchen.

To the right of the stairs, there was a hallway with three bedrooms, a bathroom, and another entrance to the kitchen. It was easy to see her mom wasn't in the living room. As usual, a stack of romance books sat precariously piled on the table beside her favorite lounger in front of an old-school brick fireplace. There were more on the floor and probably a bunch on hold at the library waiting for Lexi to pick them up.

Lexi's stomach rumbled audibly. Damn. She really wanted that sandwich. Tomorrow. If she remembered to pick up the groceries.

"Lex? Is that you?" her mom's soft singsong voice called from down the hallway. Lexi headed that way. Should she cancel with Will? Of course she should. What was she thinking going to a party with people she wasn't even friends with anymore? It wasn't like showing up with a guy she barely knew was going to make her fit in again. Anywhere. No matter how good he looked. Or sweet and funny he seemed.

When she entered the space that used to be her dad's office, some of the tension in her shoulders loosened. Gwen's most animated moments were when she worked on her miniatures. Scene after scene of moments she'd read decorated the walls of shelves. Story snippets. Lexi could lose herself looking at them as easily as her mother got lost in making them.

When Lexi was restless or couldn't sleep, she'd come in here to focus on the intricate details of the creations, labeled neatly by the book that inspired them. *The Kiss Quotient* by Helen Hoang, *Twice Shy* by Sarah Hogle, *Happily Ever After* by Nora Roberts, and so many more. Lexi hadn't read all of the books, but the miniatures shared the essence of the moments that really tugged at her mother's dented heart. While it was an outlet—an amazing one at that—Gwen often leaned on the activity like a crutch to keep to herself, avoid social engagements, and focus on something other than missing her husband.

"Hi, honey," her mom said without lifting her head.

"Hey." Lexi wandered in, noting that her mom hadn't changed out of the pajama bottoms or ancient Eagles T-shirt she'd been wearing when Lexi left that morning. "What are you working on?"

"Dinner scene from the book I'm reading. He reaches for her hand across the table and she just tells him absolutely everything. Like he released something inside of her, you know? It was adorable. Reminded me of my first date with your dad." The table was strewn with tools, miniature pieces, clay, paints, brushes—everything a craft enthusiast could imagine.

Lexi's heart flinched. She squeezed her mom's shoulder, knowing where this was headed. It seemed she was destined to get stuck in the past today. *Who are you kidding? Your past and present have merged forevermore.*

"We went to see the Eagles. First and best concert I've ever been to. Oh, sweetie, Don Henley has the most beautiful voice." Gwen used the tiniest of tools to manipulate the clay. Usually, Lexi's mom bought miniature items she found at craft stores, like tables, benches, books, fruits, vegetables, little glasses that looked like they held liquid, and so much more, to create her scenes; for the characters, she often made her own. "We sang along to every single song and then went to this diner after. We had apple pie and I felt like I could tell him anything. This scene, it just got me, you know?"

She knew her parents' story. All too well. They'd also shared a chocolate vanilla milkshake. When the band's "Peaceful, Easy Feeling" came over the speakers, they'd declared it their song and never spent another night apart. Until.

The mixture of sadness and wistfulness in her mother's tone dug beneath the crack in Lexi's heart that never quite healed.

"Have you eaten today?" Lexi asked when her mother fell silent. Lexi couldn't count how many times she'd heard the first-date story.

"Don't mom me." Gwen set her tool down, rolled her shoulders, and spun around on her chair. Her once dark hair had liberal streaks of pale gray, almost white. The tiny-framed glasses she wore to see things up close were perched too far down her nose. She removed them with a deep sigh.

"Don't give me reason to," Lexi reminded her. When Lexi did anything even slightly mom-like, Gwen brought out her *I'm serious* tone. In truth, she loved the way little flickers of her mom's old self came through when she told Lexi to knock it off.

"Have *you* eaten today?" Her mom's brows arched. She stood

and stretched her hands over her head. Despite the drawstring being cinched, the pajama bottoms hung loose on her waist.

"Well played. Why don't I make us something?" *Do it. You're stuck in as much of a rut as she is.* "I'm going to go out for a while tonight." Lead by example. Another old favorite among Coach's sayings.

Her mom lowered her arms, a small smile gracing her lips.

"That's good, honey. That makes me happy. You should get out more. You spend all your time working or here. It's not healthy."

The weight of irony in her mother's words sat like an angry gorilla beating its fists on Lexi's chest. She shook off the feeling, the pressure. Lexi rolled her eyes as she turned and headed for the kitchen. "Don't mom me."

"That's my job. You're almost thirty. You shouldn't live at home." Her mom followed behind.

"I'm twenty-five." She couldn't argue with the rest. She shouldn't live at home and if she thought her mother would pay her bills, feed herself, and remember to pull herself out of bed on the bad days, Lexi would move out. Though Gwen's depression wasn't nearly as bad as it had been during the first year following her husband's death, Lexi still did most of the things that were necessary to keep them afloat.

"Almost twenty-six. I was married to your dad by that age. For four years," Gwen reminded her, taking a seat at the breakfast bar.

Lexi rooted through the fridge, found some eggs, ham, and cheese. Omelets would do. Not pastrami, but she'd settled for less.

"Make you a deal: You get out more, I'll get out more. Besides, times have changed. People don't get married so young anymore."

Though it wasn't stopping her former classmates apparently. Lena couldn't have been much older than any of them and she was making partner in her law firm.

Maybe Lena didn't have everything fall apart. Or maybe others were better than her at rebuilding. "I placed a grocery order. Why don't you come with me to pick it up tomorrow? Stop for a piece of pie."

Her mom shook her head. "I'm reading tomorrow. I wouldn't mind a nice walk, though. By the river, maybe?"

Lexi snorted. "You're reading every day, Mom." She only picked activities that kept her in Lexi's company or her own. "Come on. Just the store then, for the ride. Twenty minutes round trip. Didn't you just say it's healthy to get out of the house?" She grabbed a pan from one of the lower cupboards, set it on the stove.

When her phone buzzed in her pocket, she ignored it in the hope of Gwen actually changing her stance on getting out more.

"Where are you going tonight?" Gwen asked. *Small steps.*

"I ran into a couple girls from high school. Do you remember Jackie?"

Lexi grabbed a bowl, a whisk, and some spices. Her mom's brows were furrowed when she set the items on the countertop across from her. "Here. You do this part while I cut the ham."

"She was another runner, right? Not like you but she did track with you. She used to come over after school?" Gwen cracked the eggs, added some spices, and picked up the whisk, moving it around the bowl. If there was one thing her mom had a firm grasp on, it was the past.

"Right. Well, she's getting married." Lexi started chopping the ham across from her mom. Gwen was pretty absentminded about eating but once Lexi got things going, she chipped in. "She's having an engagement party."

"That's nice that you're going. You should bring a gift."

Lexi stopped chopping, irritated by the idea that not only had she been roped into the party but she might have to spend money she didn't have. She hadn't thought of that.

Gwen watched her carefully. "Just something small, Lexi. Doesn't have to be expensive." She pushed the whisked eggs toward Lexi. When she wasn't lost in memories or busy with her miniatures, Gwen was pretty astute at reading people's moods. Too bad she hadn't been great at recognizing her husband's money problems. He'd hid it well, and Gwen had been happy to defer to him.

Washing her hands at the sink then drying them, she set a hand on Lexi's shoulder as she walked by. "I'm glad you're getting out more, sweetie. Call me when it's ready."

Lexi closed her eyes, pressing her palms flat to the cool counter. She counted to ten, breathing in and out slowly. *Focus on what you can control.* She set about making a meal that she'd eat alone. She'd leave her mom's in the fridge because Gwen would fall back into the scene she was creating and not want to stop again.

Doing her best not to let the events of the day take her legs out from under her, Lexi grabbed a soda and her freshly made omelet, taking the seat her mother had vacated.

Since she was alone, again, she pulled her phone out of her pocket as she took a huge bite of her eggs. New texts were on her screen, making Lexi smile her first real smile in hours.

The Man You Share Everything With

She hadn't checked his entry in her phone. Definitely funny. Lexi swiped the text open.

> My older sister says we need to bring a gift.

Lexi

> Who is this?

Her lips twitched with amusement as she imagined his response.

The Man You Share Everything With

> Do you have more than one man you share everything with? Sorry. I should have been more descriptive when entering my contact.

Lexi

You could have gone with Will.
I don't know any other Wills.

The Man You Share Everything With

My ego almost took a hit there, thinking you'd
forgotten me so quickly. I don't let just anyone
eat my fries.

Lexi scooped up a bite of omelet while she considered what to say
next. Since she didn't know him well, it seemed prudent not to take the
conversation right into the gutter.

Lexi

It was one fry and I think your ego will live
long and prosper. My mom says we should
bring a gift too. I think we should bail.

The Man You Share Everything With

On the party or each other?

Her stomach wobbled. Setting her fork down, she thought about
that. Was he regretting his insistence on their meeting up tonight? She
hadn't been looking for a date but now that it was up in the air, she
realized she very much wanted to see him again. And not while he was
relying on her for food.

Lexi

Which would you prefer?

The Man You Share Everything With

> Neither. Let's go to the party. I'll take care of the gift.

The silence in Lexi's house reminded her that staying home would just be another night of the same. Alone. Bored. Wishing she could make time go faster or accomplish more in the moment. She had a paper on the best social media apps for marketing due in a week. She'd done the readings, taken notes. Just needed to actually write it. It was taking her longer than she expected to get back into the groove of being a student. Even a very part-time one.

Lexi

> I'll meet you there.

The Man You Share Everything With

> I can pick you up.

Her thumbs hovered over the screen. She was so tired of over-thinking everything. Why did he want to go? What did he get out of it? Would the night just make her feel worse about herself than she already did? She liked controlling what she could.

Lexi

> I'll meet you there.

She texted the address. She wasn't backing out. With literally nothing else to look forward to—unless she counted the definite possi-bility she'd be fired soon and therefore have more free time—Lexi fig-ured tonight could tide her over socially for a while. It might even help her find that girl she used to be. Worst case, given the size of Jackie's ring, the food ought to be good.

Five

In his everyday, predictable life, Will wasn't a second-guesser. Apparently, Alexandria . . . shit, what was her last name? Probably not actually *The Great*. He smiled at the thought, straightening his tie in the mirror.

Should he wear a tie? He wore ties every day and to most formal events. What kind of party was this? See? Lexi brought out the second-guesser in him. His phone continued to buzz but he ignored it. As expected, his mother hadn't been happy with him canceling on dinner. She requested (her word for "demanded") monthly dinners with several courses meant to have them linger, but it usually just made him feel trapped. She claimed they were a way to reconnect and bond away from "societal pressures." The Grand siblings found it ironic that she was usually the one putting said pressure on them. Those dinners were often headlined by their mother telling each of her three children ways they could improve their lives and social standings. And hers in the process.

To that end, the last several, his mother had "unexpected" guests join at the last minute. Conveniently, these guests tended to be single, attractive women who ran in the same social circles as his mother and her friends. She'd gone so far as to make a folder in her photos app of "eligible women." A shudder ran through him at the thought of his mother obsessing over who he spent his time with.

He'd made it abundantly clear that he didn't need or want help in his dating life. He wanted to make her happy, so at first he'd gone on a few dates. But it quickly became clear that what he wanted and what his mother wanted for him were entirely different things. So he'd asked her to stop. His mom had selective listening when it came to her children, watching her salt intake, and flying economy. Will didn't want to be rude to any of the women his mother introduced him to; some of them were nice enough. But it all just felt forced, rightly so. Looking good in a photo op together didn't make a couple compatible. He wasn't going to marry a woman and settle down because his mother thought she came from a good family. He'd been throwing himself into work more and more as a result and not just because of his desire to add to the company's success. If he was at the office, his mother tended to leave him alone. Dating could be nice but relationships took effort and right now, or for the past several months, he'd been too busy to make the time. *You had no problem making it for Lexi tonight.*

Will yanked the knot on the tie, opened the first couple of buttons on his Ralph Lauren dress shirt. He glanced down at his dark-gray dress pants. Huffing out a breath, he grabbed a pair of dark jeans from his hardly-ever-worn drawer. This was more difficult than the last actual executive decision he'd made.

Tonight was an opportunity to think about something else— something that wasn't wrapped up in his family, his grandfather's legacy, and his future. Will needed a break from his father's burning desire to enter into a large-scale partnership with the international chain store Home Needs. Despite having a degree in finance and economics, Jackson Grand held an unofficial role in the company. He paved his own path, considering himself in charge of idea and product development, possible merger and acquisition opportunities, while also dabbling in marketing.

After playing several rounds of golf, and maybe sharing one too many drinks at the nineteenth hole, with Fredrick Banner, the CEO of Home Needs, Jackson decided this was the very thing that Grand Babies needed to really launch themselves into being a household name.

In return for a sizable investment that would allow for the opening of two new Grand Babies stores, Fredrick Banner wanted the prestige that was associated with the Grand family name. The universally respected Grands—who'd once been dubbed Seattle's royal family—looked a hell of a lot better in the media than Fredrick's own clan.

With his son making headlines for bad choice after bad choice, Fredrick had stalled discussions and negotiations by demanding a surprising number of social engagements that shone a spotlight on the two families spending time together.

Which meant Will, the CFO and face of Grand Babies, who just happened to be Nolan Banner's age, was banking a lot more hours outside of the office than he wanted, spending time with someone he didn't particularly like. *This* would be a welcome reprieve.

A sharp beeping sound let him know someone had opened his front door. Served him right for giving his sisters keys.

"You home?" his younger sister's voice called out. Will groaned and yanked on his stiff jeans, hoping like hell they relaxed, and buttoned them quickly. Kyra wasn't big on privacy. She barged in anywhere she wanted like they were all still kids. Though in her case, she *was* still a kid. At twenty-two, she was the baby. A bit of a surprise for his mother. Will was in the middle at thirty. Madeline—Maddie—was the oldest at thirty-two.

"Be right out. Why are you here?"

Will nearly tripped over her when he opened his bedroom door. She stopped in front of him, gazing up with a wide grin. She'd changed the star nose stud to a shiny diamond. The tips of her long side bangs were purple while the rest of the short, blunt cut was blacker than a starless night. Her eye makeup made her look older but Will always saw the kid she'd been underneath all of it.

"What if I'd had company?" Will asked, keeping his tone brusque as he shoved his phone and wallet in his back pockets.

Kyra laughed. A full-out, loud belly laugh. "Right. Then I would have alerted the media. All hail, the Grand Babies bachelor is off the market, ladies. Dry your tears on our ultra-absorbent, earth-friendly disposable towels."

"That's a long slogan, brat," he said, nudging her shoulder on his way by. He should eat something. The pastrami sandwich was surprisingly filling but once he got back to the office, he'd worked for hours without a break. His focus was interrupted more than once by thoughts of Lexi. He couldn't remember the last time a woman had occupied that much space in his brain from just a brief meeting.

"I'm on my way to *la parents*. Why aren't you coming? Once-a-month mandatory dinner. Touching base, a civil game of Monopoly, and a thorough review of what we're doing with our lives," Kyra said, doing a poor job imitating their mother's lecture voice. Put like that, it sounded boring as hell. He was definitely in for a better night with Lexi.

"*Les parents,*" he corrected. "Or *mes* if you want to call them yours."

"No way, dude. I'm adopted."

He laughed. "You wish." They joked but they loved their parents. Sometimes they just spent a little too much time together.

She trailed after him, making him smile. She'd been doing that since she could crawl. Kyra was 100 percent not adopted. He remembered how fascinated he'd been when his mother was pregnant. And with Kyra as a baby. His sidekick growing up despite their age gap.

"Anyway. I'm busy tonight." He continued to the kitchen, the familiar pride filling his chest. The house was more than an investment to Will. With three thousand square feet spread over two floors, it was his *home*. He'd grown up with a proverbial silver spoon in his mouth and knew he was beyond privileged. That didn't mean there weren't other challenges. Despite the fact that he wasn't the oldest, he had an extra layer of duty placed on his shoulders by his parents that included everything from watching out for his siblings to excelling academically. There was an aloofness to his parents' mansion that meant he'd never been able to relax there even as a child. Will and his sisters were loved but their parents were not affectionate or effusive. The three siblings, despite their age differences, made up for that with one another. They'd always been close.

"*Busy* isn't a synonym for *work*, just FYI. And work isn't an excuse to skip dinner."

Will shot her an amused glance, saying nothing.

"Seriously, if I have to listen to Mads and Rachel talk about their trip again, I'm going to drown myself in my butternut squash soup."

Will pulled open the fridge and grabbed a couple of bottles of water, passing Kyra one. "That wouldn't end well. You're allergic to squash. Though it would give your face a nice rosy glow so you wouldn't have to wear all that makeup."

She stuck her tongue out at him because despite being twenty-two, she was his baby sister.

Kyra opened the bottle, took a long drink—their mother wasn't around so out of the bottle was fine. She set it down and Will knew the second she figured it out.

Her eyes went rounder than dinner plates, her long lashes lifting. "You have a date. Oh my God. Did hell actually freeze over? Did you lose a bet? Did Mom pick her? Does she have good teeth? Strong child-bearing hips and an incredible pedigree?"

Will nearly snorted the water through his nose. "Stop. I don't have a *date*. I'm going to a get-together. Speaking of which, I need to *get* going so you should stop stalling and head to dinner. Give Mads a break. She put off their honeymoon for months. Now that we're closing this deal, she and Rach deserve to have some time to themselves."

His oldest sister had married her high school sweetheart just over a year ago. They'd both been born into families who put business first. Rachel even more so. Her family owned a chain of coffee shops that she was heavily involved in. Both of them had understood needing to postpone the honeymoon to work around other things. With Will buried in numbers for a possible merger, the birthday party for the company's fiftieth, and Kyra still in school, they couldn't get away right after the wedding. No, it was a perfect time for Maddie and Rachel to travel. Before they all got even busier.

"I know. I just hate that everyone is moving forward, doing exciting things, and I'm not allowed to do anything." Kyra sulked, leaning against the white marble countertop.

He tapped her nose, set his drink down. Hopefully there would be food at the party. "Don't pout. You're starting the way we all did. Interning while finishing college and learning the different areas to figure out which one you want to focus on."

She straightened, cautious optimism dancing in her blue eyes. "I already know it'll be product development. I'm telling you, one day all of our products will be completely organic and earth-friendly."

"You need to do your time in each section to be sure. There's no rush, Ky. I know it feels like there is, but don't be in such a rush to grow up."

She glared at him, her dark brows drawing together. "I *am* grown up."

He smiled at her, gave her a side hug. "You'd be surprised how much who you are changes between twenty and thirty."

Kyra poked him in the belly. "You're right. I don't want to rush becoming boring like you."

He gave her a gentle mock shove toward the doorway. "Time to go."

"Blah, blah, blah," Kyra returned, putting the cap back on her water to take with her. "If I end up in the hospital with a butternut squash reaction, I'm blaming you."

It wouldn't even be a thought if their mother changed the menu now and then, but she liked consistency and making her husband happy. Kyra grabbed her boots on the way to the door. Will grabbed his keys and a thin leather jacket.

"I'll take the risk."

She kissed his cheek and walked down the stairs to his circular driveway where she'd parked her Mercedes.

"Have fun on your date," she called, closing the door before he could reply.

He chuckled, walked to his own Mercedes, a dark-blue sports model. He didn't feel the need to rush life forward like Kyra and wasn't ready for kids like Maddie, and he didn't really care about image like his parents. Will was content making work his focus, though it occurred to him that maybe he ought to make more time for social outings that had nothing to do with his family or job.

He'd wanted to pick Lexi up, maybe go for a drive, grab something to eat before they went to confront her past. Today had sort of snowballed into an adventure. Maybe he was a little like Kyra. He had no idea where tonight would lead but he'd known, with a certainty he usually only felt for business, that he needed to see Lexi again.

Anticipation hummed in his veins and he knew part of that was basic attraction because she was gorgeous. But there was more. The way she had every intention of getting better at her job but wasn't willing to admit to old friends she worked there. It made him curious. There was nothing wrong with waitressing, and she seemed to have a strong work ethic, so what was it that made her sit down with him? He didn't think it was an image thing in the same way his mother liked them all to have a matching color scheme at holiday events. It went deeper. And he wanted to dig into the layers beneath the woman.

She was different from any of the other women he'd dated and certainly not a woman his mother would have set him up with. Will chuckled as he drove. Maybe *that* was her appeal.

Six

The list of stupid decisions was getting infinitely longer as the day went on. Sitting down at Will's table, not telling the truth, pretending she was with Will, leaving work early—she hadn't even cashed out and now her pay would be docked a couple of hours—agreeing to go out with a man who was far too sexy for her to make smart decisions around. And now she was here. Lexi stared at the bottle of wine she rested against the steering wheel. She couldn't show up with nothing even if Will brought something. Especially if he brought something. She'd bought the most expensive cheap bottle she could find. And was seriously contemplating taking a swig. When was the last time she'd even been to a party?

Flashbacks of high school flitted through her head. She didn't want to be a Bruce Springsteen song but she truly felt like her glory days were long gone. Life had passed at a molasses-like pace for a while after her dad died. She'd slipped under the surface of her own life only to drown in the depths of her dad's debt—which her mom had known nothing about—and her mother's profound sadness. By the time Lexi emerged from the weight of all of that, someone had pushed the fast-forward button. Everything spiraled at an alarming speed and most days, Lexi was still trying to catch up. She'd tried to keep the company going at first but when it became clear she couldn't, one of her dad's employees agreed to pay off the business debt in exchange for the business. She'd had no choice, and it meant they'd kept the house.

Which means you're entitled to some slips and slides.

The path was clearing, there was an actual chance of her becoming her own person again. But not tonight. Tonight, she'd do what she did best: pretend everything was okay. That she was okay.

Her lips pursed, moved back and forth. No one would notice if she opened the bottle. She didn't usually need liquid courage but she wasn't sure she had it in her to put on another show. This afternoon's had drained her. Would they have even invited her if they'd realized she *was* their waitress? Would they have had the same level of excitement? If she walked through that door tonight, she had to keep up with a charade she shouldn't have started. Lexi just wanted to be herself. Or at least, figure out who her self was now.

Her phone buzzed, making her jump.

The Man You Share Everything With

> Are you contemplating life or
> opening that bottle of wine?

Her head snapped up, her gaze locking with Will's. Mortification swamped her. Had he seen her talking to herself?

He stood at her driver's-side door, knees bent, grinning at her. That little dimple in his left cheek popped and his dark eyes sparkled with mischief. God. He was gorgeous. Or maybe his smile was just so great, it transformed him. No escaping now. Unless she told him to jump in and drove them up to the bluff where she'd hung out with Jackie and Becca when they were younger. She and Will could polish off the wine under the stars. *Sounds almost romantic.*

She didn't particularly need romance. Definitely didn't need the happily-ever-after her mom craved from her books, the kind she'd lost with no warning. No, Lexi didn't know who the hell she'd turned out to be but she knew she didn't want to love someone so much it would tear her apart if something happened. *Stop worrying about the past and the future. He's gorgeous, funny, sweet, and could be anywhere else he wanted tonight but he chose to be with you.* Maybe pretending wouldn't be so bad if she got to laugh and have fun with Will. No strings. Just a break from regularly scheduled programing.

Tugging her purse over her head, shoving her phone inside, she gripped the neck of the bottle in one hand, keys in the other, and got out of the car.

She leaned against the door, shivering in the night air, drinking him in. Spending time with him, despite the circumstances, would not be a hardship. Will stared at her. He'd dressed in seemingly ironed jeans—a sight she'd never seen before—and a gray buttondown that somehow looked casual, sophisticated, and sexy AF. Yes, she'd said *AF* in her head. His thin leather bomber jacket looked soft and expensive. Judging from the neighborhood, he'd fit right in at the party.

"Hi," he said. Just that, paired with his half smile, amused gaze, and that damn shirt, was enough to make her wonder what she was really getting herself into.

"Hi."

"That is an excellent bottle of wine," he said, gesturing with a chin nod.

She glanced down at it, tilted it to see the label. "Really?" Wine wasn't her thing but maybe she was better at choosing than she thought.

"Not at all but it'll get you nice and drunk if that's what you're after."

Despite the bouncy-ball feeling in her stomach, he'd made her laugh. Again. And that felt good. She didn't do a whole lot of it these days and it was strange to realize she missed it. She met his gaze. "Maybe I'll hang on to it and see how the night goes."

"Good plan. You should have brought a bigger purse. Stashed it inside." He shook his head with a mock frown, like she'd let him down by not thinking ahead.

"I clearly didn't think that all the way through," she said, falling into step beside him as they crossed the quiet street. Both sides were lined with elegant, new-looking family homes. No fixer-uppers here. The house was a two-story Colonial with more windows along the front than Lexi's whole house had.

"You look *really* good," he said.

His emphasis on the word *really* made her heart and stomach spasm in tandem. So did the way his eyes roamed over the high-waisted black jeans that she'd paired with a slightly bulky, off-the-shoulder dark-green sweater. She didn't run the way she used to but she kept in shape, and thanks to yoga her arms and shoulders were sleek. Will's obvious appreciation made her happy she hadn't bothered with a jacket even with the bite in the air.

Stopping at the start of the cobblestone path leading up to the door, Lexi tipped her head back to look up at him. "So do you. Really good. This is a strange not-date date, isn't it?"

He nodded, firming up those full, alluring lips. "We don't have to label it." His lips twitched. "But should you give me a little background? If we're supposedly together for the night, they might think we know something about each other."

She pursed her lips again. An age-old habit she'd shared with her dad. When her dad was sorting through something, he'd always push his lips together, twist them side to side. Her mom would see and pop over to kiss him. Said he was asking for it. Lexi flattened her lips.

"Hmm. Okay. Fast five. I'm twenty-five, a former track star, current waitress slash Dress Hut manager. I've worked there since high school so I've come a long way, baby. I live in Astrid Park and my favorite color is amaranth."

"You made that last thing up."

She held up two fingers. "Scout's honor."

His brows lowered. How could eyebrows be sexy? "You definitely weren't a Scout."

She laughed. "It's a shade of reddish pink. It's unique and beautiful. Your turn."

"Fine. But only because we'll draw attention if we don't go in soon. Thirty. Played varsity basketball. I'm the financial officer at my work. Worked my way up since high school so we have that in common. What color would you say Lay's potato chips are? That's my favorite color."

Letting out a snort-laugh embarrassed her but he didn't seem to mind. "That should cover it. What else could real couples possibly know about each other?"

He grinned before they walked side by side, the backs of their fingers brushing, to the door. "I can't think of anything."

His easy acquiescence and humor dulled some of her nerves. Will used the brass knocker, which was nestled in the middle of an oversized wreath with a variety of leaves in different shades of red, yellow, and orange. Little acorns and pinecones were tucked into the foliage. Within seconds, Jackie opened the door. She wore a pale-blue silk top with a strand of pearls around her neck. Her hair was up in an elegant chignon and her linen pants, like Will's jeans, showed not one wrinkle. *This is what perfection looks like.*

Before Lexi could dwell too much on that, a tall, dark-haired, dark-skinned man came to Jackie's side. His eyes were a different brown than Will's. If she were poetic, she'd call them dreamy. And his smile? Those straight white teeth, the easy curve of his lips, he could be a mouth model. Was that a thing? Great. Not enough that Jackie O was beautiful, well off, and successful, but she was marrying a movie-star-handsome man with shoulders wide enough to block the doorway.

Jackie squealed. "You came!"

Will nudged her forward by touching his hand to the small of her back, and instead of focusing on how all of her nerve endings suddenly moved beneath his palm, she listened to his smooth reply. "Of course. We appreciated the invite."

Not a slouch in the looks department himself and quick with responses, her not-a-date date surprised her again with his ability to roll with what Lexi threw at him. She wasn't looking for a picket fence and babies but there was a lot of room to play between whatever tonight was and that destination.

"Honey, this is my high school bestie, Lexi, and her sweet fiancé, Will."

Will's and Lexi's gazes locked. It was a toss-up whose eyes went wider. *That escalated quickly.* She bit her lip, her brain tumbling with responses. When she shrugged, he mimicked her and increased the pressure of his hand on her back, heightening her awareness of him even as the touch calmed her heart rate. Weird.

"This is *my* fiancé, Nigel. Please, come in. Lexi, you didn't have to bring anything."

They stepped back, revealing a gorgeous curved staircase in the center of the chandelier-lit foyer. Laughter and conversation floated from the back of the house. The scent of cinnamon and vanilla wafted in the air like the music that played softly.

"It's really nice to meet you both," Nigel said, shaking Will's hand then Lexi's before taking the bottle from her. He didn't even glance at the label, which was probably a good thing.

A nervous kind of energy vibrated over her skin. She recognized it from her track days. Before meets, her body had buzzed in exhilaration. She loved that feeling. Craved it. Now she wasn't entirely sure what to do with it. How to channel it. Or how to ignore it.

Jackie went to a table nestled into the curve of the stairs, picked up two small envelopes, and brought them over. Before she could give them to Will and Lexi, Will pulled an envelope from his back pocket.

"A little something for the two of you," he said with the same ease and polish as the man who'd gotten her out of a tricky situation today. He was well practiced and though she had no reason to doubt him, it made her wonder how he'd attained such . . . skills. *CFO of a company. Probably not his first time with "situations" or events.*

Lexi noticed the With This Ring logo and her wine suddenly seemed much cheaper. That was a hip boutique in downtown Seattle where only the most hoity of the toity registered. Nigel offered to take Will's jacket and Lexi's purse. They did that while Jackie set aside Will's gift and came back to stand in front of them.

"You didn't have to bring us anything. That was so generous of you both," Jackie said, leaning into Nigel's arm.

"Thanks, man. That's cool." He kissed the top of Jackie's head, careful not to disturb her hair.

Lexi started to say it was from just Will because she didn't deserve credit but Jackie shook her envelopes.

"We have a little something for each of you." Jackie passed one to each of them, and sweat started to pool in uncomfortable places on Lexi's body. She didn't love spur-of-the-moment surprises.

What on earth could they have for them? It'd been a while since she went to a party, but she didn't remember gifts for showing up being a thing.

"It's a game. We wrote the names of famous and influential people, alive and dead, on labels inside. Put them on each other's back but don't look at your own. Everyone gives clues until you figure out who you are."

She said it so excitedly that Lexi felt bad for her internal groan. Couldn't they just gossip over cheese dip? The last game she'd played was Trash with Bitsy and her friends during a slow spell at the dress shop. She'd lost. Dramatically. Those women took their cards, regardless of the game, seriously.

Nigel must have mistaken her silence for misunderstanding. "You'll see once you get out to the party. It's an icebreaker. Get in there. Have fun. There's a great spread of food, music playing, and lots of wine."

Jackie's smile was contagious even if her enthusiasm for guessing games wasn't. Jackie gave a bouncy wave before she and Nigel mingled into the crowd. Will moved around Lexi, lifting her hair off the nape of her neck. His fingertips brushed her skin and she shivered involuntarily. The little hum in the back of her throat almost made an escape. She swallowed it down.

"I'll put it below your hair so it can be seen," he said, leaning down so his breath traveled over her ear.

Okay. Her not-date date was hot. Never mind forever and always. How about some here and now? It'd been a long time since she'd felt anything like the sensations Will caused with just a touch, a look, or a glance. She bit her bottom lip, hoping she wasn't sweating through her shirt.

When he smoothed the label over her back, she did her best to ignore the tingles spreading down her legs and turned to do the same for him.

His back was wide and muscular beneath her fingers. She may have lingered over smoothing out his shirt before unsticking the label and pressing it to his back. It said MICHELLE OBAMA, which made Lexi smile even as she spent more time than needed making sure it was secure.

When he turned to face her, he was grinning. "It's been a long time since I went to a party with games."

"We used to do game nights when I was younger but it's been a while for me, too." She cleared her throat when her mind wandered. "Are you a sore winner or sore loser?"

Will took her hand as they walked down a somewhat narrow hallway where people didn't seem to mind stopping and chatting, essentially creating a maze of bodies. Clearly, his hold was to keep them from being separated, so she didn't pull away but she was definitely very aware. When they reached the end of the hallway, he dropped her hand, but her awareness lingered. "Both. You?"

For a minute she'd forgotten what they were talking about because she was struck by how nice it'd felt to have his hand surrounding hers and the heat between their palms. There wasn't a lot of hand holding in casual hookups. Not that she'd had one in a long time. And not that this was one. Which was why it felt strange. It'd felt comfortable and a little *too* enjoyable.

"The only game I really play is Trash. It's a card game and I'm positive my boss, Bitsy, cheats. She's old enough to be my grandmother and if you call her on it, she gives you puppy eyes. It's like saying no to an aging hound dog."

When Will laughed, it felt, oddly, like a win of its own. She glanced his way. His gaze met hers and he smiled. A boyish grin that made her forget she hadn't wanted to come. One that made her pulse speed up.

The hallway opened to a gleaming white and stainless-steel kitchen. There were dozens of people, each with a sticker on their back. Will and Lexi were surrounded by all of history. Everyone from Cleopatra to Elton John was either in the kitchen or spilling out onto the lantern-lit patio. She didn't recognize some of the names and she recognized none of the faces. The table was filled with food and a gorgeous centerpiece that looked similar to the wreath on the door. Leaves and foliage were interwoven with the dishes along the ivory-colored table runner as well as artfully placed wide, low candles.

Will stepped closer, and Lexi told herself that the way her breath and heart both hiccuped when he was close enough to smell his faint cologne was just science. *Yup. Even though you've felt attraction before and it's never felt quite like this, it's just basic science. Science and something a little woodsy and warm. Something you wouldn't mind leaning into and inhaling deeply. Nothing to worry about.* Lust wasn't a concern. It was just love she planned to avoid.

"This is interesting," he whispered, his breath tickling her ear.

"So much for showing up and being myself," she muttered.

He laughed. "Look at it this way, now you can be whoever you want."

That definitely held some appeal. She looked up at him. "Who am I?"

Will shook his head. "No way. I'm not spoiling the fun. But I will tell you that you're very neighborly."

She scrunched her brows. "What?"

He chuckled, then stepped closer when someone passed behind him.

Heat flushed over her skin. She wanted to press into him and forget about everything else. When he dipped his head, she lost her breath. *Not a date. Not a date. Not a date.* But oh . . .

"And you pull off a cardigan like no other."

Now, why did that sound sexy? Will. She'd bet that Will saying anything—describing the weather, reading a grocery list, citing facts—would be sexy.

She poked him in the chest. "Two can play at this game. I can tell *you*, you're an incredible woman."

He frowned. "I'm a woman? That's it? That's not a clue."

Lexi smirked. "An incredible woman who impacted the world for a lot more than eight years."

"Hmm. Maybe this is harder than I thought," he said, facing the patio doors.

Lexi couldn't help but stare at his profile thinking the exact opposite.

Seven

Jackie, Becca, her boyfriend, Lena, her wife, and a couple of other nameless faces formed a half circle around Will and Lexi. Music pumped through the speakers outside while the space heaters glowed orange, making the crispness of the evening air tolerable. The stars wouldn't show themselves for a bit but the lanterns cast twinkling lights all around them.

"Jackie said you two are engaged as well. Tell us how you met," Lena said, her voice soft. She glanced pointedly at Lexi, then added, "Were you two *neighbors?*"

Lexi was stuck on the clue but also sidetracked by how quickly Jackie had passed that little bit of gossip through the crowd. Lena's wife, Amelia, gestured to her wife as she spoke to Lexi. "She's giving you a clue but we still want to know the story."

Lexi looked up at Will, eyes wide as her mind scrambled for something believable. And how was "neighbor" a clue? *Famous neighbors?* All that came to mind was *Friends*, which she and her mom frequently watched old episodes of.

Little creases formed at the corners of Will's dark, expressive eyes. Only the slightest twitch of his eyebrows revealed his uncertainty at how to respond. He smiled at her, their arms brushing casually. A nothing touch that felt like a hell of a lot at the moment. Her mom might have been right about getting out more. If every whisper of a touch set her skin alight, she was spending too much time alone. Or maybe it was just her—he didn't seem affected by their casual touches. From the little he said, he spent a lot more time socializing at functions like this than she did. Her socialization tended to come from apologizing to customers in between making them laugh, texting with her bestie, convincing seventy-year-old women that any age was a good age to wear what you wanted, or working in small, online groups for her class. She was too tired to do more at the end of most days so it surprised her to feel somewhat energized in this setting even if the low-key anxiety never fully faded.

All eyes were on her, including Will's.

His fingers brushed hers; maybe an accident, maybe a show of support. Maybe a reminder to say something so people would stop staring at them. She was starting to when he linked their hands together, lifted them, and pressed his lips to the back of her hand. Her lungs filled but didn't empty out. Her breath froze in her chest painfully. It was one of those things long-term couples did without thinking because it was part of who they were. That simple kiss reminded her it'd been a hell of a long time—too long—since she'd gotten lost in a man, felt the pressure of his mouth on hers, his body against hers, skin to skin. The gentle press of *Will's* lips to *Lexi's* skin felt like fireworks dancing in little bursts of light up and down her arms.

Will's arched brows suggested he had some insight into where her brain had wandered but was also waiting for her to fill in the blanks.

How had they met? She took her hand back and looked at the group. "It's a funny story, actually. We were both seated at the same table in a restaurant. The hostess mixed up and thought we were together even though we were both alone."

Jackie's eyes widened as Nigel came up and wrapped his arms around her from behind. "That's so adorable," she said, looking back and forth between Will and Lexi.

Lexi nodded in agreement. It was somewhere in the vicinity of the truth. "A classic meet cute." Just because she didn't gush over romance books or build little scenes out of them like her mom didn't mean she was completely unaware.

"A what?" Nigel asked.

Lexi grinned. "When two people meet and it's cute and the start of their story, it's called a meet cute. Sorry. My mom reads more romance novels than anyone I've ever met so I'm familiar."

"An apt term," Will said, taking a sip of his beer.

"Speaking of," Becca said, her voice soft, especially in the crowd of partygoers, "I'm so sorry about your dad. How is your mom?"

Before Lexi could answer or swallow the lump that immediately lodged in her throat, Jackie reached out, squeezed her arm.

"Me too. I'm sorry we couldn't come to the funeral."

Lexi hated the uncomfortable looks, the mood shift, and the piece of her heart that still felt so goddamn fragile.

She felt Will's solid presence more acutely than she had seconds before, like he'd stepped closer when he heard. She didn't look at him, knowing, though not knowing why, that if she did she'd lose her weak grasp on composure.

Instead she smiled, nodded her head. "Thank you. I understand. You were at Stanford. That's a far way to travel and it was honestly so unexpected."

Becca stepped closer to Lexi and she realized that these two women were genuinely sorry for her loss and not being there. Lexi forgot that at one time, she'd had a wide support system and it wasn't entirely their fault it disappeared.

"I don't think it makes it easier even if you see it coming. Is your mom doing okay? I spend most of my day online and I have to say, your social media is seriously lacking, girl." Becca added the last part in a teasing tone that lifted the mood again.

Lexi laughed as Becca had clearly meant for her to do. What did she do all day? Hang out with sassy geriatrics who thought spandex was a cure-all? Spend her evenings with a woman who preferred romance books to reality?

Stories weren't her thing but it didn't mean she couldn't spin one. "I work a lot. It took time to sort through my father's business before making the decision to sell it." She placed a hand on Will's chest, moving into his side, looking up at him through lowered lashes. "And of course, I spend time with this guy."

Will's lips quirked but like a perfect date-not-date-boyfriend-turned-fiancé, he kissed her forehead and smiled at the others. He was *really* good at playing pretend.

Argh. Forehead kisses. A definite weakness in her shield. Before anyone could ask for more details, she switched the focus. "What about you? Book deal, social media guru. I'm terrible at social media. I can't see people wanting to know what I ate for lunch or how my cat is doing. Not that I have a cat." *Smooth. Really smooth.*

"I just love seeing what other people are up to. I started out sharing my own journey of ups and downs, dating, finding clothing that suited me, getting caught in ruts, you know? After graduating with my psych degree, I wasn't sure about doing my master's and started playing around and voilà." Becca laughed and lifted both hands, palms up. "I started gaining followers, sharing more specific content. I did a series of posts last year under the hashtag MakingItLookEasy. A couple of local brands asked me to be an ambassador and it snowballed. Now I write for different online outlets just as a guest contributor, doing the social media gig while working on my book. Honestly, I just love the whole vibe. All of it. I could scroll through profiles for hours," Becca said, leaning into her boyfriend in a casual, enviable way.

"You *do* scroll for hours," he said affectionately.

"And she makes more than me doing it," Jackie said with a laugh.

Becca tilted her head to the side, arching her brows at Jackie. "Please. This from the woman who runs her own art gallery downtown?"

Jackie preened a little, looked up at Nigel. "Where I met this guy who was outfitting his new condo."

They continued to share their stories, their successes, and though Lexi liked hearing that they'd all made it out okay, it was another reminder that when the chips had fallen, she'd left them there in a big pile on the floor. She'd been too busy trying to hold it together to pick them up and move forward.

"Hey, let's get a post-high-school group shot," Becca said, turning her phone and pulling the six of them together.

Jackie shook her head but got right in there. "Make sure you tag us all."

Nigel and Jackie were in the middle, Darcy and Becca on one side, with Lexi and Will on the other. Will was on the end, his arm moving around Lexi's shoulder when he leaned down a bit. "You okay?"

She nodded, not trusting herself to speak. Once the picture was taken, more jokes and laughter were shared, and Lexi waited for her moment to announce she needed a drink. Instead of heading toward the selection in the kitchen, she found the small bathroom down the hallway, closed herself in, and leaned on the door.

Because she was better at avoiding things than facing them, she pulled her phone out to check on her mom and saw Maisie had messaged. Opening the text, she saw the gorgeous photos her friend sent of the wedding venue she was working. Maisie Smart was an amazing photographer. And a kick-ass best friend who would give her shit for hiding in the bathroom instead of enjoying the party, the people, and the exceptionally hot and sweet guy she'd somehow ended up here with.

Maisie

This wedding is incredible. They released doves. Actual doves.

Lexi smiled, typed back:

> As opposed to fake ones? Plastic ones? Those would probably fall flat.

Maisie

> Hey. Home now, curled into my couch with a good book. How's the party, funny girl?

Of course, she'd quickly updated her bestie on the events of the day. Lexi sighed, looked up at the ceiling before answering.

> Will is like a made-for-TV date. He's perfect. My old friends are successful, happily in love, and doing great.

Maisie

> I want a picture of Will.

Lexi snorted.

> NO.

Maisie

> Picture or it's not real

Lexi could hear the music and laughter through the door. It didn't feel real anyway. For her, none of this was. Just a weird sidestep the universe thought she should take to remind her that she hadn't lived up to her full potential.

Putting her phone back in her pocket, she went back to the party through the kitchen, intending to grab that drink.

She found Will by the food, putting tiny little pastries on his plate. His gaze brightened, flickering like the candles, when he saw her coming toward him. A warmth pooled low in her belly. She very much didn't want to be charmed by this man, but she wasn't superhuman.

"Why do they make these so tiny?" He asked it quietly, almost conspiratorially. He held the pastry between his thumb and forefinger. "Do you think anyone eats a couple of these and then says they're full?"

Lexi laughed. She was here having some sort of quarter-life crisis and he was contemplating hors d'oeuvres.

"Maybe so you don't feel bad trying some of everything? You know, overeating is an issue here in the States and you're a very strong advocate for healthy eating and lifestyles. You even worked it into legislation." She took one of the pastries he had on his plate and popped it into her mouth while he contemplated her clue.

He pointed at her, then himself. "Am I Michelle Obama?"

Lexi nodded, surprised by how excited and happy it made her for him to have guessed on her clue. Proof she needed to throw a little more fun into her daily routine. "You are. Now tell me who I am."

She turned and let him see her back just in case he'd forgotten. Her breath hitched when he stepped into her, his hand on her hip.

"No cheating, Lexi." The way he said her name sent shivers through her but he stepped back before she could move away (or worse, completely into him).

She turned around slowly, hoping her expression didn't give away her thoughts. They stared at each other a moment, their gazes locked like some sort of staring contest where whoever looks away first likes the other more. When he looked at her, everything around them blurred and he became her entire focus. Ironic since that was the very reason she avoided relationships.

She grabbed another one of those little pastries, popped it in her mouth. Couldn't say too much if your mouth was full. She chewed, pretty sure it was quiche. The tiniest quiche ever.

"By the way, I bet you my younger sister could rival your mom for romance reads and romcom movie marathons."

Happy to focus on something other than the attraction making her skin feel too tight, she finished her food. "Oh yeah? Do you watch them with her?"

He laughed. "I do." He winced like he was embarrassed. "I totally knew what a meet cute was."

Laughter burst from her chest, surprising her with its intensity; it nearly felt foreign, but damn it felt good.

"We do weekly movie nights and she gets to pick. She says it's because women don't have enough power in our business and this is her way of exercising it, but really, she's just bossy."

"I think I'd like her. One sister?"

They wandered away from the table, finding a little corner to chat.

"Two. I'm in the middle. You?" He leaned against the frame of the archway leading to what looked like an office.

"Only."

"I'm sorry about your dad."

Lexi looked down. "Long time ago now." Long enough for her and her mom to have moved on. She forced a smile when she met his eyes again. "I was twenty-two. Finishing school."

"On a track scholarship," he said, his gaze never leaving hers.

"I used to be great," she said in a teasing voice.

"I think you still are."

Before her insides could flutter from the sincerity of his tone, he asked, "How fast are we talking?"

She stood straighter. "National champion. My last two-hundred meter was twenty-three seconds."

"Holy shit," he said, pushing off the wall.

Little flickers of pride she'd forgotten existed inside her flared to life. "Long time ago."

"You still run?"

Had he moved closer? "No."

Music floated through the patio doors, something up-tempo with a heavy amount of bass. Or maybe that was her heartbeat.

His fingers brushed hers. "It's been a while?"

She nodded slowly. Running. They were talking about running.

"Do you miss it?"

She hadn't thought much about running or its absence from her life but she realized that yes, she really did. "I do."

He nodded decisively. "If I can beat you at a race, you go out with me on a date-date."

She grinned. "What, like now?"

He shrugged.

"You are an intriguing man, Will." That was putting it mildly, but she didn't want to acknowledge all of the other adjectives running around in her head, never mind admit them out loud.

The air grew thick between them, and for a minute Lexi thought about what it would be like to find her other half. To have a person to hang on to, share stories with, end the day with. Maybe not everyone got that. She could be one of the ones who didn't. Then she thought about how her mother ended every day since she'd lost her person. Being alone didn't seem so bad. But neither was this. Maybe life offered something in between.

Eight

Cocktail parties, get-togethers, and social engagements were part of the job in Will's family. Sometimes they attended as a whole group, sometimes a couple of them, depending on the event and the guests. Will wasn't thrilled to admit he was the unofficial "face" of Grand Babies. He'd argued that it didn't seem right for the finance guy to be the face guy. But he was single, not in school, the same age as many of the people attending. He'd lost that battle.

Which was usually okay because he didn't have a ton of hobbies. He worked, liked to read, swim, and watch sports or reality television. Having to socialize a bit got him out of the house. As long as his mother didn't pull her matchmaker card, which she'd done more than once, he was good with things as they were. But this evening hadn't been like any of those *show your face, shake some hands* events. Tonight was a fucking blast.

Lexi was funny and thoughtful, beautiful and humble. Smart and a little sheltered, like she'd kept the world at bay. She didn't spend most of her day on social media; she hadn't immediately asked him to follow her on any platforms. Though she tried to guard her expressions and responses, her eyes spoke like pages of beautiful literature. She was amazing.

Their conversation on running got sidetracked when Jackie brought out cake and Lexi nervously declared that she never said no to cake. He'd keep that in mind. Though they chatted with others, getting caught up in a few conversations, they kept finding quiet pockets of time and space with just the two of them, and Will liked those moments best.

They'd found an area of the patio where the music was softer, the lights dimmer. He was listening to her words but also captivated by watching her mouth move. The hazy glow of the moon washed over them, adding a shimmer to her gaze.

Will was doing his very best to focus on every word she said but the more time he spent with her, the more he wanted to kiss her. Touch her. Of all the things he'd expected when he sat down at the restaurant today, this was not one of them.

Will leaned in and Lexi's speech faltered, her chest lifting with a deep inhale.

"Are you listening?" The curve of her lips hinted that she knew he'd lost the thread of their conversation.

Reaching out, he trailed his hand up her arm slowly, watching her reaction, holding her gaze to make sure she wasn't uncomfortable. When she stepped into him, he sucked in a sharp breath, intoxicated by her perfume. Or maybe it was her body wash.

She tapped his chest with her index finger. "A good fiancé listens."

Will let out a low laugh, his fingers trailing over her shoulder, up to the spot where her neck and shoulder met. He pushed his hand into her hair, cupping the back of her head, nearly freezing when her tongue darted out to lick her lips.

"Sometimes even the best fiancés get distracted." He shifted closer, the music, the lights, and the people fading away.

Lexi put one hand on his hip, the other flat on his chest. He wondered if she could feel his heartbeat. It felt like his heart was trying to fist-bump her palm. Cool air rushed over his skin but he felt overheated.

"Your hair is the softest thing I've ever felt," he said. Clearly his brain was short-circuiting because he wasn't even sure if that was a compliment. It was, however, the truth. And he wanted to bury his face in it.

When she pulled her bottom lip between her teeth, he almost groaned out loud. Desire hummed through him, sharp and strong, nearly knocking the breath out of him.

Glasses clinked in the background, noises filtering in the night air. Chatter, laughter, melodious music that seemed to amplify the electric energy between them.

"Thank you," she whispered.

Their mouths moved closer, barely brushing against each other like a phantom caress. Because he wanted to savor everything about her, he kept a bit of space between them. Just enough for him to speak and her to feel his words.

"When I saw you today, it was all piled on your head. Little tendrils were trying to escape. It was sexy."

She huffed out a breath he felt everywhere. "Sure."

His free hand moved to her cheek, his thumb stroking along her jaw. "I wondered what it felt like. What it would look like, tumbled around your shoulders."

Lexi's breathing turned choppy, short, sharp little bursts. "Then you thought, maybe I shouldn't order soup?"

He laughed, aware of the way she tried to deflect compliments. He smiled, his face coming closer, his thumb stroking her cheek in a mesmerizing back-and-forth. "Maybe. But I also thought you were beautiful and focused. Determined."

Her fingers flexed against his chest. "Clumsy."

Will shook his head. No. He wouldn't let her see only that. He hated that she did. She was a hell of a lot more. People milled around; he didn't know anyone so he didn't really care but he didn't want to make her uncomfortable. He started to step back, just to give her some air, but her fingers curled into his shirt, keeping him close, making him grin.

He pressed a kiss to the corner of her mouth, enjoyed her hiss of air. She tried to turn her head to meet his lips but he pulled back, touched the tip of his nose to hers, moving up to press a kiss to her forehead.

"Not clumsy. Determined. Strong. Fucking beautiful and completely unaware of it."

The hand in her hair slipped down her back, over the curve of her hip. He used it to pull her against his body but he had a feeling that with Lexi, close wouldn't be enough. And that was something he could say he'd truly never felt or thought about a woman before. She dropped her forehead to his chest with a small thud.

She groaned, soft but audible. "This reminds me of what running feels like."

He leaned back, forcing her head to leave his chest. "What? How's that? Clearly, I've been doing running wrong."

Lifting her head, she held him captive with those expressive eyes. "I'm no expert anymore but this slow burn? The buildup?"

Her fingers danced up his neck, along his nape, and he shivered. Actually fucking shivered.

The proof that she felt it was in her sultry smirk. "Your blood warms up, your muscles relax, your limbs loosen up." She pressed herself closer. "You get in the zone. There's nowhere else you want to be. Then it starts to get really good. Your blood starts rushing so hard you can feel your heartbeat everywhere in your body."

Holy fuck.

"Jell-O shots," someone behind him hollered.

He and Lexi kept staring at each other, their breath seesawing back and forth across the small distance between them.

She stepped back as more people crowded the patio. Someone came around with a platter of mini cups filled with orange and green Jell-O.

A tall redhead in sky-high heels and a body-molding black dress stopped beside them, holding out the tray. "Take one and pass it around."

Lexi shook her head. "No thanks. Love your dress. It's gorgeous."

The woman smiled, met Will's gaze. There was something familiar about her but he couldn't place her.

"How about you, handsome?" She moved the tray closer to him.

He frowned. He was very clearly *with* Lexi. Sure, no one knew the dynamic between them, but it was impossible not to see the chemistry firing around their little bubble. Jesus, he could *feel* it.

"No. Thank you."

"You look so familiar," she said, tilting her head as if trying to place him. She took one of the shots, downed it, set the cup on the tray, and passed it to the next person.

Lexi stiffened even as she fidgeted with the hem of her sweater. He felt her discomfort as if it were his own.

"I must have one of those faces," he said, hoping she'd move on to another group. Though, to be polite, they should really rejoin the party. *Or you could go somewhere with just the two of you.*

The woman set her gaze on Lexi, smiled. "Turn around. Let's see who you two are."

"I'm Michelle Obama," Will said, hoping his voice didn't sound rude or dismissive. He'd recycled his card.

Lexi turned around and though the redhead glanced at her back, her focus went back to Will almost immediately. The interest in her eyes made him reach out, grasp Lexi's hand as soon as she spun around.

"Hints?" Lexi asked, squeezing his hand.

"I'm not surprised you wouldn't have a Jell-O shot. You're very wholesome. I *am* surprised you aren't singing 'Won't You Be My Neighbor.'"

Whether she realized it or not, Lexi moved closer to Will, maybe recognizing this woman's too-obvious interest in him. It made him smile and want to hug her close. He was no stranger to being hit on.

He'd done an interview a few months ago in the *Seattle Times*, talking about working at his family's company, being a bachelor in a busy city, and what being a wealthy man meant to him. It was supposed to be flattering. His mother had been thrilled by the recognition, but Will felt . . . exposed. He could talk business all day, to anyone. But that didn't feel like the tone of the article. More than one woman had brought it up since at various social functions.

Lexi's arm shot out and for one brief nanosecond Will thought she was going to punch the woman out of jealousy. The thought was so ridiculous he snort-laughed.

At that same moment, Lexi loudly proclaimed, "I'm Mr. Rogers!"

The group of people on the patio cheered. Lexi laughed.

"Yes! I give great clues. Nice to meet you, *Mr. Rogers*. I'm Carolyn." She turned to Will. "I'm positive I know you from somewhere. I'm good with faces and yours is great."

Lexi's brows rose, her nose scrunching. It was such a genuine response he almost laughed out loud. Instead he squeezed her hand.

"Not sure what to say. I'm Will, if that helps. And this is my *fiancée*, Lexi."

Lexi side-eyed him with a half smirk. Will bumped her with his hip, slipping an arm around her shoulder.

She turned her head and looked at him, the amusement in her gaze shining brighter than the moon.

Looking back at Carolyn, she gave a little wave. "Nice to meet you."

Right. Enough of this. "We should get going, honey," Will said, hoping his beseeching look would hammer the plea home.

Lexi bit her lip, then nodded and put an arm around his waist so they fit together like interlocking puzzle pieces. "Yes. Yes, we really should. Good night, Carolyn."

Lexi turned them, maneuvering them around Carolyn and a few other guests, right through the kitchen, down the hallway, and to the closet to grab his coat and Lexi's purse. By some unspoken agreement, they kept going, walking right out the door. It wasn't until they were back close to her car that they stopped. They looked at each other and both released pent-up laughter.

"Wow. Let me just say, as a waitress, I get hit on frequently and some of it is pretty unpleasant but I didn't know that happened to guys too."

"Not usually so blatantly but when it does, it doesn't feel great. I hate the thought of you feeling uncomfortable when you're working."

She turned to face him, setting her hands on his chest again like that was where they belonged. He put his hands on top of hers, holding them there.

"Do you think that's the only place it happens?"

He frowned. "I'm not naive, and I have two sisters and a sister-in-law. I hate that it happens at all. To anyone. But I appreciate you playing along."

Her lips lifted in a soft smile that twisted something in his chest almost pleasantly. Like when he got a massage and it hurt a bit but it also felt great.

"You saved me," he said quietly, his tone playful.

"Now we're even. *Honey.*"

God, he liked her. When was the last time he'd laughed and had this much fun? Felt this good?

"Lexi," he said, his heart beating loud in his ears. "Go out with me again. On an actual date. Just the two of us."

Her gaze moved down. "I don't know, Will."

With one finger, he lifted her chin. "I like you. It feels like it's mutual."

In a swift move, she went up on her tiptoes, pushed her arms around his neck. His went around her waist, his hands resting on her lower back.

"It's definitely mutual. I just don't know if it's wise."

Before he could list the reasons it would be smart for both of them, she muttered, "Neither is this."

Then she pressed her mouth against his, her lips soft and sweet, not one hint of their earlier teasing in the move. His arms tightened around her as she angled her head, pressing closer. Will groaned, one hand sweeping up her back, into her hair as they learned the shape and feel of each other. When her tongue touched his, he couldn't hold back the low growl that left his throat. She didn't seem to mind, tangling her fingers in his hair, tugging a bit as they held tighter.

Gentle presses, demanding ones, their mouths moved apart and together over and over until he thought he'd actually lose his breath. Kissing her was better than having oxygen.

When she pulled back, lowered herself to the ground, Will's brain was foggy.

"Jesus Christ. You cannot deny we have chemistry."

Lexi reached up, ran her thumb over his bottom lip. He took her wrist, kissed her palm, then held her hand.

"No. I can't. And I won't. But I'm not sure there's room for this in my life, Will."

He hated the hint of sadness in her tone. "Room for what? Fun?"

She smiled but it didn't reach her eyes. "You. You're not just fun. You're sweet, sexy, and smart."

"So far I see no reason not to date me."

She laughed even as she moved back. "I'll think about it. Thank you for tonight."

"Trust me," he said, hating that they were saying goodbye. "It was my pleasure."

She opened her door, got in, and looked up at him through lowered lashes. "I'm very glad I sat down at your table."

When she pulled away, he stared after her car a minute before heading to his own.

"You and me both, Lexi," he said to himself as he got in. "You and me both."

Seattle Times

ENTERTAINMENT

Top Stories

- "Barbie" sequel in the works?
- Rock and roll memorabilia donated to Museum of Pop Culture
- Seattle's own Grand Babies bachelor off the market?
- Pike Place hosting special holiday visitors this year

Nine

If Will didn't find a way to wipe the wide-ass grin off his face in the time it took to walk from his parking spot to the boardroom, everyone in his family—his sisters in particular—was going to be all over him about the source of it. He'd had such a good time with Lexi. She made him laugh, in person and through messages. They'd texted throughout the day on Sunday, just going back and forth about random things. He liked talking to her and definitely liked looking at her. She was real, sweet with an edge that was wrapped in a hint of vulnerability. He wanted to know more.

But right now, he needed to get to the Monday meeting. His phone buzzed again. If he weren't waiting on Lexi to text back about taking her out to dinner, he'd have silenced it. News outlets were calling, which was a concern. Will didn't have much to do with the downtown Seattle socialite scene unless it was to build connections in the community or for work—it'd never been his thing.

Drinking and hanging out with other people his age who only knew each other because all their parents had money wasn't his idea of fun. Since discussions of a merger had begun with Home Needs, the CEO's immature and impulsive son, Nolan Banner, had been calling him nonstop for advice on "living in the limelight under so much pressure." Will scoffed. The guy spent more time drinking than he did in the boardroom and if Will was honest, Nolan was the real source of his reluctance to keep moving forward with the merger.

The two had been photographed a few weeks ago outside a downtown nightclub. Nolan had asked Will to meet him there because he needed some advice. Will had tried to befriend the guy but they just didn't connect. The guy was an ass.

Most likely, Nolan had gotten himself into some trouble over the weekend and wanted Will's suggestions on how to keep it under the rug. Which he clearly hadn't done himself if the news outlets, who'd gotten wind of the merger, were calling Will.

Danielle, his secretary, smiled at him as the elevator doors slid open on the third floor of the building where the offices were housed. Floors one and two were the store, three the offices, and the fourth was his grandparents' penthouse.

"Good morning," Danielle said, picking up the to-go cup from his favorite café and holding it out to him. "Seems like someone had a good weekend."

Will winced. Shit. If even his secretary noticed his aura of Lexi-induced happiness, he was going to have to work harder.

"I did. How was yours?" He wasn't sure why she was staring at him with a smirk.

"Not as good as yours. Everyone is waiting on you. Your mother is in a mood."

Will laughed, thanked her, and took his coffee. If anything could sour his own mood . . .

Sure enough, his entire family was sitting around the large, custom-made walnut table that resembled the dining table in his grandparents' home. His older sister, Madeline, sat next to Kyra on the far right. His mother and father sat on the long side of the table, closest to the wall of windows. His grandfather, who usually sat at the head, on the far left of the room, was standing by the window looking out at the view of the harbor.

All eyes turned his way and Will's muscles clenched, his jaw tightening. What the hell was going on? If Home Needs was pushing on the contract again, he was going to suggest they walk away. Will had their lawyers going through the terms and he wouldn't be rushed. They weren't the only option.

Everyone spoke at once, inundating him and confusing him more.

"What the hell, William?" his father boomed as Madeline and Kyra let out actual whoops of "Congratulations!" His mother shook her head while telling him to close the door so the world didn't hear about their drama. The only drama he could see was right in front of him.

"Good morning," his grandfather said in his typically smooth voice, now leaning against the window ledge, an unusual glint in his astute gaze.

Will closed the door. "What is happening?" His phone buzzed again. He tossed his messenger bag on the table, pulled his phone from his pocket, and set it on top. "What's going on?" He looked to his grandfather, who was always the quickest source of accurate information.

"We should be asking you that question. Though it doesn't need a lot of explaining, I suppose. I knew immediately with your grandmother. One dance and I was done. No one else would ever do. Took a little longer to convince her but for me, I just knew. I didn't even know you were dating someone."

What? How do you know now? Will stared at the man whom he'd idolized growing up, continuing to wonder what the actual fu—

His father stood up quickly, knocking his chair back. "You didn't think this was something you should tell us?"

Will looked to Kyra, wondering if she'd spilled about his date. She just looked back with an almost giddy grin on her face, Maddie beside her with a nearly identical expression.

"I repeat, what is going on?" Will raised his voice slightly, gripping the back of the chair in front of him.

His mother stood, her dark hair pulled into a tight bun that made her angular face seem sharper. "What's going on? We're trying to figure out why our only son would ask a woman no one knows to marry him when he says he's too focused on work to even show up for a date with the *respectable* women from families we *know* that I've kindly tried to arrange."

Dates, marry, respectable. What. The. Fuck? He looked back at the door, wondering if he'd maybe walked into some bizarre alternate reality, then back at his siblings.

"Please tell me what's happening. Am I being pranked?"

Maddie slid her always present iPad across the table. Will glanced down to see the entertainment page of the *Seattle Times*. He scanned it, trying to see what would be there that would explain his family's behavior. *Holy shit.*

SEATTLE'S OWN GRAND BABIES BACHELOR OFF THE MARKET?

Will's mouth went dry. He clicked the link, his brain and body buzzing like they were gearing up for fight or flight.

Rumor has it that the speculated merger between two Seattle founded companies isn't the only merger happening for the Grand family

William Grand, CFO and grandson of Jeremy Grand, the founder of Grand Babies, two locally owned and operated baby product stores, is said to be engaged. The hard-to-reach-for-comment bachelor was seen at a party in the Seattle Heights area to celebrate the pending nuptials of former pro football player Nigel Warrington (click here to read about Warrington's retirement and move from New York to Seattle) and local art gallery owner Jacqueline O'Dell. Grand is pictured below with the happy couple, along with author and social media presence Becca Kramer, her date, and one Alexandria Danby, an otherwise unknown who partygoing sources revealed was introduced as his fiancée. Dubbed one of Seattle's finest bachelors, William has been seen

around town as of late with Nolan Banner, whose father owns
another locally started company, Home Needs. While the two have
a few things in common, the friendship has come as a surprise
(<u>click here</u> to see a timeline of Nolan Banner's troubled early adult
years). No one in the Grand family could be reached for comment.

Will stopped reading. The picture was the one Becca had taken, and there were links to other articles and probably whatever Becca had posted on social media. Holy shit. Holy shit. He lifted his head, met the gazes of his family, all looking at him with varying degrees of surprise. Except Kyra. She looked like she was holding back delighted laughter.

"This is not the sort of thing you keep from your family, William. Your mother has been getting calls all morning from news outlets asking for a statement," his father said, running a hand through his wavy salt-and-pepper hair as he stalked back and forth along the bank of windows, stepping around his own father to do so.

"I just can't believe you'd ask a woman none of us know to *marry* you. Are you trying to get back at us for something?" His mother's expression was tortured, and Will's stomach twisted.

"Fredrick Banner called early this morning," his grandfather added. "I didn't answer but I'm sure he's thrilled as it's likely this news will push his son's weekend of debauchery under the radar."

Maddie stood up, came around the table. "I don't know what's going on with you. The news was shocking but if you're happy, I'm happy." She rubbed his shoulder in support.

Kyra came around and hugged his arm tightly. "When you know, you know." The tease in her tone, and their close relationship, told him she knew something was off. And she was enjoying it way too much.

His grandfather rubbed the weathered skin of his chin while Will's dad continued to pace and his mother typed something on her phone.

"I suppose we can spin this, highlight our dedication to family.

What do we know about this woman? Alexandria Danby. She looks attractive but I can't find any information about her. She has no social media," his mother said, not looking up. "I'll keep digging. No one has to know you care so little for your family that you couldn't even be bothered to introduce us to the woman you're going to spend your life with."

Will groaned. He needed out of here. He needed to sort through this disaster. Holy shit. He needed to talk to Lexi. Had she seen this?

"I have to go." Will picked up his phone and his bag.

His mother's head snapped up. The dark eyes she'd passed on to him narrowed. "You can't leave us with this media nightmare. When are we meeting this woman?"

"What? You're not going anywhere," his father said at the same time.

"Let him go, Jackson. Maybe all this badgering is why he didn't tell us," his grandfather said.

"Everyone says no comment until I have more time to look into this woman's past," his mother said, setting her phone down with a look of utter disappointment and a dash of hurt. "Really, William. I hope you know what you're doing."

Leaving. That's what he was doing. He walked out and wasn't one bit surprised when his sisters followed him to his own office.

Maddie shut the door behind them after they'd gone through. Kyra flopped down on the leather couch that sat along the wall.

"That must have been one hell of a first date," Kyra said, kicking off her high heels.

Will bit back a snarl. "Don't you have classes?"

Kyra grinned. "Not until this afternoon."

Maddie put her hands on her hips. "First date? Excuse me? What's going on?"

Will told them as quickly as he could that it was all a big misunderstanding. That Carolyn—who he realized later had been in some of the photos his mother had shown him of possible dates—had likely called the fucking news outlet the second they left. The other option was that

Lexi's friend's post had caught the attention of either the *Times* or another outlet and it snowballed. Must have been a slow news day.

"Wait. You're *not* engaged?" Maddie stared at him.

The oldest of them, she was always well put together, well mannered, even tempered, and reliable. She held the position of chief operating officer at the company, ensuring everything ran smoothly among the departments and among the staff.

Their parents had high expectations of all of them and put a lot of pressure on Will but they often overlooked the amazing contributions his sister put in. She was a large part of why their company continued to thrive. At least their grandfather recognized it.

Will flopped onto his leather rolling chair. "No, I'm not fucking engaged. I can't even get a yes on a second date from this woman. Who I *really* like and *want* to go on a second date with. What am I going to do?" He leaned forward, put his head in his hands.

"You could call the paper. Ask them to print a retraction." Kyra sat up on the couch, losing the teasing smile.

Will sat back, looked up at the ceiling.

"If he does that, we don't control the narrative," Maddie said. "If he makes any statement, good or bad, they'll run with it. Even if it's retracted, it's already out there. I think we should ignore it."

"What about Mom and Dad? Should he tell them?" Kyra asked their sister, discussing his life like he wasn't in the room.

"If he tells them the whole truth, Mom will be all over him to make a splash with whichever woman she's got on her roster this week. Carolyn, most likely."

Will groaned and stood up. What were the chances Lexi hadn't seen this yet?

"I need to go. I'll be back this afternoon."

"Where are you going?" both of his sisters asked.

"To see my fiancée," he muttered, hoping like hell she wouldn't tell him to get lost. Hoping even more that she'd agree to a second date.

Ten

Lexi stared at the screen of her laptop, which sat on the counter next to the cash register at Dress Hut on Monday morning, trying to think of what else she could sell on Marketplace to come up with cash. Fortunately, and predictably, the store was quiet. Uploading a picture of some of her dad's tools she'd held on to, she posted a price and details. She had about ten tabs open at the moment while she jumped back and forth among course reading, updating the store website, practicing graphics on Canva (homework), and searching Marketplace. She'd purposely kept her phone under the counter, tucked into her purse. Will was more charming than she'd expected. Not that she'd expected anything. She wasn't opposed to dating even though her schedule was stuffed like an overweight suitcase, but she wasn't looking to get attached. Add his kissing skills to his humor and charm and that made him a dangerous distraction she didn't need.

She was wondering about a third job when her bestie, Maisie, strolled in like a welcome breeze. Her adorable jet-black hair, cropped just a bit shorter than a bob, peeked out under the blue knit cap she wore. With soft features, big brown eyes, and love of makeup, she had a *girl next door with an edge* vibe. Like a Disney princess gone rogue. In her hands was the very thing that was going to get Lexi through the rest of her shift: two large take-out drinks from her favorite coffee shop.

"Hey there, bestie," Maisie said as she strode over to where Lexi stood behind the counter. Her black wool jacket reminded Lexi that autumn in the Pacific Northwest could be unpredictable.

Lexi took the drink Maisie passed her with both hands, letting it warm her fingers. Bitsy, her boss, kept the temperature in the store low because she was always overheated. She popped in and out when she felt like it or when she wanted to use the back room to host card games for her gal pals, whom Maisie referred to as the Crazy Eights.

"You're a wonderful human being," Lexi said after her first sip of the vanilla chai latte with just a hint of cinnamon.

"As are you. Anything you want to share?" Maisie set her own drink down, removed her coat, picked the cup up again, took a sip, and eyed Lexi with a strange sparkle in her gaze.

Lexi frowned. Could her friend read her that well? She'd told her about the world-rocking kiss in detail. Even if she did feel a little perkier than usual today, Lexi didn't think Maisie was referring to her mood.

She shrugged. "Nothing good, honestly. Bitsy wants to close the store on Mondays because—" She stopped, glanced around at the empty store. "Obviously. So I called Brett to tell him I could now work any and every Monday, only Reese—that's the waitress he always gets to shadow my section—answered and said that she'd tell him and that was good news because get this: They're running a special now. Bring in a friend on Mondays for lunch and get half off your meal."

Maisie let out a sharp gasp. "That was your idea."

"Yup."

Setting her cup down, Maisie reached out, squeezed Lexi's arm, then leaned on the counter. "I'm sorry. That sucks but that job isn't forever. What else? Anything to *report*?"

Lexi's brows furrowed. She took a sip and shared the rest. "I just posted my dad's tools on Marketplace. If I can sell them all, I'll have enough to pay for the rest of this marketing class. Speaking of, I need to interview someone who works in the field for my final project. You know anyone?"

Other people were doing internships and making connections while attending classes but with Lexi doing her course online and part-time, she didn't have the same opportunity or advantage.

"We'll get back to that. What I'd really like to know is how one date to a party you didn't want to attend and one kiss—even if it was amazing—ends with you engaged to one of Seattle's finest bachelors. Especially since you, my lovable best friend who is supposed to spill every ounce of tea the second it's poured, are averse to such things as marriage and forever after."

Lexi set her cup down a bit more abruptly than she intended, grateful she hadn't been drinking when Maisie spoke. "What are you talking about?"

Shaking her head, Maisie pulled her phone out of her back pocket, tapping the screen. "I'm not sure if I want to be maid of honor or photographer. Maybe both. I'm a hell of a multitasker."

Maisie passed her phone for Lexi to read. If she were a cartoon, her eyes would have doubled in size and bounced out of their sockets.

When she looked up at Maisie, her friend was smiling so wide it looked unnatural. "What the hell happened at that party?"

Engaged . . . eligible bachelor . . . Seattle royalty . . . who is this nobody?

Lexi shook her head, words stuck in her throat as she clicked one of the links. It brought up Becca's Instagram, but since Lexi didn't have Instagram, she couldn't see the full post. Just the picture and part of the caption.

Going back to the previous article, she read aloud, "An anonymous source says that Alexandria Danby was introduced as William Grand's fiancée. For those of you not following Seattle's local gossip, the Grand family is well known in Washington not only for their strong family values and commitment to quality but for their generous work within multiple charity organizations. There has been a lot of speculation lately about William Grand and whom he's choosing to spend his time with. He's been spotted with Nolan Banner, the son of major chain store owner Fredrick Banner. This unlikely friendship— see Banner's history of trouble with the law here—may be one of many surprising connections William has formed lately. Who is Alexandria Danby and how did she hook one of Seattle's hottest men in business? (See *People* magazine, June 20, 2022.)"

The store felt like it was about a hundred degrees. Lexi continued to struggle to find words as she set the phone down, stripped off her cardigan, and picked up the phone again.

"You failed to mention a few things," Maisie said, a happy hum underlying her words.

"I don't." Lexi shook her head, the phone shaking in her grasp. "I can't. Holy shit. What's Grand Babies? Who is this guy?"

Like she'd summoned him or as if he had decided to answer her questions for himself, Will came striding through the door of the dress shop, looking very hot and very much out of place.

Maisie squealed with excitement, clapping her hands. "Yay. I get to meet the groom-to-be. Mm. The papers didn't lie. Excellent cheek-bones, great eyes. I look forward to photographing you both for your engagement pictures."

"Knock it off, Maisie."

Will's gaze was locked on Lexi. "Lexi."

Despite the chaos swirling in her head and her gut, she took a moment to drink him in. She hadn't imagined those gorgeous, intense eyes or the wide set of his shoulders. He looked like *GQ* personified in his dark suit, lightly pin-striped tie. His hair was a little mussed from the wind and she had vivid images of mussing it another way.

She kept her voice even, holding his gaze as she set Maisie's phone on the counter. "Mr. *Grand*."

He winced. "You saw the articles?"

"Articles?" As in more than one?

"I showed her," Maisie said with too much pride. She held out a hand, which Will shook as if this were a normal introduction. "I'm Maisie Smart. Her bestie and your worst nightmare if you hurt her. I'd ask your intentions but it seems a little late for that so why don't you two kids tell me what's going on."

Lexi wanted to laugh and tell her best friend to shut up in the same breath. Her heart was beating dangerously fast. Hadn't it just been cold in here?

Will's lips twitched as he dropped Maisie's hand and glanced at Lexi. "She's good. We could use her on our contract team."

Lexi picked up her drink, mostly to keep her hands busy. She wasn't well practiced at playing it cool. "This is one hell of a way to get a second date."

His cheeks flushed. "I'm so sorry."

He was sorry? She'd sat down with him, roped him into her drama. It was her friend who'd posted the photo. Though he'd failed to mention a few key things about himself. Not that she'd asked. CFO. *I'll say.*

Lexi set her drink down, inhaling slowly, purposefully, before exhaling. She moved around the counter. "I'm sure you can ask for a retraction." Just a little mix-up. No harm, no foul. Not for her, anyway. For him, it probably didn't look great to be linked to someone so . . . underwhelming. *Who is this nobody?*

"How did this happen?" Maisie asked, leaning against the front of the counter.

Lexi told her about the mix-up during introductions, the overeager redhead who'd needed a little diverting. Shit.

She looked at Will. "Wonder if our anonymous source was a certain redhead."

Will's lips tightened. "Carolyn. That was my guess too."

"You do make an adorable couple," Maisie said. "And as far as second dates go, getting engaged is unique."

Lexi glared at her. "Don't you have somewhere to be?"

She grinned back. "Hell no."

Will stepped closer to Lexi, dipped his head to give them the illusion of privacy. "Can we talk? Please."

"Will." She made the mistake of inhaling. The scent of his cologne and fresh air went to her head, made her think about the kiss.

"Lexi. Let me take you to dinner tonight. We need to talk."

"Wedding plans?" Maisie asked.

"I'm going to poison your latte, Maisie." Lexi didn't even turn around to threaten her friend, and she could see by his small smile that Will found it amusing. She liked the feel of his hand on hers too much so she pulled away. His proximity, his stare, and the way he smelled were all muddling her head.

"I don't think we need to have dinner to get a retraction. If anything, that might fuel the fire."

"Alexandria." One word, that dark gaze rooting her to the spot and making her wish she could let herself fall down the rabbit hole of love that so many craved.

She felt her resolve crumbling like brittle leaves. "I can't. My mom . . ."

"I'll hang with Gwen tonight," Maisie said. "I need to talk to her anyway."

Lexi turned. "What do you need to talk to my mom about?"

Maisie lifted her drink in one hand, waving away Lexi's concern with the other. "Gwen and I are friends. You two go out. Socializing two nights in a month is a new record for you."

Will let out a small laugh. "Best friend, huh?"

Lexi shook her head, met his gaze. "She used to be."

He took her hand again. "Please? Dinner. Drinks. Whatever you want. I really want to see you again. I know it's complicated but I . . ." He glanced at Maisie then back at her.

"Do," Maisie said in a stage whisper.

"Maisie!" Lexi turned to glare at her friend.

Her friend covered her mouth.

When Lexi turned back, Will looked like he was fighting a laugh. "Say yes. Please?"

She was almost positive Maisie gave a muffled *please* behind her.

Lexi took a deep breath. "Fine. Dinner."

Will's grin knocked the air out of her and she knew she should change her mind, tell him she couldn't.

"You won't be sorry," he said, leaning in to kiss her cheek.

The touch of his lips sent her brain tumbling again like it remembered, all too vividly, the way it felt to have his mouth on hers. It was intoxicating. *He* was intoxicating. Which made him dangerous.

"I'll pick you up," he said. "Text me your address."

He left as quickly as he'd come and Lexi stood there wondering how the hell she'd gotten herself into this mess.

"I have to say, your fiancé is fine as fu—"

"Shut it, Maisie."

Her friend laughed, wrapping her arms around Lexi's shoulders as they watched Will's fancy car pull away from the curb in front of the Dress Hut.

"Just go with it. It'll be fun. You could use some fun more than anyone I know. Besides, hot guy paying for dinner? What's the worst that could happen?"

Lexi leaned her head against Maisie's, staring out the wide window with the store logo on it that she should probably wash. She kept her thoughts to herself. A random hookup? Fine. A couple of dates? Okay. But a man who made her heart speed up just by standing in the same room? One who looked at her like she wasn't the mess she felt like on the inside? What was the worst that could happen? She could fall in love.

Her shoulders stiffened. No. She wouldn't. She was stronger than that.

Eleven

Will walked into Side Tap, the brewpub his friend Ethan Reynolds and Ethan's brother owned. They were in the process of opening another location and Will couldn't be happier for them. He hadn't seen the new location yet but this one, the flagship near the university campus, would always be Will's favorite.

Its high ceilings and wrought-iron light fixtures gave an air of urban class that meshed perfectly with the warmth of the dark wood bar, the aged-brick walls, and the variety of seating options. A couple of long farmhouse-style tables made it great for parties or even college kids meeting up to study during the affordable happy hour.

Like the restaurant where he'd met Lexi and many of the eateries around, it had an enclosed patio space, strung with twinkle lights and decked out with low fire tables. Ethan had built that long before it was necessary; it was often hard to get a seat. When the weather wasn't freezing or raining, the large grounds also offered a gorgeous outdoor seating area with picnic tables, canopied tents, and more twinkle lights for summer nights.

Smiling and nodding to the bartender and a couple of the waitresses he knew, he wove his way toward the back where he preferred to sit. He sent Lexi a quick text telling her where to find him, wishing she'd let him pick her up. He wasn't all that surprised when she'd messaged and said she'd drive herself.

Ethan walked out of the office down one of the hallways as Will spotted a seat. Will grinned when he saw his friend.

"Hey, man. How's it going?" Ethan tucked his phone away, ran a hand through his dark-blond hair.

They shook hands, exchanged the typical bro hug with a slap on each other's backs. Will waited, knowing what was coming.

Ethan put his hands on his hips. "What the hell? I'm hurt. I've been busy but you still could have told me the news."

Will shook his head. This was already becoming incredibly complicated. His mother had sent him a list of ways to spin the news in their favor. All he could think was if he really were getting married, if he'd found *the one* and wanted to spend his life with her, the last thing he'd worry about was his mother's fucking lists.

"It's complicated," Will said.

Ethan arched one brow. "Complicated as in not true? Or more the *you knocked her up* sort of complication?"

Will let out a half laugh, half growl. "Shut up, man. I absolutely did not."

"Am I the best man or is that a surprise, too? If you tell me it's that Nolan prick, we're done."

Will shook his head, made yet another split-second decision. "It was a misunderstanding that got out of hand and now my parents are losing their minds. But I like this woman and want to see where it could go. So, pretty much a PR fucking nightmare over a relationship that I don't want ruined before I get to know her."

Ethan's gaze widened. He huffed out a breath and clapped him on the shoulder. "Shit. Nothing is ever straightforward in your family. Mama Grand must be pissed about not getting to choose her daughter-in-law. You're right not to tell her the truth. Who is this woman? Are you meeting her here?" Ethan looked around.

"I only met her a couple of days ago and yes. I'm going to sit in the back."

They walked side by side to the area at the back of the room. Ethan said hello to customers on their way past the tables. Not far from the water or Seattle's downtown, the place gave out-of-towners a taste of what the locals loved—being close to the action without all the crowds.

Will followed his friend, taking the three steps up to the raised area. The seating up here was plush and comfortable, reminding Will of his father's study with high-back chairs and low tables arranged to encourage conversation. A large stone fireplace sat as a focal point, with framed pictures of Ethan, his family, and the staff on the wide raw-wood mantel. To the right of the fireplace, two deep-brown leather wingback chairs sat empty, facing each other. To the left, a group of six women laughed and chatted animatedly, three of them on a love seat, the others taking up the chairs.

"You two can join us," one of them, a blonde who looked close to Kyra's age, said.

The following giggles and suggestions made him feel older than his thirty years. Well practiced at flirting, Ethan winked at the table.

"Not this time, ladies, but enjoy yourselves."

Will shrugged off his thin leather jacket, hanging it on the little hook attached to the chair. When he sat, Ethan took the seat across from him, pulled his phone out, and frowned at the screen.

Looking up, he shook his head. "I have to deal with something. Give me the lowdown. Where'd you meet this chick?"

"Jesus, man. Grow up. Her name is Alexandria. Lexi. She's incredible. I met her at a restaurant. She was the waitress and . . ." There was no easy way to explain it. Will sighed. "It's complicated."

Ethan whistled. "Papers didn't say much about her. Your parents know she's a waitress?"

Will shook his head. Ethan knew how judgmental his parents could be about family backgrounds, education, and employment. It didn't matter to Will. "The chemistry is off the charts. Things got messed up in the news and now I'm just trying to get her to see I'm worth a second date. Honestly, I feel like I'm spinning out of my depth." He spoke low and fast because even though Ethan was busy, he was also Will's best friend and Will needed someone other than his sisters to know the truth.

"Wow. Listen to you. You really like her. Maybe things didn't get so messed up after all. Just because you didn't write it down first doesn't mean it's a bad idea."

Will didn't like how much his friend made him sound like his parents but he was able to shrug it off when he saw Alexandria weaving her way through the crowd.

"That's her," Will whispered, his heart rate speeding up. He waved at her, feeling like a fifteen-year-old with his first crush.

He met her at the stairs, leaned in to kiss her cheek, inhaling the sweet scent of her shampoo or body spray or whatever it was that made her smell so intoxicating.

"Hi."

She leaned back. "Hi. Is this a college bar? I think we're the oldest people here."

Will laughed. The only other people who made him laugh effortlessly were his siblings, his grandfather, and Ethan.

"I'm older than you so maybe I am but you aren't. It's a great place. My buddy owns it. Come meet him."

He heard the low groan under her breath and laughed again. When he took her hand, pleasure unfurled inside him. He recognized the punch of lust that hit him square in the gut—it'd been a while and he couldn't remember it ever being quite so sharp. However, the warmth and happiness that filled his chest, just from seeing her, were completely foreign to him.

"I had to meet your best friend," he reminded her, happy when she laughed. It was a great sound.

Will caught Lexi's glance toward the women, a couple of whom were watching them. Whether she realized it or not, Lexi moved closer to him, like she had the other night when Carolyn had been too friendly. It tripped something inside of him. Something protective and unfamiliar. He put an arm around her shoulders, all too aware of the way she fit so well against him. His pulse raced, anticipation humming over his skin. When was the last time a woman made his heart beat harder? Quicker? Made him so aware of everything he was feeling? Dangerous, he thought. And yet he couldn't stop himself.

"You look beautiful," he said before they reached Ethan.

"Thank you," she said, looking up at him. "So do you." She bit her lip. "Good, I mean. You look good. Really good."

Will bit back a laugh. "But not beautiful?"

Ethan grinned. "Throw him a bone. You're beautiful to me, Will."

Lexi and Ethan laughed, which made it impossible not to laugh along with them.

Ethan stood, held a hand out. "I'm Ethan. Owner of Side Tap, best friend to this guy. He was just telling me about you. Alexandria, right?"

She shook his hand. "Lexi is fine. This place is beautiful." She dropped her hand, looked around before meeting Ethan's gaze again. "My friend Maisie is a photographer. She loves architecture but mostly does people." Lexi's eyes widened. "Photographs people."

Ethan's bark of laughter made Will's shoulders relax. "I look forward to meeting her. With you two being engaged and all, she and I should probably connect." He gave an exaggerated eyebrow wiggle that probably charmed women.

Will glared at him. "Off limits."

Lexi laughed. "Great, glad the news is spreading."

He was a little surprised that she wasn't mad. Put off. But she seemed to be rolling with everything that had happened a hell of a lot better than he had. At least she'd agreed to a second date.

"I'll bring her by sometime."

Ethan's phone lit up in his hand, and his grin faded. "I wish I could stay and chat with you two, get to know you better, Lexi, and give you the dirt on Will."

Lexi laughed while Will frowned. "I'd like that, too."

Ethan held up his phone. "Unfortunately, I have a mess to deal with. But I'll send over our Fall Flight. It's our newest selection of IPAs to celebrate the season."

"Thanks. Everything okay?" Will asked, not liking the worry creasing his normally easygoing friend's eyes.

Ethan shook his head. "Trickier when family and business overlap."

Will gave a humorless laugh. "Don't I know it."

Saying goodbye, Will gestured to the seat, waited while Lexi removed her jacket and purse, hung them on the chair. He sat across from her. Her hair fell in soft waves around the shoulders of her cream-colored sweater. Like him, she wore jeans. Soft makeup and a slightly wary expression made her all the more intriguing.

"I hope your friend is okay. He seems nice."

Will settled back in his chair, trying to appear more at ease than he felt.

"He's a great guy. He and his brother own this place, and they're in the process of opening a second one in southern Washington. Not as far as it sounds—about an hour from here. I'm sure everything is fine. Nothing about starting a business is easy."

"That's what my degree is in, actually. Business administration with a focus on operations."

Will's jaw dropped. "Shit. You should have said that when he was standing here."

Lexi shook her head, her cheeks going pink. "Ha. I don't think he needs anything a mature college student in her final courses might have to offer."

Will leaned forward, rested his elbows on his knees. "Don't do that. Don't diminish how hard you're working or what you're working toward."

Her smile was small, her gaze unreadable. "Thank you."

The moment hummed between them. "Now, back to more important things. What's this about me not being beautiful?"

She leaned forward, glanced toward the women for a second, then reached across and took his hand, much as he'd done to her the other night. She lifted it and kissed it, met his gaze through lowered lashes.

"You know how good you look." She dropped his hand while it still tingled from the press of her lips and subtly hooked her thumb toward the table of women. "If not, they'll reassure you."

God, he liked her.

"I'm perfectly happy right here with my fiancée," he said.

What was it about this woman? He spent his life interacting with people in a business, personal, and social capacity. But this woman with her cautious gaze, her gorgeous smile, her unparalleled laugh made him think about things he hadn't given much thought to. Like what he really wanted. More, *who* he really wanted.

"Smooth. Speaking of that," she said, pausing when a waitress dropped off their flight. "We should talk."

He wanted to do a hell of a lot more than talk, but first, he needed to figure out how to get a third date. She was a complete surprise. Will didn't like surprises. He liked planning things out, knowing the path he was on, and making the decisions for himself. But everything about Alexandria Danby made him feel like he wasn't driving this vehicle. He was simply along for the ride. Instead of fighting it, he just wanted to see where it took them.

Twelve

It took effort to keep from fidgeting as Will looked at her across the small table. She wasn't even sure why she'd come, other than sorting out the whole engagement thing. And the fact that something about him—the way he looked at her like he really wanted to see her, the way he listened like what she said mattered—soothed and excited her at the same time. She liked him. There was a lot of space between alone and never falling in love. Perhaps she could dabble in the middle.

A waitress far more proficient than she was dropped off a selection of beers in small glasses. "Ethan said to send this over. Nice to see you, Will."

"You too," he said. "Thank you."

When she left, heading to the table full of women who'd checked out Will more than once, Lexi tried to figure out what to say, coming up blank.

To distract herself, she looked at the selection of four beers in varying shades of amber, like a liquid color palette designed especially for fall.

Lexi stared at the beers, picking up the little cards with their names. "I've never done a beer tasting."

Will leaned in. "I have but I haven't tried any of these. They're all new. Alexandria." Her full name on his lips slid over her skin delightfully.

She looked at him. "Can they print a retraction? An apology to your family?"

"I want to date you. I like you and would like to get to know you. We could go the retraction route but it'll make things more complicated when I convince you to keep seeing me."

She laughed, played with the little card in her hand that read: APPLE ORCHARD. "What if I came to break up with you?"

Will smiled, picked up the short glass, smelled it. "Ouch. I think you're honest enough with yourself to admit to both of us that you're interested."

He started to take a sip when she said, "Maybe I just want to sleep with you."

Coughing, he widened his eyes. Lexi felt a bit bad for blurting it out like that but he was right about being honest with both of them.

Amusement sparkled in his gaze, his eyes crinkling at the corners. "I think that would require a third date." He took another small sip.

When he set the glass down, she picked it up, smelled, watching him over the rim as he watched her, coughed a bit more.

"Hmm," she said, after a sip. "It actually tastes like apples."

Will cleared his throat. "Granny Smith."

She nodded, set it down. "Yeah. A little bitter but I like it." She smiled at him. "You okay?"

Heat underscored the amusement in his gaze. "I'm good."

"How did your family take the engagement?" She picked up the next glass, the scent of citrus and cinnamon mingling together in a welcoming mixture.

"Shock, irritation, amusement, support, and skepticism. That would be in order of person. Mom, dad, grandfather, younger sister, older sister."

"Wow. That's a lot of people. Did you tell them it was a mistake?"

He shook his head. "My sisters know. And your friend. And now, Ethan." He leaned forward, touched his hand to her arm. "I'm sorry about this. I truly am. But I'm not sorry I met you or that I'm spending time with you."

He was so sincere. It tugged at places in her heart she thought she'd closed off. "It's likely Becca's post was the start of it so I should be apologizing to you. She sent a text today apologizing that she shared without making sure I didn't mind first." His thumb stroked over the sensitive skin of her inner wrist. She startled and the beer sloshed over the rim. She set the glass down, licked her fingers, and became all too aware of Will watching her.

Heat blazed between their locked gazes. Lexi looked away first. "Maybe I should ask for the retraction and make an apology statement." She sipped the beer. "This one has cinnamon. It makes it too spicy. Less natural." She passed it to Will, their fingers touching. Her body shouldn't feel all shimmery from a touch.

"You have nothing to apologize for," Will said.

"Uh, sat down at your table, dragged you to a party, fake engagement news. There might be a few things."

A waitress stopped by their table with a large platter of appetizers. Her bright smile and ease holding the huge dish made Lexi want to ask for pointers. "Ethan thought you might be hungry so he ordered you a Side Tap Platter." She set it down with plates and napkins, glancing at Will. "Congratulations on the engagement."

Will gave a tight smile so Lexi thanked her. "I really love your top," Lexi said.

It was a cute T-shirt with a cartoon graphic of an apple tree, an apple in the midst of tumbling down while saying I'M FALLING FOR YOU.

The woman smiled. "Thank you! We actually sell them at the bar. They're really comfy."

When she walked away, Lexi smirked at him. "I don't think most of the women who say congratulations to you will mean it but she might have."

Will set the beer down. "I'm only looking at one woman right now and I have a proposal."

Lexi arched her brows and laughed. "Another one?"

He chuckled but she could see from the set of his shoulders, the line of his jaw, that he was nervous or tense about what he was going to ask.

"Go out with me," he said.

She leaned in. "I *am* out with you."

Will shook his head. The delectable scent of fried foods—cheese sticks, wings, onion rings, chicken fingers—wafted between them, complementing the harvest smells from the beer.

"Most of my family thinks we're engaged. Lots of others think we're engaged. I want to date you. I had more fun with you the other night than I can remember having in a long time. Letting the news of the engagement just die out rather than denying it would get my mother to stop foisting women on me."

She wondered what kind of woman his mother thought suited him. She was pretty sure she wouldn't be on such a list. "Aw, poor Will."

He flushed. "Sorry. I don't mean it like that. I just . . . Lexi, you're the first woman I've met who I can't block out. I don't want to. I think you're sexy as hell, you're funny and sweet. I want to get to know you. I know the engagement thing puts an awkward spin on it but it doesn't change the fact that there's something between us."

Lexi sipped the apple beer. She liked that one. "My mom *has* been nagging me to get out more."

Will pointed to himself, passed her a side plate. "Built-in date, right here."

Putting a couple of wings, a chicken finger, and some of the fries on a mini plate, Lexi considered his suggestion. She liked him. She liked him a lot and wanted to sleep with him. Most of her life was spent just trying to get through, get to the next step, or figure out the one she was on. Would it be so awful to date Will under the guise of a fake engagement for a bit? Just see where it went? He'd obviously move on and marry someone his mother chose but didn't she deserve a bit of fun? Maybe if she went out more, her mother would too.

Will pointed a fry at her before popping it in his mouth. "You're thinking about it."

"You're a hard man to say no to, Will. But you have to know, on paper, and *in the papers*, we're not a great match."

He frowned, added a couple of chicken wings to his plate. "Why's that?"

"Tell me about the women your mother sets you up with."

Instead, he ate one of the wings so Lexi did the same. Her nerves were erratic but there was something simple and comfortable about sitting across from him, sharing food and beer.

He set his plate down, wiped his hands on a napkin. "I get that you're not like them, Lexi, and I won't lie and say that isn't part of the appeal. But the truth is, I just like you. We can print a retraction and I'll still ask you to go on a third date."

The thought sent warmth through her chest, down to her stomach. "If we date under the guise of engagement, what happens when it ends?"

Will was quiet. He tossed his napkin on his plate. "Let's talk about what happens next and not think about the end."

Needing to avoid the intensity of his gaze, she picked up the pumpkin spice beer, smelling it before letting the flavor notes sit on her tongue. "Kind of like pumpkin pie." She took another sip. "I'm not overly fussy about beer. Not really a wine drinker. I do love a good margarita, though."

He grinned, his eyes still serious. "Good to know. We could have ordered one of those."

She smiled back, hoping it hid her nerves. "Nah. Margaritas need chips and salsa, maybe some tacos. We have wings and mozza sticks. Beer is a better match."

When they'd snacked a little, finished most of the beers, she wiped her hands and set them on her lap. If she really wanted to have some no-strings-attached (at least not real ones) fun, she wanted to do it with a clear conscience and as much of the truth between them as she could.

"Why would you want to date a woman who is floundering? I looked you up so I'm sure your family and you have done the same. There's not much to go off, but I can fill in the blanks. I'm three classes short of a degree, I work the same job I did in high school, I have a second job I'm not great at yet and am considering a third. Today I put my dad's tools on Marketplace, probably for less than they're worth. I hated doing it but I know he'd want me to finish my degree and I can't pay for it otherwise." He started to speak and she held up a hand. "Don't even try offering anything—I can see it in your face. I don't need charity. My mom has shut down since my dad died. I'm having a harder time getting her out of the house. She spends all day reading romance novels or making little miniatures of scenes she's read. Don't get me wrong; they're incredible. She's truly talented but it's another way to block out the world. She ignores the fact that the house needs repairs and won't talk about selling it. That's me, Will. That's who I am. What about that is appealing?"

In a move that surprised her all the way down to her toes, he stood up, pulled her to her feet, took her seat, and pulled her down onto his lap. Not that she didn't go willingly but that didn't mean he hadn't shocked the hell out of her. Or that she didn't *really* like it a lot more than she should. One of his arms wrapped around her waist and he took her hand in his, settled them both on her lap.

"You. You're what's appealing about all of this. The way you talk, the way you brush off compliments but give them freely. The way your hair curls around your face and your eyes light up when you're speaking about something you care about. The fact that you didn't care who I was or what my last name was when you stepped closer to me the other night after you realized Carolyn's interest made me uncomfortable. When you talk about your parents, your tone changes, gets sad, and it makes my heart hurt. There's a lot to like, Lexi. Don't sell yourself short. You're a beautiful, funny, caring woman with a work ethic I admire."

He trailed a finger over her hand. "And I've never had a kiss knock me on my ass the way yours did, if I'm being honest."

Lexi felt like her insides were trembling. She put her hand to his cheek, rubbed the barely there stubble, letting it rasp under her thumb.

"You're a very strange man, Will Grand. I like you back and can promise absolutely nothing. This will probably end badly. Mostly for you because no one knows who I am." Her hand moved down, her fingers trailing along the neckline of his shirt, making his eyes go impossibly dark. "But I'm in if you are."

They moved in tandem, his hand coming up to cup the back of her neck, her head dipping to meet him halfway. The second their lips touched, her other hand went to his neck and she pulled him in closer, falling into the kiss in a way she hadn't known was possible. Life changed in seconds. She'd forgotten some of them could be good.

His mouth moved over hers like he knew exactly how to kiss her to drive her crazy, like he knew how long it'd been since she'd been kissed or touched this way. The answer was never. Never like this. The slant of his mouth, the pressure of his hand moving down over her back, urging her closer, his tongue touching hers, retreating, touching again. Teasing and tormenting in the most delicious way she'd ever experienced. What the hell had she been doing all those other times if just kissing could be like this?

Time spun out and she was drowning in a completely new way. A way she was happy to sink down into. His other hand cupped her cheek with a softness that contradicted the ferocious feelings inside of her. Lexi gave him back everything she had. Apparently, she'd been storing up, waiting for this moment, with this man.

He pulled back, whispered her name, a plea full of reverence as his fingers journeyed, brushing over her face. She'd lost so much, and in this moment, it felt like he'd found her.

His lips traced over her cheek, along her jaw, his teeth nipping at the spot where her shoulder met her neck, then soothing the sting with his tongue. His mouth came back to hers, deepening the kiss and softening it at the same time so it became almost leisurely. Seductive, decadently sweet and slow. When he pulled back again, she was grateful the high-back chair and its position pointing away from others kept this moment between only them. Lexi's breath was as unsteady as Will's and both of their gazes were hooded.

"Jesus Christ," Will whispered.

"I'll say." It took effort to form words, to think of anything but kissing him again. She really wanted to kiss him again. And again.

Will pressed a kiss to the tip of her nose and Lexi closed her eyes, hoping this moment stayed with her no matter what lay ahead. He whispered her name again so she opened her eyes, stared into his.

"I'm in."

Thirteen

She couldn't call him a unicorn because, let's face it, unicorns were majestic and pretty. Will was neither of those things. He was rugged, in a refined sort of way. Sexy, handsome, and kind. Genuine and funny. He'd kissed the life back into her, walked her to her car, and made plans with her for the weekend.

He wasn't pretty but he might just be a unicorn. Lexi's body still buzzed like it was infused with static electricity. She couldn't imagine what it would be like if they actually slept together. Which she definitely wanted to do. Maybe should have suggested it for tonight. If they made it physical, maybe she could focus on that piece and lock down the pesky emotions wanting to surface. She could do this. Date him, have some fun, and put her life back together. As she drove, she passed her old high school track. Without meaning to, she pulled over, got out of the car. Walking onto the grassy hill, she stood there staring down at the ovals that had once ruled her life. Determined it. Shaped it. Defined it.

She sat on the grass, thinking about where she thought she'd be right now. Twenty-five, almost twenty-six, she never thought she'd be living at home. Though the strange thing was, if her dad hadn't died, she wouldn't have found out about his debt, wouldn't have been able to save the house. At this point, she wasn't sure it was a good thing she had. But her mom loved the connection to him.

Lexi pictured herself running this track, hanging out on the bleachers with friends, amping some up, talking others down. A smile ghosted her lips. She'd had a race the weekend her dad died. Obviously, she never ran it but she didn't realize until this moment that she hadn't run since. Will was the first thing to make her feel alive since she'd given up running, something she hadn't really intended to do. Lexi stood up, brushed off her butt, and walked back to her car. As she drove, she reminded herself that Will wouldn't always be there. But running could be. And tomorrow morning, she was going to let it back into her life.

Charged with pent-up energy from Will, gratitude for her friend, and worry for her mom—she definitely shouldn't tell her about the engagement but she'd be happy Lexi had a "boyfriend"—her body and brain felt like they were spinning in two different directions. Her phone buzzed with incoming texts but she ignored them, too antsy to focus. Letting herself into the house, she forced deep, slow breaths. Maisie would see through her in seconds, but Lexi wanted to at least attempt the appearance of chill.

When she arrived at the top of the stairs, the first thing she saw was her mom curled up, as usual, in the dark-gray recliner they'd had as long as Lexi could remember. A worn but cozy flannel throw was tucked around her lower half. Alexa Martin's *Better Than Fiction* was open on her chest, the back flap fluttering with Gwen's exhales.

"Hey," Maisie said, coming in from the kitchen with a mug between her palms.

"Hey, yourself. Thank you for this." Lexi wasn't sure why but a small part of her felt like crying. Her eyes even watered.

"How was it?"

Gwen stirred so Lexi took the book, set a bookmark in it, and put it on the side table. When she turned back, Maisie was grinning like an overeager kid. Lexi was pretty sure that if her friend weren't holding a hot drink, she'd be bouncing.

"Was it good? Was it amazing? Did your bones melt? When's the wedding?"

A laugh-snort escaped Lexi as she walked past her friend to the kitchen. "We didn't do anything. Well, we kissed." Damn, they'd kissed. That alone was better than anything she'd experienced in years.

The water was still warm in the kettle so Lexi thought about the details of her evening while she made herself a cup of decaf tea.

"Start with the good stuff," Maisie said when Lexi was quiet.

"He wants to date me so he doesn't think there's any point in refuting the engagement. In fact, he said it'll keep his family from bugging him." She turned, leaned against the counter, smiling when she saw Maisie eyeing her expectantly. "The kissing. Good God, I felt like I could combust from that alone. Kissing him is better than anything I've ever experienced. He wants to go out this weekend. I honestly don't know if I can handle more." *But I want to.*

Maisie waggled her eyebrows. "Oh, you can handle it. I love that he's pushing you out of your little scaredy-pants cave."

"Hey!" Lexi turned back, added an extra helping of sugar to her mug.

"Hey, nothing. Excuses are fine if the guy isn't worth it but your fiancé sounds amazing. Completely worth it."

Lexi shushed her friend, turning to make sure her mother was still asleep. The engagement shouldn't impact anything in her life. Her mother didn't go online for any reason other than to order books and was unlikely to find out. Why complicate things further?

Her phone buzzed again with an incoming text and like her heart was already trained to respond, it squeezed tightly at the thought of it being Will.

"Is it him?" Maisie tried to peek as soon as Lexi pulled her phone from her pocket.

Lexi laughed. They were older but maybe there were still pieces of high school girls inside of them. Which could explain why she sighed in disappointment when it turned out to be Brett asking if she could pick up an extra shift the following week. She also noted Jackie and Becca had started a group chat, insisting the three of them needed to get together again soon and asking if she was having an engagement party and wasn't it just fate and good luck that had them all together again?

Lexi typed out a quick "let me check my schedule" that she hoped would suffice for her friends. Then she said yes to Brett and slipped her phone back in her pocket.

She settled into the stool beside her friend, who had already sat, with her tea. "I really like him, Maisie. His family isn't happy about things but he doesn't seem to mind that. His best friend is a cutie. You should see his pub. We'll have to go sometime."

Maisie nudged Lexi's shoulder with her own. "We will. How cute are we talking?"

Lexi laughed. "Let's not complicate this further. I should have walked away. My first interaction with Will was a disaster, so we're starting from a foundation of misunderstandings. I've got another paper due in three days that I haven't started, I'm not getting better at waitressing, I'm so tired of working at the Dress Hut. I'm tired of this house, of running on empty." She heaved out a large sigh, exhausted by herself and her list of complaints.

Maisie put a hand on Lexi's back, rubbing slow, soothing circles. Lexi had to stop herself from purring like a cat. "You need something stronger than tea. Like an entire night with Will. Like you said, it won't impact you much except you'll be dating a gorgeous, funny man, getting out of this house a bit. Maybe it'll remind you that you're young and deserve good things. I know you're tired but it's because you're so close to the finish line."

Dig deeper.

"I know you're already busy but I could use a hand with a job this weekend. Just for a few hours. It's an engagement shoot out by Lake Union. I'll pay you what I'd pay my assistant, and that combined with the tools should cover the rest of your tuition."

Lexi picked up her tea. "I don't want you paying for my stuff."

"Don't be an idiot, Lexi. I'm paying you to do a job I pay someone to do. I need help; you need money."

She had considered a third job. She was being silly. Her friend wasn't giving her charity and so what if she needed a little help? That's what she told herself, but it still made her feel heavy.

"Can you pay me in advance?"

Maisie laughed. "You're doing better than you think. You won't work at either of those jobs forever. I know you're tired. Give yourself this. You like him. You know he likes you. See where it goes."

Setting her tea down, she leaned her head on Maisie's shoulder. "Sorry. You're a good friend."

"I know. So I'm going to add a little more happiness to your day."

Lexi lifted her head. "What is it?"

"Gwen is really talented."

Lexi smiled, gave a half laugh. "She's getting really good at the figures and the scenes, isn't she? When I'm restless, I go in there and stare at them."

Maisie nodded, her smile widening. "So good I'd like to hire her to create a cake topper for one of my clients. She was talking about not being able to find exactly what she wants."

A strange sense of pride and a small kernel of hope stirred inside of Lexi. "Really?"

"Really. Gwen's got a great eye and her details are exquisite. When I brought it up, she seemed really excited. She started throwing out ideas, almost talking to herself like she could see it in her head."

The thought made Lexi happy.

"It'd be good for both of you to have more to look forward to. To see outside of this grief funnel she's in."

Nodding, Lexi stared at the wall. *Grief funnel.* That was a good term for it. "I'm going to go for a run tomorrow. Maybe I'll see if she'll go for a walk."

"I talked to her about counseling too."

Lexi sucked in a sharp breath. When she brought up counseling, Gwen's body went rigid and she typically walked out of the room. According to her mom, talking to someone wouldn't fix a broken heart.

"When I bring up therapy, she says she's not crazy, just broken."

"Therapy is for everyone. Broken, glued back together, sagging in the middle, whatever. Your mom used to love socializing. She's a people person at heart. More than you are." Maisie poked her in the ribs and Lexi knew she was aiming to lighten the mood.

A little prickle of pain rippled through Lexi's heart. "She was. Now I can barely get her to go to the grocery store." Swallowing down her sadness, she gave her friend the truth. "I can't afford therapy for her."

Maisie gave her a soft smile, hopped off her stool, and disappeared, only to return a minute later with a brochure. "One of my new clients is hosting a grand opening for her clinic. I did all the photos for the brochures and the interior. She's a therapist and they have all these programs for people in need. As a widow, your mom counts and can have access to a few sessions on her own before they recommend free group sessions in the community."

Lexi took the pamphlet, opened it. Her mom had sunk into a deep depression after her dad died. She'd come out of it bit by painstakingly slow bit. But she'd never fully recovered. How did anyone when they'd lost a piece of themselves? Lexi loved her dad and missed him every day but her mom and dad were more than a married couple. They were soul mates. Best friends. Each other's everything. And when you lost *everything*, what were you left with?

"Thanks," Lexi said, closing the pamphlet, a lump forming in her throat.

"It's worth a try."

The words echoed in Lexi's ears, seeming to resonate over every aspect of her life right now. Worth trying.

"Tell me more about your man. I should do engagement photos. His family will likely expect it."

Lexi slid off her stool, picked up their cups. "No thank you. He's not my man. Definitely no photos."

"If you attend events with him, people will photograph you."

She considered that. "That's different than setting up photos. How about I go on another date with him and see if there's really something there and not just a bunch of lust wrapped up in misunderstandings?"

Maisie bit her lip, and Lexi could see she was measuring her words.

"I think you're more like your mom than you want to be," Maisie said quietly.

Lexi's hand froze on the dishwasher handle. "How do you mean?"

"Aside from the obvious stubbornness, you're a romantic at heart. You don't want to be. You'll fight it with everything in you, but the reason Will scares you so much is because you know you could fall the way your parents did. You have so much love to give and you're so afraid to let it go. To not get it in return."

Lexi covered her emotions by focusing on her task and avoiding eye contact. "Maybe you should be my mom's therapist."

"Nah. I'm too busy with you."

After a few more minutes of chatting, Lexi walked her friend to the door, hugged her hard, and said good night.

Upstairs, she pulled the blanket from her mom, nudged her awake softly.

As her eyelids fluttered open, Gwen's soft, sleepy smile faded.

"Hey, Mom," Lexi whispered.

"Hi, honey." Gwen sat up. "Did you have a good night?"

"I really did. He's really nice. He's funny and smart."

Gwen's smile turned genuine, no hint of shadows in her gaze. "Someone's got a crush."

As much as it pained her to admit it, Lexi nodded.

Gwen clasped her hands together against her chest. "Oh, that's the very best part. The beginning before you even know who you'll be together."

Definitely a romantic. Her mom, not her.

As she walked her mom to her room, Gwen stopped, gave her a hug. "I'm glad you're seeing someone. You deserve to be happy, honey."

Lexi's eyes burned with tears. She hated that. Blinking rapidly, she hugged her back, whispered, "So do you. Maisie says she's commissioning you for a cake topper."

"Yes. She described the couple's relationship to me, showed me a picture. I think I can do it." Even half awake, excitement laced her tone.

"I know you can. It's a great project for you, and you'll make money doing something you love. Mom, Maisie told me about the therapist. You could probably consult with her on Zoom. I'm asking you to try. Maisie thinks she'd be a good fit for you."

Gwen pulled back her covers, crawled in, saying nothing.

Lexi leaned on the doorjamb. "I'm going to start running again. I didn't realize but I haven't done it since Dad died."

Gwen rested against the headboard. "That can't be true."

"It is."

"But you love running."

Lexi nodded. "We're stuck, Mom. I hate how you're feeling but I can't fix it and you can't fix it so we need to learn how to move forward. Not just exist."

Her mother tilted her head, staring at her, and for a flash it felt like the old Gwen looking at her, assessing her. In high school, she'd never gotten away with a thing. Her mother had never been harsh but she'd been honest and perceptive and told Lexi the truth even when she didn't want to hear it. It was her turn to give that back to her mom.

She continued. "You need help. You're young and beautiful and I miss him too but he wouldn't want this for you. This ache you carry around like a lead balloon."

"When do you see Will again?"

"Never mind Will."

A small smile lifted Gwen's lips as she scooted down in the bed. "I'd like to meet him. You'd like me to talk to someone. Seems like a pretty fair trade."

Lexi's jaw dropped. "You can't use your mental health as a bargaining chip in my dating life, Mom."

Gwen smiled. Honest to God smiled. "Oh, honey. I'm a mom. We can use whatever we have in our bag of tricks."

Shaking her head, Lexi leaned in, gave her mom a hug. "You'll meet him this weekend. You're booking that appointment."

"Yes, *Mom*."

Walking to her own room, she changed for bed. As she crawled between her cold sheets, she realized that today had given her a lot of reasons to smile. Maybe things were finally starting to look up.

Maybe there was life after high school and heartbreak.

Seattle Times
ENTERTAINMENT

- Nolan Banner, son of Home Needs CEO, and former actress arrested over the weekend
- UW offers lineup of student-directed short films
- Theatre Under the Stars back for another fall season

Fourteen

Just because they'd been texting each day, several times a day, for several days in a row, didn't mean she was becoming reliant on him. She liked texting him. So what? She liked texting Maisie. Hell, she *loved* her best friend and that didn't scare her at all. There was nothing wrong with being attracted to someone and wanting to see them again. That didn't equate to an *I'd die without you* type of passion. Even if she couldn't think of Will and the word *passion* without coming up with some pretty detailed scenarios. She burrowed into her pillow, awkwardly yanking on her own hair. Repositioning herself, she smiled at her phone screen. She could hear Gwen puttering in the room next to her but told herself that if working on those miniature scenes calmed her mom, then where was the harm?

Lexi

You should go to sleep. Don't you have math meetings early?

The Man You Share Everything With

Math meetings?

Lexi

The F in CFO is for Finance, correct?

The Man You Share Everything With

Correct

Lexi

And Finance is math. I'm
in university. I know things.

The Man You Share Everything With

Do you know you make me laugh?

Lexi

Which is all me because I'm not
taking any classes in humor.

The Man You Share Everything With

It'd be a waste of money.
You don't need it.

Lexi

Full circle: don't you need to sleep?

The Man You Share Everything With

There's a woman on my mind,
keeping me awake

Her heart tripped. Stupid heart. *You're not in charge here, Heart. Go back to sleep. This game is strictly for the libido.*

Lexi

She's trying to let you sleep

The Man You Share Everything With

What are you doing tomorrow night?

Lexi

My social life being what it is, I'll be doing one of any of the following: homework, housework, watching reruns of shows I've seen too many times.

The Man You Share Everything With

Would you have time to stop by Cordero's? It's a small wine bar near the university.

Lexi

You doing a wine tasting?

The Man You Share Everything With

I have a meeting with someone. He's bringing his wife. I thought maybe I could bring my fiancée.

Why did that make her smile?

Lexi

And so it begins 😉

The Man You Share Everything With

I don't want to pressure you

Lexi frowned at the screen. It'd be a lie to say she didn't want to see him.

Lexi

What time?

The Man You Share Everything With

7. I could do something for you in return

Lexi

It's not a trade-off. It won't suck to see your face

The Man You Share Everything With

That's a hell of a compliment

Lexi

Don't let it go to your head

The Man You Share Everything With

Hard not to. How's the homework coming?

Lexi

> Still waiting for Maisie to let me know if she has any contacts who could help me out with my marketing interview.

Had she ever had a relationship like this? If that's what this, in fact, was? It was weird to be in a place where she had all those tingles and stomach spins from the *get to know you* stage while also being linked to this man, on paper, as so much more. He was easy to talk to, fun to flirt with, and God, was he easy to dream about.

The Man You Share Everything With

> See! I can do something for you. Interview me

Lexi

> You really need to look up your job description. You're not in marketing

The Man You Share Everything With

> We own the company. All of us are part of everything. 😁

Lexi

> Really?

The Man You Share Everything With

> I'd never lie to my fiancée

Lexi

> I think you like saying that

The Man You Share Everything With

> More than I expected. Get your questions
> ready. After wine and a bit of conversation,
> you can ask me anything

Lexi

> Enticing. About marketing?

The Man You Share Everything With

> Anything

———

She'd worried about being overdressed for the Dress Hut in the flowy, knee-length black skirt she'd paired with a dark-green blouse, but as she walked into Cordero's, she realized her mistake. She should have worried about being *underdressed* for the wine bar. Low lighting, high-top tables, and clean, sleek lines shouted elegance in an understated way. Lexi smiled at the hostess even as she spotted Will over near the bar.

"Good evening. Do you have a reservation?" The hostess, dressed in a sparkly black tank top, tight black jeans, and mile-high heels that made her tower over Lexi, looked like a runway model.

"She's with me," Will said, walking toward her, his gaze fixed on hers, an appreciative gleam shimmering there.

His words and the way he said them sent a shot of adrenaline through her system. She was with him. For now. As long as she remembered the *for now* and *for fun* part, she'd be okay.

"Of course. When the rest of your party is here, we'll seat you, Mr. Grand."

Will took her hand, leaned down to kiss her cheek. She turned her head, brushing his lips, relaxing when he hissed out a breath, slipped one arm around her waist.

"You look amazing."

She smiled up at him, running her hand down the silver tie on top of his crisp white dress shirt. "You look beautiful."

He tipped his head back and laughed. Lexi's heart and stomach danced around, giddy with the kind of joy she didn't recognize.

Nudging her toward the bar, he asked if she wanted anything to drink. Settling onto the stool next to him, aware of the murmured conversations, soft instrumental music, and high-end feel of the surroundings, she shook her head.

"I can wait."

He ran his fingertip around her palm. "Have you eaten?"

She nodded, the steady motion of his finger making her lose focus. "I grabbed a burger at a drive-through."

He frowned, his eyebrows moving together in that way that made him look far too thoughtful and really fucking good. "We could have grabbed dinner. Did you come straight from work?"

Sort of. She'd read her marketing homework in the car while eating her burger. "I didn't want to go home first and risk traffic."

Will reached out, touched a strand of her hair like he couldn't not touch it. "I'm sorry. I didn't mean to add more to your day."

She smirked, the worry over whether she was dressed well enough slipping away. "I suppose I can forgive you seeing as, like I expected, it doesn't suck to see your face."

He laughed, moved his finger so his whole hand cupped her neck. Instead of kissing her lips, which she all but craved at this point, he pressed his to her forehead. She closed her eyes, sighed deeply. When he pulled back, she shook off the onslaught of feelings.

"Who are we meeting?"

Will dropped his hand, picked up a glass of water, and took a drink. "Holden Wright. He's the owner of Comfort Plus. It's a small, fairly new, family-run company that focuses on making eco-friendly blankets, towels, washcloths, and other linens."

She shook her head. "Haven't heard of them."

"Long diatribe short, my father has us looking at a partnership with some people I'm not sure we should partner with. It's not my role in the company to pull in prospective partners but I'm taking a chance here because when I tell my family I don't think we should partner with Home Needs, I want to have an alternative."

"I read that that Nolan guy got arrested. That's the son of the CEO of the company?"

Will's jaw tightened. He set his glass down on the bar top. "Yeah. That's him. Sometimes, you don't need to know someone long before you get a feeling for who they are. You know what I mean?"

She wanted to reach out and smooth the tension in his face, run her fingers along his high cheekbones, along his striking jaw. "Yeah. I think I do."

He smiled at her, everything about his posture and expression softening. "I guess we both do, don't we?"

She nodded, not trusting herself to speak with the level of attraction and energy buzzing around inside her.

"I don't have a good feeling for the Home Needs deal."

"Have you told your family that?"

He lowered his chin, staring at the bar for a moment before looking up again. "A couple of them are a little frustrated with me and recent decisions they believe I've made. Which is why I want to have something in hand when I talk to them."

"Then I guess we better charm the pants off this Holden guy, huh?"

Will smiled. "He's closing in on seventy, his wife is with him, and I want to work with them. I think it's best if he keeps his pants on."

Lexi laughed loud enough to turn a few heads. She leaned into Will. "Are you taking humor classes? That was funny."

Coming close enough that they shared the same air, he shook his head. "Must be the woman I'm falling for rubbing off on me."

She bit her lip, hard, doing her best not to think about rubbing and Will in the same breath.

"Mr. Grand. The rest of your party is here," the hostess said beside them.

Lexi moved back, looked over to see an elegant couple watching them with pleased expressions.

"Do you remember what it was like to be young and falling in love, Holden?" Average height with silver-blond hair shimmering around her shoulders, diamonds glittering in each ear, in a lovely blue cocktail dress, the woman beamed at them.

The man, Holden, lifted his wife's hand, kissed it. "Young, not so much. Falling in love? Yes. I do it every morning when I wake up and see your face."

Even the hostess sighed. Lexi's heart turned over in her chest. If her dad had lived, had grown old beside his wife, that's the sort of thing he would have said.

"Holden," Will said. "It's a pleasure to see you again." He shook the man's hand, reached for the woman's. "I'm William Grand. This is my fiancée, Lexi Danby."

"Lovely to meet you, dear. I'm Bethany. Holden and I read about your engagement online. Congratulations."

Lexi shook off the discomfort of the conversation and focused on the prospect of spending time with a charming couple and a man she truly enjoyed. There were worse ways to spend an evening. Like sitting at home wishing life would move faster so she could get to the good stuff. This right here was pretty damn good.

Fifteen

Will didn't have much of a temper. He got irritated the same as any other person on earth. He disliked when people weren't prepared for meetings, judged others unfairly, or used anyone in his family as a means to an end. His grandfather was a smart man so Will didn't understand why he was letting Fredrick Banner and his asshat of a son run the meeting. After meeting with Holden and his wife the other night, he was certain Grand Babies was currently moving in the wrong direction.

"Listen, we want to make this fair for everyone but if we're investing in *you,* we need a higher percentage. Having Grand Babies products in every one of our stores is going to quadruple your income. I know you've got some personal stuff going on." Fredrick Banner paused, his too-wide smile turning Will's stomach. "Congratulations on that front. We could be capitalizing on your son's fantastic news, Jackson. He's getting married; we're entering a marriage of sorts. I'm tired of going through lawyers and secretaries for the details. I want this sorted sooner rather than later and quite honestly, we could use a little positive press. As you know, Nolan recently had some trouble when he got pulled over by the police."

"Wouldn't have gotten in trouble if you hadn't had drugs on you and you weren't driving under the influence," Will said from his seat next to his grandfather.

"It was weed. Big fucking deal. You and I aren't so different, Will," Nolan said, his thin mustache over his snarling lips making him look like even more of a jerk. "People are always trying to capitalize on shit that doesn't matter. Who cares if I had some weed, I got drunk at a party, or you're marrying some nobody? Everyone just wants to see and be seen."

Before Will could react, his grandfather put a hand on his wrist even as Fredrick chastised his son. Will's phone buzzed but he was too worked up to check it. He didn't know why his dad wanted to work with these men, and couldn't fathom why his grandfather *would,* but Will couldn't keep quiet anymore.

"I think we should all take a step back and reconsider whether or not our path and values line up," Will said.

His grandfather's manicured white brows lifted.

"William," his dad said sharply.

"We've already been leaking information to the press about a possible partnership," his dad continued. "It's what's keeping our name in the local news. Well." He looked Will's way, his lips tugging into a frown. "That and other recent developments."

Fredrick stood up. He was a big man, a cross between imposing and caricature-like in his navy suit and black cowboy boots. "We'd like to capitalize on the holiday season. We're less than a month out from Halloween. This should be signed and sealed. There are already Christmas decorations up at some of our stores, for Christ's sake."

Jackson stood up as well, leaning his hands on the tabletop. "As much as I want this partnership so we can grow Grand Babies to the level it deserves, we don't need to rush, Fredrick. There's no harm in waiting a bit longer to iron out all of the details."

His grandfather, unusually quiet, leaned back in his chair. "In the meantime, it'd be a nice idea for Nolan to think about the image he's creating, the reputation he's building for your company. When Jackson brought this idea to the table, you wanted to join forces for our mutual benefit, but right now, I don't like the terms or the temperament."

Like a sullen teenager, rather than a grown man, Nolan got up and walked out of the boardroom. The lines around Fredrick's mouth tightened but he followed after his son.

Will's phone buzzed again. He pulled it out and checked it.

Mom

> I'm meeting with an event planner at Mika's. Your sister is in a meeting. Please join me ASAP to finalize details for anniversary.

Sighing, Will typed back that he'd be there shortly, wondering why they didn't delegate some of this stuff while also realizing that he was atypically pissed off.

His grandfather folded his hands on the table. "What are you thinking?"

Leaning forward, Will gave him the truth. "I'm thinking we're not stupid but partnering with those two is. I don't understand, Gramps. What are we doing? You can't possibly think that us joining forces with them, no matter how much money they invest, is a good idea for our solid name and reputation." He kept his voice low even though his father had called after Fredrick, then followed him.

Will didn't like acknowledging that his grandparents were aging. For as long as he could remember, his grandpa had been his rock, his friend, his mentor. His guide. Somehow, affection and warmth had skipped a generation and what Will once craved from his dad, he got from Gramps. They'd always been close and Will hated that he couldn't get a thorough read on the man who'd molded him. Something else was going on.

"It started out on a lot more even footing. I'm in agreement with you about them. On the other hand, their capital would go a long way to opening more stores."

"Why do we need more stores? I have to go meet Mom to talk about the anniversary party. We're spread so thin as it is. Is having more worth risking what we've got?"

A slow smile spread over his grandpa's face, making his eyes more youthful. "You're a good man, William. I think I need to think about that question and talk to your grandmother."

Will nodded and when he got up, he squeezed his grandpa's shoulder. "I know you want to solidify the Grand name, Gramps, but I think we're more solid on our own than you, and certainly Dad, give us credit for."

Will was on his way to the upscale eatery his mother had summoned him to when he realized there was something—someone—who would lift his mood. It almost felt like he missed her and he was regretting saying they'd wait until the weekend to go out. She picked up on the first ring.

"Hi, honey, how was your day?" Lexi's voice filled his car as he stopped at a light and his grin was instantaneous.

"I knew you'd make me smile," he said, his shoulders immediately loosening.

"Smile maker. I'll add it to my résumé."

"What are you up to?" Someone honked behind him before the light even turned green.

"Just locking up the store and heading home. I wasn't entirely joking. How was your day?"

"Interesting. It'd be a hell of a lot better if I didn't have to wait until Saturday to see you."

She laughed and the sound washed over him like a touch. One he wanted badly. "You just saw me. It's only Thursday. Needy, aren't you?"

He never had been. "I have to stop by Mika's. It's a small restaurant—"

"I'm a local too, Mr. Grand. I know it. It's not far from work."

Was she eager to see him as well? *She won't be when she realizes your mother is there.*

"Meet me there."

There was some shuffling through the speaker as he turned onto Pine Street and he wondered for a moment if she'd heard him.

"I'm not dressed for fancy. Despite the other night, I should probably tell you now, I rarely am."

"I just want to see your face."

He heard the sharp intake of breath and smiled.

"Will."

"Lexi. My mother is requesting my presence to go over some things for a celebration we're having for the company in a couple of weeks. I'd like you to go as my date. My *fiancée*. I do like saying that—you're right."

"You want me to meet your mother before we've had our fourth date?"

He pulled into the parking lot, found a spot. "You want me to meet your mother this weekend. In two days, actually." She'd texted him yesterday and told him about her mother's negotiating tactic. "Plus, our situation is unique. Once my mom meets you, she can stop giving me the cold shoulder, truly stop setting me up. Plus, I'd rather you met her in a less intimidating venue than the gala."

"Gala? You said party."

"Will you meet me at Mika's? Please?"

"I will but only because I still need to interview you."

"That's right. We didn't get to it the other night. I'm sorry."

They'd had a hell of a good time with Holden and Bethany, though. They'd moved through conversation topics with an unexpected ease considering the age gap between the two couples. Holden reminded Will of his grandfather and being there with Lexi, letting his hand rest on the small of her back, pulling her close, had felt thrilling and comforting at the same time.

"You don't need to apologize. Are you sure you don't mind? It's a weird comparison sort of thing where we need to find out if what we're learning is as transferrable as the instructors hope."

"It's not a big deal." He got out of the car, locked it. "I enjoy talking about business and talking to you so I'm looking forward to it."

The cool breeze reminded him that colder days were quickly approaching as he walked toward the front entrance. "Are you driving here?"

"No. I walked to work. It's literally around the corner from the shop. I'll be there in ten minutes but I can't stay long."

"I can drive you home."

"I'm okay. Stop stalling. Go meet your mom. I'll save you soon."

He walked through the door smiling. A host in a crisp, white dress shirt and black pants greeted him immediately. Will was pretty sure his name was Lionel.

"Mr. Grand. Nice to see you. Your mother and her guest are this way," he said.

Trying to remember the kid's name, it took Will a second to register what he'd said. "I'm sorry, did you say 'guest'?" Their event planner was known by name to the staff here as much as his family was. That was strange.

He saw his mother and her *guest* before Lionel answered affirmatively. Son of a bitch. Approaching the table, Will's jaw twitched as he leaned down to kiss his mother's cheek.

"Mom."

He nodded at the sultry redhead who looked at him like she wished he was on the menu. "Carolyn."

"So lovely to see you again, Will." Carolyn's voice was a low purr when she set her hand on his arm. He pulled back, moved around the table to sit on the other side of his mother.

"Carolyn's been helping me with the party planning. She said she saw you at an engagement party the other night, dear. She reached out to say how lovely that was and we got to talking," his mother said.

I bet you did. Will held Carolyn's gaze, worried she was up to something, but for the life of him he couldn't figure out what. She was an attractive woman, she wouldn't want for company, she came from a good family and knew all the people in the same social circle he did. He'd made it clear he wasn't interested, hadn't he? *Maybe your ego is too big. She could just be helping your mother.*

"Yes, I knew I knew you from somewhere. I wish I'd had more time to chat with you and Mr. Rogers," Carolyn said, laughing at her own not-funny joke.

His mother laughed, meaning Carolyn had filled her in. The thought of this woman and his mother possibly laughing at Lexi stirred something dark in him. They knew nothing about her except maybe what they'd gleaned off the internet. There wasn't much. He'd looked because he hadn't wanted Lexi to be bothered by being linked to him when all he wanted to do was date her.

Before he could respond, he felt a hand on his shoulder, saw his mother's and Carolyn's faces shift.

"We did have to cut it short, didn't we? That was such a great night, though," Lexi said, her voice an octave different from usual as she came around to sit beside him, her gaze locked on Carolyn.

"Oh. I didn't realize you were joining us. I've forgotten your name," Carolyn said.

Will clenched his teeth, helping Lexi out of her long wool jacket. She had her long hair tucked into a side ponytail. She wore very little, if any, makeup, a simple pink T-shirt, and a pair of dark jeans. She looked beautiful.

"It's Alexandria Danby," Lexi said, reaching a hand beyond Will, toward his mother. "It's a pleasure to meet you, Mrs. Grand."

His mother blanched a moment but immediately put her mask back in place and smiled, shaking Lexi's hand.

"How nice you could join us," his mother said. Anyone who didn't know her would believe she meant it.

Lexi dropped her hand and glanced at Will. He saw the nerves dancing in her gaze along with a bit of fire. She was protective. And for some reason, he fucking loved that she felt that way about him.

A waiter brought waters and asked for drink orders. His mother ordered a bottle of wine and a cheese platter for the table. Will reached for Lexi's hand, settled his on top of hers on her thigh. Her quiet smile felt like a victory.

"I'm not sure if you're aware, Lexi, but we have a very important party coming up. Our company, Grand Babies, is turning fifty. Carolyn has been helping me with the planning but I wanted Will's input as well."

Will wondered if Maddie was actually in a meeting as his mother claimed or if this was just a ploy to set him up.

"He did tell me. I'm very much looking forward to attending," Lexi said smoothly, squeezing his hand.

"I couldn't find any of your socials, Lexi. After we met, I thought I'd follow you on some," Carolyn said as the waiter set down their drinks.

Lexi didn't appear bothered by the conversation but her thigh tensed under his hand. "Maybe because, as you said, you forgot my name."

Carolyn's nostrils flared. Will wanted to fist-bump Lexi but gritted his teeth instead, pleasure simmering inside him right alongside the irritation.

His mother rested her palms on the table. "I know very little about you, Alexandria. Perhaps you could tell me what you do."

Shit. Will had brought her here because he wanted to see her. He hadn't guessed his mother would, once again, be trying to set him up.

"I'm a purchaser for a retail shop. I'm also finishing up my business degree."

Smooth. Will smiled at her. She was good at coming up with something on the spot. And he liked the fact that she didn't cower under his mother's somewhat snooty tone.

"A degree is so important," Carolyn said, lifting her wineglass, swirling the white liquid. "I finished mine about eight years ago. I actually double-majored. I didn't need to, of course, as I work for my father's design company, but I believe in being well prepared."

Will's jaw tensed again and he decided he'd had enough playing nice for the day. "I forgot your mom has that appointment tonight." He stood up, pulling Lexi with him.

She looked at him, eyes wide. "What?"

"Mother, Carolyn. Sorry to do this but we'll have to reschedule. But I more than trust your judgment on the final details for the party."

"William, you're being rude," his mother said, glaring at him. *I'm being rude? That's fucking rich, even for you, Mom.*

He widened his smile. "It's not my intention, Mom. But we need to get going."

"It was nice to meet you, Mrs. Grand, and to see you again, Carolyn."

Carolyn simply nodded. His mother stood up. "I'd like to know more about you, Alexandria. I'll ask William for your number and we can arrange a lunch. After all, if you're going to be part of our family, I should have some sense of who you come from."

Who. God. His mother irritated the hell out of him.

"Of course," Lexi said as Will helped her with her coat.

He kissed his mother's cheek. "I'll bring her for dinner soon." No way was he letting his mother get Lexi alone.

They were outside before Lexi pulled her hand out of his. "Whoa. Slow down. What's going on?"

Will turned, looked at her. "That was a nightmare. I'm so sorry. I had no idea my mother had Carolyn here. I never would have set you up for an ambush."

Lexi stepped closer to him. "I've met mean girls before, Will. I can handle Carolyn. I'm sorry if I didn't make a good impression on your mom, though. I can see why you want her off your back and out of your love life. She's not going to be happy when she realizes how much I exaggerated with my job."

"Your job shouldn't matter."

She stepped closer and Will inhaled, catching the subtle scent of vanilla and something else sweet. Something very Lexi. She put her hands on his chest like they belonged there, and he wished they were alone. At his place.

"Maybe it shouldn't but it does to your mom. And probably the rest of your family. Are you sure this is worth the hassle?"

"What?" He slipped his hands inside her jacket, which she hadn't done up, resting them on her waist, pulling her a bit closer.

"Dating me. You really could just tell your mother it was a mix-up. Might save the family drama."

Will dropped his forehead to hers, closing his eyes so he could just . . . absorb the way she made him feel. Excited, settled, eager, peaceful. Such a blend of emotions that he didn't know what to do with them all.

When he opened his eyes, she was staring at him. "I want to get to know you, spend time with you. None of this has been conventional or even ideal but I don't want to walk away from you. You promised to be my plus-one to this party, and you dealt with my mom, so it's only fair I meet yours. I owe you that favor." He ran the tip of his nose along the bridge of hers. "Plus, you're an excellent kisser and I can't get you out of my head."

She grinned, slid her arms around his neck. "I do want to get a good mark on my project."

His laugh was cut off by her mouth moving against his, her fingers sliding through the hair at the nape of his neck. His body molded against hers like there was nothing outside of them. She breathed a soft sigh into his mouth that lit a fire inside him. He wanted all of her sighs. He wanted her in a way he wasn't familiar with. It should have scared him but instead, being with her made him feel alive. He hadn't realized he was missing anything in his life until she sat down with him. Maybe the best things in life weren't planned down to the minute.

Sixteen

It was silly to be nervous. It was a date. With a man she enjoyed. One she was pretend-marrying, one whose mother hated her, one who was wanted by other women. One who looked at her like she mattered even after a short period of time.

Lexi logged on to her bank, transferring the money a lovely woman, Danielle, had e-transferred her this morning after picking up her father's tools. She said they'd make a great gift for her husband and it was such a great deal.

It was good for both of them since Lexi's tuition was now paid. Brett texted as she was staring at her school account balance in another open tab, enjoying the statement: BALANCE OWING: 0.00. That meant any extra shifts she picked up at the restaurant could maybe go toward purchasing something for the party Will also called a gala that she was mildly freaking out about.

Brett

> Can you work? We need someone ASAP.

She stared at her phone. Shit. She'd never be in a financial position where she *shouldn't* say yes. But Will was due in half an hour. He'd put time and energy into planning a date. She'd ended up emailing him her interview questions and they'd spent their texting time going back and forth with him teasing her about what they were doing.

She started to text back, paused. If she said she was sick, she'd definitely run into someone who could tell him because that was how life worked. *Your tuition is paid. Say no.*

Lexi

I can't. I'm sorry. I have plans.

Brett typed back immediately.

Brett

Fine.

Lexi pushed away the niggling sense of irresponsibility. She was reliable almost 100 percent of the time. She could take this one day. Even if she was losing her Monday shift at Bitsy's. Heading out of her room, she found her mom hunched over her worktable, sketching out a drawing.

Lexi took a breath before braving the topic she rarely brought up anymore. "You know, if we sold the house, we could find you an apartment. I could even get one close by." She couldn't leave her mom alone in this huge house. The mortgage was too much. The bills on her dad's business were finally paid but the house needed work and was basically a money suck.

Her mother didn't even lift her head. "Lexi, you know I don't want to leave. Please don't start on me."

Stepping into the room, she pushed just a little more. "It's getting harder to keep up with the house, Mom. Dad's insurance barely made a dent, we barely broke even on selling the business, and I'm barely finished scraping together and paying off what he owed around town for supplies and stuff." Construction made good money and there was plenty of work. But not if you kept spending in the time between jobs. Which her father had.

Despite being the office assistant, her mom had known nothing about the bookkeeping and only continued to shy away from the truth every time Lexi brought it up. When Lexi was young, her mom was full of life, like a glitter bomb adding a sparkle to everything. Nothing would be the same now, of course, but was it asking too much to get a little more of her back?

Gwen stiffened her spine, her gaze brimming with tears. "It'll all work out somehow. I could sell some of my pieces on the internet. Maisie said she'd make me some sort of online shop."

Lexi smiled, tried to be gentle. "I think an online shop would be wonderful. You're very talented. But Mom, we can't afford to stay here."

"You have a friend coming over. I need to get ready." Gwen lowered her head as she left the room.

Lexi closed her eyes, leaned against the work table, and counted to ten. *You're pushing too fast.* It was true. She'd gone running every morning since she'd promised herself she would and it was as if she'd lit a fire under herself, a drive to . . . not get back to who she used to be, but become the person she wanted to be. Lexi went to her own room to get ready but her thoughts refused to settle.

Will's mother had been no peach but she wondered how he'd react to Gwen. He was clearly no stranger to the wear and tear parents could create on a grown child's life. Maybe they weren't so different in that respect. The realistic part of her figured she was just shoving the final nail in the coffin. He'd see she wasn't his type. She had too much going on and if he was going to date a high-maintenance woman, it might as well be one with a pedigree so he could get his mother off his back.

But damn she liked him. Liked the way she felt when she was with him. Her mother wasn't the only one who'd lost the person she used to be. Will made Lexi feel like her old self again. Older, wiser, a little more sarcastic and realistic, but *her*.

"Do I look all right?" Gwen's soft voice, like a scolded child, came from the archway between the hall and the kitchen.

Lexi turned to see her mom in a pair of soft, faded blue jeans and a navy-blue cable-knit sweater, her hair brushed so it looked like dark silk and a hint of makeup adding to her delicate features.

"You look beautiful, Mom."

Gwen wrung her hands together, looked at the floor. "I don't mean to make your life harder. I'll try, Alexandria. I will. I've got an appointment with the counselor for next week. But I'm not ready to let go of the house. I know we can't afford it. I'm not completely unaware. I just . . . need more time."

Lexi nodded, tears stinging her eyes. They didn't have any more time. It'd been over three years. They were floating on the surface but the undertow was hovering. They'd be no match for it.

Walking over, she pulled her mom into a hug.

"Let's just get through today. One step at a time. I love you."

Lexi held tighter as Gwen cried softly against her shoulder, apologizing and breaking Lexi's heart a little more.

Lexi hated feeling unsettled. And she was. The *tummy tangled in knots, checking her makeup thirteen times* kind of unsettled about a guy meeting her mother. It was a first. Track had kept her too busy to maintain a steady boyfriend and while she'd had a few crushes, she'd never brought a boy home to introduce him. In college she was even more focused, because keeping her scholarship was everything. She knew she couldn't run forever. Athletes had a sweet spot. She'd met a few guys, hooked up a couple times, but she'd never found a guy who made her want to wander off her path.

When Will knocked on the front door, she was already standing there, waiting to open it. Staring at the wood separating them, she smoothed down her pale-yellow sweater. She'd gone with a sweater, jeans, and a pair of cute, dark-brown ankle boots with cozy beige cuffs. She closed her eyes, inhaled deeply, held it, let it out softly.

She opened the door telling herself it was just a date. She could admit to the term this time while also acknowledging that a date was no big deal. Then she looked at him, felt her heart thump like an over-active puppy tail, and knew she was lying to herself. Will Grand was not just a date.

His eyes widened with obvious pleasure, those kissable lips tipping up in a smile warmer than her sweater.

"You look amazing," he said, his gaze roaming down, then up to meet her eyes.

"Thank you. And hi."

She caught just a hint of nerves in his laugh. He leaned in, kissed her cheek. "Hi," he whispered.

She wished she could settle her pulse. Closing the door, she gestured to the stairs. "Come on in."

He let her go first but with every step, her feet grew heavier, the nerves acting like cement, slowing her down. About halfway up, she turned and faced him. They were eye-to-eye.

"My mom," she whispered. "I told you; she hasn't gotten over losing my dad. I just want you to know that in case she says anything weird or—"

Will pressed a finger to Lexi's lips, and she resisted the urge to bite it.

"We love our moms. We don't have to explain them."

He made everything seem so easy. Lexi nodded and Will replaced his finger with his mouth, giving her a quick, bolstering kiss.

When she turned, he patted her butt, nudging her up the stairs, once again making her laugh.

Gwen was in the kitchen, sitting ramrod straight on a stool, her hands cupping a mug.

"Mom, this is Will Grand. Will, this is my mom, Gwendolyn Danby."

Setting her mug down, her mom got up from the stool.

Will stretched his arm out, a sweet smile on his gorgeous face. "Mrs. Danby, it's a pleasure to meet you."

Her mom's cheeks pinkened, her gaze happy as she shook Will's hand. "Please, call me Gwen. It's so wonderful to meet you. Lexi's never brought a boy home. Though I guess you're not a boy. You look like a male model on one of my romance books. Though, these days, more and more of the covers are illustrated, which I love." Gwen trailed off, dropping Will's hand to clasp her hands together.

Lexi groaned and Will laughed.

Will's hand settled on Lexi's lower back. "I'll take that as a compliment. I think you and my sister Kyra share an affinity for the same books."

"Oh, I mean it as one," Gwen said. "Can I get you something to drink, Will? We have coffee, orange juice, soda, and water."

Lexi's gaze widened. What the hell—Gwen was playing hostess?

"I wouldn't say no to coffee. Black, please."

A wave of dizziness washed over her when her mother all but pranced to the cupboard to get a mug.

Will leaned down, his lips brushing her ear. "Relax, Alexandria."

Fuck. The way he said her name made shivers race over her skin, making it hot and uncomfortably tight. *Relax. Yeah. Okay.*

"So, Will, tell me about yourself."

Lexi watched with low-key fascination as her mother served Will his coffee and listened intently while he told her about his two sisters, his grandfather, and Grand Babies, all of which he clearly loved.

"Oh!" Gwen clapped both of her hands together under her chin. "I bought from there when Lexi was a baby."

Will smiled, winked at Lexi. "My family would be happy to hear that."

"What are you two up to today?" Gwen asked.

Lexi hadn't seen her mom filled with this much energy in months and months.

"I thought I'd take Lexi apple picking," Will said, finishing up his coffee.

"How fun." Gwen tapped her fingers on the counter before adding, "If you bring back some apples, I'll make a pie."

Grateful she wasn't drinking anything because it would have been spewed all over the counter, Lexi gaped at her mom. "You will?"

Gwen tipped her head to the side. "Sure, sweetie. Don't you remember how good my piecrust is?"

Nodding, not sure why her throat felt tight, Lexi could only stare. Of course she remembered. That and a whole lot of things. Piecrust, pumpkin carving, holiday parties, after-school snacks full of protein, her mom at track meets. She'd placed memories of that Gwen in a box labeled: BEFORE DAD LEFT US.

"I'm going to go look up a recipe right now. Will, it was wonderful to meet you."

"You too, Gwen. Truly."

When Gwen left the room, Lexi stared after her, still dazed.

Will squeezed her shoulder. "You okay?"

She turned to him, tipped her head back. "We never have visitors. Just Maisie. I haven't seen her like that in a long time." Her chest felt tight but in a good way.

He smiled, pulling her closer with a hand on her waist. "That's a good thing, right?"

Lexi narrowed her gaze. "Are you magic, Will Grand? Some sort of sorcerer?"

Will laughed, lowered his head so their noses almost touched. "No, but I'm happy to let you think so."

In the quiet of her kitchen, she fell a little more. She reminded herself that athletes knew how to fall in a way that helped them avoid injury, but she wasn't sure that applied to what she was feeling.

Will kissed her like he wanted to keep kissing her, like he had all the time in the world but not nearly enough. It was intoxicating.

When she pulled back, her fingers clutched his sweater. She laughed and smoothed the fabric. "Apple picking, huh?"

He nodded, his gaze darker, crackling with warmth and something deeper.

"Alexandria?" Gwen said from behind her, from the doorway to the kitchen.

Lexi looked back, over her shoulder. Gwen had her phone in one hand, a look of something Lexi couldn't read on her face.

"Mom, what's wrong?" Lexi turned away from Will.

In that moment, Lexi watched a little piece of the woman her mom had once been fill this version with light. Her smile was nothing short of luminous.

"I had my phone turned off. I mean, I don't use it all that much anyway, but." Her mom's voice softened as she took a deep breath. "Louanne, do you remember her? I haven't seen her in ages. She texted me."

Lexi felt like her breath was trapped in her lungs. "Okay?"

"Oh, honey. You said it was a date. You're engaged? Why didn't you tell me?" Gwen looked at Will, tears shimmering in her gaze, happiness emanating from her core. "William. Welcome to the family." She drew him into a hug, murmuring, "You're engaged. You're engaged. Lexi's father would be so happy." He hugged her back, a look of uncertainty on his face. Yeah, she didn't know what to do either. She shouldn't have assumed her mother would remain clueless about it.

Gwen stepped away from Will, turned to Lexi, and put both hands on her cheeks. "This is why you've been talking about moving forward. I'm so happy for you. I'm so sorry you felt like you couldn't tell me."

Lexi was incredibly torn in that moment. Part of her felt like an absolute monster letting her mom believe a lie. But the other part of her was staring at something she hadn't seen in a very long time: true happiness in her mother's teary gaze.

"Mom," she said, pulling her into a hug, fighting back tears of her own. She didn't know what to say, how to say it.

She met Will's gaze and the softness, the sweet understanding in it nearly leveled her. It was too much. She should end this now, while she could still pick up the pieces of her mom's disappointment when she told her the truth. And Will. She should end that, too. Because the way he was looking at her right now, a little part of her wanted all of it to be true.

Seventeen

Will had a few serious relationships under his belt. He'd known love, heartbreak, disappointment. He'd even thought he'd found the one when years ago, on break from college, his mom had set him up with the daughter of a friend. When it turned out the family was having severe money problems, Will found the security of his bank account had been more appealing than he was.

Still. None of what came before had prepared him for being with Lexi. For how much he wanted to be with her while at the same time worrying that all of this was too much on her. On her mother. Lexi stared out the passenger-side window, quiet and incredibly still.

He reached over, loving the feel of her fingers automatically curling around his when he touched her hand. "Are you okay?"

Stopped at a light, he looked over at the same time she turned to face him.

"I am. It feels strange. All of this. Honestly, since the second I sat down with you, I've felt like I'm in some sort of play or television show. I can't tell if it's a comedy, drama, or farce."

"Life is all of those, right?"

She smiled at him before he turned back to face the windshield.

Traffic was slow on a Saturday morning but he liked having her to himself right now.

"Maybe it's too complicated," she said quietly, tracing her finger up and down the back of his hand.

"Probably. I was just thinking that myself. I don't want to hurt your mom. Or my mom. It got tangled pretty quickly, but I don't want to stop seeing you."

She was quiet so long his gut cramped.

"I don't want to stop seeing you either." She said it so softly that he wondered if she was just admitting it to herself and he was lucky enough to overhear.

"It might be an accident but outside of the mama drama, it's been a happy one."

Lexi laughed, the sound filling him with unexpected lightness. "Mama drama? You could have shirts made."

"There's that marketing brain. I wish it'd happened in an easier way where the lie wasn't wrapped around the truth. But let me just say, pretending to be your boyfriend, fiancé, significant other, doesn't matter. If it means I get to spend time with you, I'll take it. But I understand if you're worried about your mom. About the fallout from all this at some point." It surprised him how very much he didn't want to think about that. About the idea of them ending. "If you want, I can and will tell my parents the truth, and then we can print a retraction."

"Your family would be okay with that?"

He shook his head. Not her problem. "I'm starting to realize that I can't live my life making sure my family is happy at the expense of my own feelings."

He'd sat down with his family, minus Kyra, who'd been at school, yesterday to go over their options in terms of moving forward with Home Needs. Will had stayed in touch with Holden Wright and even talked to Kyra about seeing some of her long-term ideas about being earth-friendly coming to fruition through this possible partnership. But his father hadn't been in any mood to hear about what Will had to say. He was as caught up in opening more stores as his grandfather had been.

"That sounds like it's bigger than just what's happening between you and me."

He liked having someone to talk to. *No. You like talking to her.*

"It is. I don't want to go through with the merger with Home Needs. My grandfather and father think opening more stores is a must and I'm not sure I agree. My mom is so worried about our image and being on the list for every social engagement, I don't think she cares which direction we go as long as she gets invites. I tried to bring up Comfort Plus but my father wasn't in a headspace to hear it."

"For what it's worth," Lexi said, reaching out for his hand, "I got a really good feeling from the Wrights. They're a wonderful couple and their business model, as well as their values, seems to be more in keeping with your family's."

He parked in the back of the Side Tap lot, cut the ignition, and released his seat belt. Putting a hand to her cheek, he pulled her closer. "Your opinion is worth a lot to me. And I agree. Look, I know what we have has been brief and unconventional, but I care about you and I'll do whatever you want. Tell the paper myself, say no comment to anyone who asks. I just want to see where this goes." He pressed a light kiss to her lips, pulled back. "What do you want, Lexi?"

She took a deep breath, and he felt the soft, sweet warmth of it when she exhaled. "Right this second? You. I want today with you."

Eighteen

One day. That's all she wanted. Like a spa day but different. Lexi wanted to enjoy this man and pretend that everything would be okay. Technically it would be even if it wasn't, because she'd dealt with getting knocked on her ass before and she was still here. She might be setting herself up for some heart hurt but there was also a high probability of what she suspected would be excellent sex. The prospect of that was enough to make her push every other little worry aside. She *liked* this man. And she deserved a day to turn off the worry switch. From the sounds of it, he did too.

Lexi was on a date with a gorgeous, sexy man who looked at her like he wanted to comfort her in one breath and rip her clothes off in the next. She was down with both ideas.

She spent every day getting through, one step to the next, telling herself eventually life would settle and she'd get the brass ring. She wasn't sure she believed in fate or karma or any of that stuff but life had thrown a brass ring in the form of William Grand directly into her path and she was too damn smart not to grab hold.

Giving herself a few seconds to catch her breath, she waited for him to open her door, which he rounded the hood to do. Because on top of everything else, he was a gentleman. *Yes, please.*

Will held his hand out and as she slipped her palm into his, she felt little pulses of electricity tickling her skin. She wondered what he had in store besides apple picking.

When she turned to walk with him toward the entrance, she stopped and stared. The property and building had been transformed into some sort of harvesttime wonderland. It was nearly magical. As if October had rolled in not just on the calendar, but physically into Side Tap. It wasn't noon yet but the place was bustling with people—couples, singles, families. Despite the chill in the air, the autumn sun shone bright in the sky so the twinkle lights didn't dance the way they did at night but they still looked pretty. Dreamy. Like anything could happen.

When she'd come the first time, Lexi hadn't noticed all of the picnic tables on the expansive lawn. Many of them were set up as stations for pumpkin carving, face painting, beer tastings, and leaf-wreath making. Lexi wasn't entirely sure about the last one but was 100 percent certain Bitsy would like it. So would her mom if she'd ever agree to come to an event like this. Families and friends were snapping photos by some decorative hay bales that had been set up.

"This is amazing. And busy," she said, tucking her other hand around Will's arm.

He smiled down at her and she felt a shot of contentment hit her hard in the center of her chest. Dangerous territory for a woman who'd just committed to living in the moment.

"Ethan loves this time of year. He's always looking for ways to pull in more people. Things like this are great for families."

"Smart. Really smart. And really fun." Ideas spun in her head. This space was fantastic. She wondered if he did weddings, hosted other events.

They took the path to the right of the building, which was lined with solar lights. Laughter and music mingled together as they came out at the back. There were rows of hops, apple trees, and even a small pumpkin patch.

"I really need to bring Maisie here. She would love it."

Will released Lexi's hand to pick up a basket from the stack of them on the wooden-planked patio. All of the bistro tables were full, people sharing appetizers and flights of autumn-colored beer. A few servers, dressed warmly, walked with trays of small sample cups. A photographer wove through the area taking candid shots. A couple of people on the far left side of the lawn played ladder toss. The vibe and energy were uplifting and fun.

"You're helping her out tomorrow?" He swung the basket as they walked toward the apple trees.

He listened. Lexi liked that. "I was supposed to. Basically, it's like caddying but with her camera equipment instead of clubs. But her regular assistant moved some things to make it work so I'm not needed. I've done it before though. It's fun. She's very talented."

"Maybe she *should* take our engagement photos," he said, his tone teasing as he took her hand again.

Lexi gave him a wry smile. "Don't encourage her."

Will shook his head. "I'm glad you have her. She seems like a great friend. I'm also grateful you're being so chill with all of this. There was another article in the *Times* this morning. No one's bothering you, right?"

She shrugged. "Other than Jackie and Becca, no one's talked to me about it. It's fine. Trust me when I say there are worse things that could happen to a girl like me than being linked to one of Seattle's most eligible bachelors."

He turned into her, lifted her hair off her shoulder, sweeping it behind. "I hate that label and what do you mean a girl like you?"

Why couldn't he see how different their lives were? Growing up, she and her friends were all from middle-class families; there were kids more fortunate and definitely some less fortunate. Lexi never thought much about money until her dad died and she realized how bad he was at hanging on to it. For someone like Will, who'd grown up rich and privileged, she'd expected him to be more aware of their social statuses. Especially since she'd sort of fibbed: one article she saw painted Lexi as a down-on-her-luck opportunist. She'd stopped looking after that. It wasn't like she was trending on X or Threads or whatever the hell the popular app was these days. She didn't even go on Facebook. She definitely never checked the *Seattle Times* website. Or regular newspapers. Did they even still make those?

"I'm not really a country clubber," she said, trying to laugh it off.

"Neither am I. Having a membership somewhere doesn't really make a person belong. For the record, I'd rather be here with you, doing this, than anywhere else right now."

Going up on tiptoes, she pressed her mouth to his, hoping she could get a handle on her jumbled emotions. His free hand came to her waist, holding her close.

"Keep it family-friendly," a deep voice said from behind them.

Will pulled away, taking Lexi's hand in his again. "That's as PG as I can make it, man."

Ethan strode up to them. Dressed in jeans, a sweater, a puffer vest over top, and a beanie that read SIDE TAP, he looked like a swag advertisement for his own business. Which, according to her marketing class, was an excellent tactic.

"Lexi, it's nice to see you again. I was actually going to ask Will for your number," Ethan said, which made Will frown.

"Bro code," Will growled.

Lexi laughed. Like Will had anything to worry about. Despite his mother trying to marry him off, he seemed unaware of his many charms.

Ethan laughed too. "Chill, man." He looked at Lexi. "Will mentioned you're in school for business and marketing. I wondered about your areas of expertise and whether you might be looking for some work."

Lexi glanced between the two friends. "Oh. I . . . I'm finishing my degree. I'm not done yet."

With a tenderness that flipped her stomach like a pancake, Will stroked a hand down Lexi's hair. "I told him that, too. Even though I don't think it's that big a deal. A degree isn't everything."

Lexi laughed. "Only people with degrees say that."

Ethan laughed as well. "Or people running businesses who know sometimes there's more required than just a piece of paper. Not that I'm disparaging your degree. It's an excellent path, just agreeing with Will that it's not the only thing that matters."

The muscles around her heart tightened, taking her breath away. It was one thing to say those things to herself but to have someone else validate the thoughts was almost too much. She didn't want Will clearing paths for her, but she had a feeling that wasn't what he intended. He was more genuine than anyone she'd met. In the romance books her mom read, the couple usually faked the whole relationship. But she and Will were actually dating. Weird that dating him complicated their pretend engagement.

Ethan's phone rang, drawing Lexi's attention. He looked at the screen, cursed, and shook his head. "I have to take this. Brady's wife is on bedrest. He can't oversee the new place and I'm stuck here right in the middle of all of our holiday events." He looked at Lexi, any traces of humor gone. "That's why I wanted your number. I'm in a jam. Give me a few minutes? Pick some apples, drink some beer." He put the phone to his ear and hurried off in the direction of the pub.

"Why would he want to talk to me about a woman on bedrest, and who is Brady?"

Will laughed, stepped them both to the side as another couple walked by. "Brady is his brother. The woman on bedrest, Lori, is his sister-in-law. I didn't know about the bedrest either but they have two-year-old twins so it must be pretty difficult right now. I'm not completely sure but if I had to make an educated guess, he's probably curious what area of business you're majoring in and whether or not it's applicable to what he needs. Which, while I may be biased, it sounds like it could be."

Her pulse jumped with excitement but her brain, of course, poked holes in the story. "Is it because we're together? Because we're pretending to be engaged?" She didn't want to sound ungrateful, but Will wasn't a permanent fixture and she didn't want to rely on him for things. Especially not his connections. She knew, even from their brief relationship, that he got enough of that.

Will gave her a wide grin. "Of course not. He's met you himself and can read people. You're smart and work in an area he currently needs help in. Why wouldn't he want to talk to you?"

Lexi looked around, unsure what to do with this information. With this . . . *possibility*. "I'm a Dress Hut manager and a waitress."

Will grasped her hand, pulled her close enough she had to tip her head back. "I believe the title was buyer for a retail store? Also, I don't think waitressing should be your long-term plan."

"Hey!"

He laughed. "People who plan to get married shouldn't lie to each other. As I was saying, there are lots of reasons he might want to chat with you."

Before she could respond, he tugged her hand so they were walking one of the rows. Thick, beautiful trees, heavy with multicolored, crisp-looking apples surrounded them. It smelled earthy and fresh. Lexi took a deep breath.

"He doesn't even know if I'm doing well in school," Lexi said, reaching for a shiny green apple that looked almost too pretty to eat. With a slight yank, the apple came free and she placed it gently in the basket, wondering if her mother would actually bake a pie.

When she glanced back up, Will was watching her. "Are you?"

She pursed her lips. "Yes. I work hard. I got an A on my last two assignments."

"Listen, he's in a pinch. You might be exactly what he needs. If he talks to you about it, just be honest."

Lexi paused in the act of picking another apple, turned to face Will fully. "Something we're not being with others."

A hint of sadness touched his gaze. "It's a few people in our direct circle, and like I said, we can come clean. I don't like lying as a general rule but I don't want to complicate things further."

Guilt cramped her stomach. "I've been making you lie since you met me."

The scent of cold air and fall swirled around them as Will stepped closer. "Maybe about some of the details but not the important stuff."

She gave a half laugh. "Oh yeah?"

"Yeah. I'm not lying about liking you. Wanting to know you better. Wanting to spend time with you." He leaned down, his lips brushing the outer shell of her ear, making a hard shiver course through her. "About how funny you are." He kissed just under her ear. Wow. She never would have pegged that as a sweet spot. His lips lingered just a second, as if he could read her body. "How sweet you are." His nose grazed over her cheek on the way to her lips. "About wanting you."

Lexi pressed a hand to his jacket-covered chest to steady herself. "Way to distract me from apple picking."

He laughed, the sound sending another shiver over every inch of her skin. "Anticipation, Alexandria. Let's enjoy the day."

She could do that. Absolutely. But it didn't mean she wouldn't be thinking about the end of the day. About tonight. And whether or not sleeping with her fake fiancé might deepen her already forming, way-too-real feelings for him.

Nineteen

They walked the rows, picking twelve apples in total. Lexi was tempted to grab a pumpkin but a memory of her father always choosing the largest one they could find tamped down the urge. Some things weren't the same without him.

By the time they made their way inside, finding a two-seater table in the corner of the room near the back patio, Lexi's hands were freezing. She rubbed them together, taking a seat. Her brain had gone into overdrive thinking of what Ethan might say. There was a small, deep-red glass candleholder on the tabletop, a candle flickering inside. Lexi held her hands over the miniature flame, making Will laugh.

"Let me know if that works," he said, removing his jacket and a soft-looking gray scarf before sitting down.

"I'm not optimistic."

"Maybe some hot chocolate?"

"That sounds perfect."

Will stood again, putting a hand on her shoulder. "Let me go to the bar and order. It'll be quicker." And like they were a couple who did this regularly, he dropped a kiss to the top of her head.

He'd just walked away when Ethan came from a hallway, glanced around the room, and saw her. With a smile, he headed in her direction.

Nerves assaulted her. What if he asked her questions she didn't know the answers to?

"Hey. Will grabbing drinks?" He sat in Will's seat, set his phone on the table.

"He is. We're going with hot chocolate."

Ethan nodded. "It's cold but with our unpredictable weather, I'm just glad it didn't rain."

"Very true. Your place is amazing. I really love it here."

"Thank you. It's my pride and joy. Finding this place was something that just happened at a time in my life when I thought I knew what I wanted, but it turned out not to be what I needed. I dove in and haven't regretted a single second." He leaned his forearms on the table. "Though the last couple weeks with my brother being split in two directions is a bit rougher."

Lexi was curious by nature but the ins and outs of setting up and organizing businesses, the running of them, fascinated her. She might have been taking only one class but it reminded her of how much she wanted to be part of a world that had nothing to do with elderly women's undergarments.

Still, she approached softly. "What stage are you at for the other property?"

"It's nowhere near this size but it's a similar rustic-style building with a warm feel. We didn't need a ton of construction or renovation so structure-wise, it's ready to go. That's about it, though. Brady, that's my brother, was just getting ready to order furniture, supplies, look into staffing."

Little wings flapped around Lexi's heart. "Could your brother do some of that from home?" What if Ethan just needed an extra waitress? Oh God, what if he wanted her to nanny for his nieces or nephews? Or just help out with his sister-in-law? Why would he? She was practically a stranger.

Ethan's forehead crinkled. "He can. Probably will. I don't know if

Will filled you in but his wife, Lori, is six months pregnant. She's on bedrest indefinitely, and they have two-year-old twins."

She nodded. "He said. I hope she's doing all right."

"She is. Thanks. I don't want to add more stress to them."

Was she bold enough to ask? *You have no idea what he wants. Don't make a fool of yourself. You don't even have a degree.*

"That's a lot with little ones at home." *That's it. Stay neutral. Casual. You're fine.*

Ethan shook his head like he was ridding himself of the worries. "I hate the business side of business. Not the numbers, really—I don't mind that. But the paperwork and setup and ordering. I'm the people person. I was going to ask Will for your number because he mentioned your business degree. I'm not sure what your work situation is right now." He trailed off, leaving the floor entirely open.

Will joined them, making her nerves multiply. He smiled encouragingly. Or maybe that was just his smile. He set the hot chocolates down.

"I'm almost finished with school." She cringed, feeling as if she'd yelled it like an accusation.

"You're almost there," Will said easily, resting on the arm of the chair where she sat.

"I'm in a class right now. I need two more to finish," she said to Ethan.

Nervous laughter erupted. She squeezed her hands together.

Ethan smiled. "Going to admit this might be the strangest job interview I've ever given. Tell me about your degree."

Oh God. Job interview? Is this for real?

She forced her shoulders to relax. She couldn't serve soup but she *could* do this. "It's a business degree with a specialization in operations management."

His grin widened. "You're already smarter than my brother."

Will and Lexi both laughed. When she looked up at Will, he

winked, and though she'd always questioned the wink as a suspicious form of flirting, it sent heat straight to her stomach.

Ethan leaned forward in the chair. "What do you do now?"

Hook old ladies up with grannie panties sounded wrong. She cleared her throat, noting the way Will smiled at her, like silent encouragement. "I manage a dress boutique in Astrid Park. I've been there an embarrassingly long time." *Excellent; make yourself sound pathetic. Jesus, Lexi. Pretend you know how to do this.*

"Which proves you have a strong track record. You must be an excellent employee," Will said smoothly. "Have you done any projects in operations management? Setup? Distribution? Working with suppliers?"

Lexi inched forward, a little seed of confidence nestling inside of her. "Actually, I've been doing that sort of thing for years. My current boss has done several makeovers on her business. I do the buying, all communications, most of the books. Honestly, I think she just uses the place more for socialization than anything else. I'm surprised she hasn't closed down yet. She's cutting back hours but she does have some steady clientele."

Ethan stood up, so Lexi and Will did too. "Sometimes life hands you what you need just when you need it. Mama Grand can stop setting you up and I can stop looking at spreadsheets." He turned to Lexi. "That is, if you're interested in this kind of position. Even if I just connect you with Brady and you find out where he's at, what the top priority is right now. If you could get us a staff for the new year, help us get the place up and running so he can come back to it open, that would be amazing. I'll pay you well. Benefits. Hell, I'll give you my brother's car if you want. Lori made him buy an actual mini van so he can't drive his beloved GTI."

She was nodding but words weren't forming in her brain. Breathing in deeply, the crisp scent of fall having followed them inside, she smoothed herself out. "I'm very interested. I'd love to chat with your brother and learn more."

"I'm going to call Brady right now. Start thinking about a guest list. I should throw you two an engagement party."

With almost boyish enthusiasm, he hugged her, stepped back, and then hugged Will.

When Ethan left them, a wide smile on his face, Will pulled her closer.

"Quite a day," he said, leaning in to kiss her.

"You're not kidding. My brain is on overdrive. He won't really throw us an engagement party, right? I feel like that will complicate things more."

"I'll tell him not to. He's excited. With good reason. You'll be great at this."

How could he believe in her so easily when she found it so hard to believe in herself? *Then change it. Believe in yourself. You can do this. More than that, you want to do this.*

Will ran a finger along her jaw. "And you thought the best thing about today would be the promise of pie."

Lexi chuckled even as she leaned her head against his. "Actually, the best thing about today was and still is the promise of you."

Twenty

Will couldn't remember the last time he'd enjoyed a day so much. Lexi made him laugh and forget about things that kept him up at night, like appeasing his parents, carving out his own place within the family legacy, hanging on to that legacy while also moving them into the future. He didn't do a lot of things for himself. Not that he was a martyr or anything close, but his whole life had been his family, his work, and the link between the two. He'd never met a woman who uncapped something inside him the way Lexi did. She made him want to see what existed outside the office, outside his family.

He didn't want the day to end but he didn't want to push too hard either. There was a very real possibility he could fall hard for this woman and he wasn't entirely sure of where she stood on the topic of them.

He drove through the University District, heading for the Ship Canal Bridge that would take him back to Lexi's neighborhood. The sky sported dusky shades of blue streaked with reds that promised an equally sunny day tomorrow. She'd been quiet since chatting with Ethan. He wasn't surprised by Ethan's offer. Life offered some handy coincidences now and again, but he didn't doubt that Lexi would be a great asset for his buddy. If only she could believe that herself. He was grateful she didn't really think he'd had anything to do with Ethan's suggestion. Not that he wouldn't have, but in this case timing had been everyone's friend. Well, not Lori's. He should ask his secretary to order Brady and his wife a few weeks of meals that could just be thrown in the oven. And thank her for buying Lexi's dad's tools. Something he wouldn't mention to Lexi even though all he'd done was point Danielle in the direction of the listing since she'd been in the market anyway.

Stopping at a light, he turned to see Lexi looking at him with an unreadable gaze. Desire sparked like a match, instantaneous.

"My mom is probably asleep. She sleeps a lot."

He nodded, his words tumbling around in his brain as he reached for the right thing to say. He'd never asked a woman to his place. He'd only moved there last year and it was his home. His sanctuary. And he very much wanted to see Lexi in it. To have her in his space. In his bed.

Like she could read his mind, she touched her hand to his. "You can invite me over."

His breath hitched. "I want you to be sure. I don't want to rush anything or pressure you."

She smiled and squeezed his hand before gesturing to the windshield. The light had changed. "We're engaged. I don't see any reason to wait for marriage."

In the quiet space, his laugh seemed to bounce off the interior. Fuck. Way to be smooth. "I'd like to show you my home."

"I'd like to see it. And more."

His skin felt tight for the rest of the drive. She was good at going after what she wanted. Good at making him feel wanted. He wondered what it was about her life, despite the hardships, that made her so unaware of her own appeal. What he wanted, more than anything at this moment, was to show her all the ways in which he found her appealing. On every level.

—————

Will parked in his garage, nervous like it was his first time. He'd realized, even before this, that she mattered. She'd snuck inside his heart quicker than lightning, and now she was all he could think about.

After they got out of the car, he opened the garage door that led into his kitchen, holding it so Lexi could go ahead of him. Her scent, hints of something softly floral, a little citrusy and fresh, curled around him, like a sensual dance, enticing him. He resisted the urge to lean in. *Let her get settled. No pressure. The woman could use a night off from pressure.* Even though it was her idea, he wondered what she really wanted. What she needed. Not just tonight but in life. When was the last time she'd been taken care of? Cherished? He should draw her a bath, give her a plush robe, and tuck her in for the night. As someone who took care of things in a fairly large family, it surprised him how much he wanted to take care of someone else, specifically, Lexi. To be there for her.

He closed the door behind them, tried to slow his actions and his thoughts. Soft rays of light came from the other room so they weren't in total darkness, but it wasn't until he flipped the kitchen light that he saw the counter.

Will groaned out loud at the obvious sign his sisters had been up to no good. His family was seriously out to mess up his chance at happiness.

He tossed his keys on the marble countertop, looked at Lexi's amused expression. "First chance I get, I'm taking all of their keys and changing the locks."

Lexi bit her lip but even that didn't stop her laughter. On his countertop were two framed photographs. One had Kyra blowing kisses to the camera. She'd attached a sticky note detailing her personality: I'M FUN, SMART, WICKED GOOD AT WORD GAMES, A FASHIONISTA, ROMANCE LOVER. The second was a picture of Maddie and Rachel on their wedding day, both of them in gorgeous gowns, their smiles brighter than the sun. Maddie, always the subtler one, kept her sticky note simple with both of their names, an arrow pointing to his sister on the left and her wife on the right. Between the two pictures was an enormous basket full of Halloween candies and miniature chocolate bars. It all seemed sweet on the outside but it meant they'd done some scheming and planning before coming to his house when they knew he'd be out. Total brats. All three of them. It looked like they'd bought up all of the holiday stock and dumped it in this basket. A folded card sat in front of the basket.

Will picked up the card and sighed again. "Brats. Just so you know? Sisters absolutely never stop being a pain in the ass."

Lexi moved in, sidling up close to him to read the note.

Dear William,

As your beloved sisters, we wanted to celebrate your engagement. Since you and Lexi have not yet registered, we thought we'd give you a gift we know you'll enjoy. It's best your fiancée learn early that you have the sweet tooth of a five-year-old child. We look forward to meeting her and sharing embarrassing stories of your childhood. 😉

P.S. We got your back with all of this. There's a treasure somewhere in the basket. Been a while since you've dated but hopefully you know what to do with it. Hi, Lexi. We can't wait to meet you. Thank you for putting up with our stuffy brother/brother-in-law.

Kyra, Madeline, & Rachel

Will groaned, embarrassment making him *feel* like a kid again. He looked at Lexi, only partially joking when he said, "I'll understand if you want to leave."

To his utter fucking relief, she laughed and threw her arms around him.

Twenty-one

Other than Maisie, Lexi didn't have much in the way of friends. The idea that these women wanted to meet her and obviously cared about their brother was beyond enticing. And that was a little worrisome. If she wasn't careful, she'd forget that a lot of this wasn't even real. What *was* 100 percent genuine was how much she didn't want to go home tonight. How much she wanted to explore this chemistry with Will. She might need to convince herself that she could keep her heart and her desire separate but she didn't want the fear of falling to prevent her from finding out just how sexy Will was under those collared shirts.

She pulled back from her spontaneous hug. "They sound delightful."

Will dropped the note on the counter. "Do they now?" He eyed the basket suspiciously.

She laughed again, pushing away all of her uncertainties to let herself live in the moment. Stepping into him again, she stretched her arms up to loop them around his neck. "Come on. They're having some fun with it. Which is what we should do. Right now, everyone is happy and blissfully unaware. What do you think the treasure is?"

Will's arms closed around her and he made her squeal when he lifted her, set her on the counter, and settled himself between her legs, his forehead dropping down to hers in that swooningly sweet way.

"You. You're the treasure."

Oh hell. How was she supposed to protect her heart, no matter how many layers of logic she'd wrapped it in, when he said things like that?

His hands moved, slid over her thighs, gently squeezing. "Actually, I'm scared to find out. I'm happy you find them amusing. I just don't want my family or this mix-up to wreck anything."

"Why don't we just focus on what we can control?" She kissed his neck, inhaling the scent of an almost woodsy aftershave—a tempting contrast with his designer sweater and jeans. His fingers slid to her hips, tightening, sending a thrill along her skin and through her entire being. She let her tongue touch the spot just below his Adam's apple, reveled in his sharp hiss of breath. "Let's just focus on us. On what we feel. And what we want." Her lips traveled up over his earlobe, and his shiver made her feel powerful. Wanted. "I want you." Maybe if she got him out of her system, she could keep things light and fluffy. Will Grand was an excellent distraction from reality, and if he could ignore their differences or the fact that one of their moms was over the moon and the other was unhappy about them, so could she. She wanted to live in the moment. *This* moment. This sexy, sweet man not only brought her back to life but made her smile and laugh. She deserved that.

"That sounds reasonable. Mature."

She laughed, kissed his chin. "That's me. Reasonable and mature."

Will leaned down and brushed his lips against her neck, copying what she'd just done to him, setting fire to her skin, awareness over every spot he touched.

"A sweet tooth, huh?"

He trailed up to her ear. "My sisters have big mouths. Now I need one of your secrets."

She was going to sleep with him. That was no secret to her. But for the first time in her life, she didn't feel like there was a rush. A need to reach the finish line as proof she could. Lexi pulled back.

Will stared at her, desire making his eyes darker. His hands flexed against her thighs where they rested.

"Let's play a game."

His brows arched.

Lexi laughed, twisting out of his hold to grab the candy basket and settle it on her lap. She rooted through it. "Truth or treat."

"That's not a game."

She looked up at him. "Is too. I just made it up."

He nodded, his lips twitching. "Right. How do you play?"

"You get to choose truth or treat. If you pick truth, the other person gets to ask any question they want and you have to answer no matter what. If you choose treat, you close your eyes and the other person gets to feed you any candy they choose."

Taking the basket from her lap, Will set it on the counter and helped her down. "Interesting. I like it. Should we move into the living room, get more comfortable?"

"We could. Or we could go up to your room and do it there." Lexi closed her eyes, feeling heat splash her cheeks even as the words left her mouth. She didn't look at him when she added, "The game. Do the *game* up there."

Will was grinning when she opened her eyes. "I think that sounds perfect. What pairs well with candy and chocolate? Wine? Beer? Juice? Water? Antacids?"

He set her at ease even when she embarrassed herself. "How about water for now?"

He grabbed two bottles from the fridge. Lexi carried the candy and they walked out of the kitchen, down the short hallway to the stairs. With every step, she wondered what she was doing. Was she fooling herself into believing she wouldn't get in too deep? Every moment she spent with him made her like him more. Made her like herself more.

They stopped on the landing of the second floor. It was large, big enough for a corner desk nestled in the nook. He had several books over the desk, neatly displayed on floating shelves. There were four closed doors.

Will pointed to the first, ignoring the others. "My room."

Pushing her nerves down the same way she used to when she was in her running position, her heart hammering as she waited for the sound of the gun, Lexi stepped around him, walked to his door, and pushed it open.

The room was about the size of her living room and kitchen combined. A four-poster, dark-wood bed sat against one wall, matching side tables that were both elegant and masculine. The large window had a dark-blue roll-down blind that matched the bedding. An oversized chair her mother would love sat angled toward a gas fireplace built into the wall. There were two hallways, one on each side of the fireplace.

"I want to live in this room," Lexi said, walking to the bed to set the candy down. She ran her hand over the comforter.

"Wait until you see the bathroom." He took her hand, pulled her down the hallway to the left, flipping a switch so the fire flared as he walked by. The hallway was short, leading to an arch letting them into the first area that housed two sinks built into gorgeous black cabinetry along the back wall. To the left, a slightly ajar door showed a powder room.

Will put a hand to her back, nudged her to the other side. "This way."

With two hands, he slid the opaque glass doors apart, opening up the room so she could see the rest. She walked forward, awe and envy swirling.

"It's like a spa," she whispered.

To the right was a dark-gray, tiled shower with a deep bench. A waterfall showerhead extended from the ceiling. Two other showerheads came out from lower on the walls. To her left the same gorgeous cabinetry as the other room lined the wall. The top surface was clearly meant to be a vanity with a long, thin, rectangular mirror extending all the way. Two stools were pushed under the cabinet.

Her eyes landed on the tub. Matte white, deep, and long, it was a freestanding oval that invited the bather to sink in and forget absolutely everything after a long day. There was a low, clear floating shelf against the wall that held candles and a couple of succulents; it seemed like a perfect place for a glass of wine.

"If we weren't already engaged, I'd propose to you just to get this tub."

Will's laugh settled into her soul, lighting her up. What if life were just like this? No sad moms, fake engagements, second jobs? Just her and him and this tub?

His arm wrapped around her waist from behind. "I was thinking earlier you deserved a long soak with a large glass of wine. How about after our game?"

She turned in his arms, too many feelings ricocheting in her chest. "How are you not already taken? With your face, your sense of humor, and this tub, you really are one of Seattle's finest."

Chuckling, he used his arm around her to turn her toward the bedroom. "I guess I was just waiting for the universe to throw a sexy, sweet, funny, clumsy waitress into my path."

She leaned back into him. "I promise my clumsiness doesn't extend to all areas of my life."

He chuckled, nuzzling her neck in a way that stopped her breath. "Just when carrying soup?"

"That's right. Lucky you," she teased.

When they reached the bed, he turned her again, stroked her hair back from her face, a look in his eyes that stole her breath.

"That's exactly what I was thinking, Alexandria. Lucky, lucky me."

Twenty-two

Will knew he should thank his sisters at some point but he'd wait to see what, exactly, they'd added to the candy basket. Lexi's gaze settled on his bed and he saw the quick flash of nerves. Stroking a hand down her arm, loving the feel of her skin under his palm, he smiled at her, stepped closer, lowered his head just to hear the intake of breath. She turned her face, putting their noses so close they nearly touched. Her pupils dilated, her mouth opened just a touch, her tongue wetting her lips.

She was waiting for his kiss. One he very much wanted to give. But he didn't want her nervous or thinking there was any pressure to take tonight further than she was ready for. More than that, he didn't want to rush anything with her. He wanted to savor everything about her. Her fingers linked with his, her breath accelerating.

"Tell me, Lexi . . ." he said, leaning in just a touch more, loving the way she shivered from his breath against her skin.

"Yes?" She swayed closer, her other hand coming to his waist.

He smiled. "Truth or treat?" He whispered the words and saw the surprise in her arched brows.

"Huh?" She scrunched her face up adorably. "Cute."

"You are that," he said, giving her a quick kiss through his laughter.

"Okay. Fine. Truth." She let go of his hand and went to the side of his bed, crawling up on it, settling herself cross-legged.

There were many, many other things he wanted to do with her on this bed but for now, he was surprisingly content with just this. In fact, this was probably about to get more intimate than either of them expected. The truth had a way of removing the barriers.

Moving a couple of pillows, he settled on the bed as well, leaning against the headboard, the basket between them.

"Truth. Let me think. Longest relationship?"

She smiled, fiddled with the wicker of the basket. "That's easy. Three weeks. Ninth grade."

He laughed. "No time or no interest?"

"That's another question. No cheating." She picked up a mini Mars bar, waved it around. "Truth or treat?"

"Truth."

Her smile widened. "What are you terrible at?"

Leaning forward, he grabbed the chocolate bar, opening it. "I'm bad at avoiding candy, crossword puzzles, actual puzzles, and making my own beer." He popped the chocolate in his mouth.

"That's a decent list. Do you often try to make your own beer?"

He finished chewing, crumpling the wrapper in his fingers. "I think that's cheating but I'll answer. I tried in college. In our dorm room. One batch that made Ethan and I sick for days."

"Oh no!"

"Admittedly, it tasted disgusting and we drank it anyway."

She shook her head. "Why? Why do guys do things like that?"

Making a fist, he pretended to pound his chest. "We're men."

Lexi snorted, kicking her legs out to the side and resting on the pillows beside him. "Nothing makes a manly statement like puking up your alcohol."

"Hey. We were college kids. I didn't drink beer again for a few years. Ethan ended up making a career out of it just to prove that he could do it and I couldn't."

"Then I guess it was worth it in the end."

"Your turn. Truth or treat."

Her lips curved up in a sweet smile that stirred feelings in his chest. "Treat."

His heart spasmed. "You have to close your eyes."

"Fine." She closed them.

Will pulled the basket closer, rooting through it. "Not allergic to anything?"

"Not that I know of."

His hand closed around something hard and square. Pulling it out, he bit back the swear word that popped in his brain immediately. Quietly opening the small box, he didn't know whether to be impressed or pissed that his sisters had thought to give him a ring to give to Lexi. Obviously, he hadn't been as subtle about his feelings as he'd thought through texts or at work when they asked about Lexi. He'd tried to play it off as just a reprieve from his mother's hounding and the ease of having a built-in date to the party. Kyra suggested a ring through their sibling group chat but Will had laughed it off. He should know better than to do that with either of his sisters.

He wasn't sure if it was real, but it was gorgeous. Square-cut diamond, or something that looked like one, on a thin platinum band.

"Are you choosing one or eating them all while I'm not looking?"

Chuckling, nerves suddenly making him overheated, he closed the lid on the box, tucked it on his other side. "Got one. No peeking."

He picked a Hershey's Kiss since it seemed fitting to the moment. After unwrapping it, he brought it to her mouth. "Open."

When she did, his stomach tightened. He set the candy in her mouth, watched as she tasted it, enjoyed it, and smiled.

"I love chocolate."

Unable to resist, he leaned in, pressed his mouth to hers, tasting both her and the candy. "Me too," he murmured against her lips.

She leaned into the kiss just long enough to make him want more before she pulled back, her hand on his chest. "Your turn. Truth or treat?"

"Treat."

Her smile was slow and sexy. "Close your eyes."

When he did, he heard her rooting through the basket, the crinkling of a wrapper, felt the nearness of her body when she came closer.

"Open," she whispered.

She put something in his mouth, the taste not registering as easily as the feel of her finger against his lips. Before he could close his lips around her finger, she pulled back and more flavor exploded on his tongue. Tangy. Or downright sour. His cheeks quirked, puckering. Lexi giggled.

Will opened his eyes, looked at the wrapper, not surprised to see she'd given him a Warhead. His mouth watered. Then his eyes. He grabbed her hand and yanked her closer, loving the way she laughed.

"Cruel."

"Yeah, don't give me one of those." She settled her upper body on his, fitting against him in a way he knew he could get used to.

"Truth or treat?"

Nestling her head into the crook of his arm, she tipped her head back. "Truth."

He wanted to know everything. "What makes you happy?"

She grinned, her finger absently stroking his chest. "Coffee. Tea. When my mom has good days. Maisie's pep talks." She lowered her chin, stared at her hand on his chest. "And lately, my fiancé."

He could feel the box digging into his thigh. The timing seemed right and she seemed so at ease with the whole ruse aspect of their relationship. So what was holding him back? *You're giving a woman a ring. It's okay to be a little freaked out.* What really fucking set his brain spinning, however, was the idea that he didn't mind the idea of slipping a ring on her finger. At all. "Speaking of . . . my sisters seem to have thought of everything. They're having way too much fun with this."

Lexi looked up again. "What do you mean?"

Will shifted, grabbed the box, and flipped it open with his thumb, held it out to Lexi.

She sat up fast, nearly smacking his chin with her head. "Holy shit. Is that real?"

Will laughed. "I don't actually know. Would you wear it? I mean, I suppose you would only need to when we're at events or with family."

Lexi looked like a kid in a candy store with too many options, like she wanted to snatch the offering and run just in case it was taken away.

"Okay, but what if I lose it?" Her eyes shifted from the ring to his gaze.

"Do you think you will?"

She laughed, touching it with exquisite gentleness. "No. But will I owe you like two point three million dollars if I do?"

Will plucked the ring from its case, feeling like the smile she brought out in him warmed him all the way through. "That's a very specific number." He set the box down beside him, held the ring between his thumb and his forefinger. "Alexandria Danby, I think you're amazing. You make me smile and laugh. I like who I am when I'm with you and I want to learn every one of your secrets. You take up a lot of space in my brain. Enough so that it should worry me. It would be my honor if you'd wear this as a symbol of our fake engagement. Doing so does not hold you liable should the ring be lost, stolen, or damaged."

Moving so she was on her knees, she held out her hand, spreading her fingers. "I like this pretend life of mine."

Will slipped the ring on her finger, keeping hold of her hand, and made sure she was looking right into his eyes when he spoke. "Just remember, it's not all pretend."

Her eyes widened but he didn't give her a chance to respond. Instead, he reached up, curled his fingers around the nape of her neck, and pulled her down for a kiss. Whether it was the intimacy of being on his bed, the simple allure of her, or the unexpected satisfaction of having her wear a ring that symbolized their connection, his need went from a simmer to a boil in the space of a few heartbeats.

She gave him her weight, settling against him, her soft curves aligning to his hard edges with a rightness he'd always thought would overwhelm him. Truly, he'd never expected to feel the things he was starting to feel when he was with her. That shouldn't surprise him since she'd thrown him off balance from their very first meeting. Even more surprising was how much he liked it. He just wished he knew his fiancée well enough to know how real it felt to her.

Twenty-three

The game had changed. Instead of taking turns asking truth or treat, they snacked on the candy while entwined with each other, asking for truths. They were still fully clothed and Lexi had never felt more naked. As much as it scared her, it felt right, and for once she didn't want to close herself off from possibility. It'd been so long since she'd felt it for anything.

"Second favorite color?" he asked.

It seemed like such a trivial question after asking about dating and fears. "Blue."

"There's a lot of blue in the world."

"You're right about that," she replied, referring more to the cloud of sadness she'd been living under. "Pale blue. Like the sky after rain. You?"

Will popped another Hershey's Kiss in her mouth. She'd never think of them the same way.

"Green."

It suited him. "What do you look for in a woman?"

Looking down at her, he smiled. "Seems smart to answer with something like, the one I'm currently holding in my arms."

Lexi laughed as she sat up, moving away to grab the basket again. Rooting through it, she was acutely aware of the weight of the gorgeous ring on her finger. Real or not, she was attached. She'd spend some time later thinking about how it felt to have this particular man give her something that symbolized something so special. For now, though, she wanted to do what she hadn't been able to years ago: Push reality aside. Forget it existed. This gorgeous, funny, sweet man wanted to date her. The engagement thing was a hiccup that didn't truly matter. The ring was just a ring. Will made her feel real. Made her feel happy.

"Don't be a chicken. Be honest. You've been around. You have a past. What do you like?" She went up on her knees, turned her body to face him, choosing a Kiss like he had.

Grabbing a purple sucker from the basket between them, he unwrapped it as he answered. "I think I've learned a lot about what I don't like from my past. I've had girlfriends. I thought I was in love with one of them, but it turned out she and her family loved my family's money more than me."

How could someone spend time with this man and think about anything other than how fucking awesome he was?

She reached out, kissed him. "She was an idiot."

His smile was soft. Sweet. Like something he shared only with her. He offered her his sucker, desire burning in his gaze when she took one quick taste. He pulled it back, tasted it himself before continuing.

"So I guess what I'm learning is that I like a woman who is independent but not so much so that she won't let me be a part of a solution if she's stuck. One who is kind. Funny. Honest. Someone who couldn't care less about my last name and has no connection to my mother. Someone who thinks meeting up with me for drinks after she worked all day and hanging out with a couple old enough to be our grandparents is fun. Someone who takes care of her mother without regard for her own dreams and goals. Someone who would lie on my bed and eat enough candy to make us both sick and consider it a date."

He looked at her with just a touch of vulnerability and Lexi's heart muscles spasmed. They were playing a dangerous game.

"This is the best date I've ever had."

Will's hand froze before the round lollipop hit his lips. "You're incredibly easy to please, Alexandria Danby."

Nerves pushed through her bloodstream. "You're incredible, period."

Will picked up the discarded wrapper, set his sucker on it on the bedside table, then moved the basket there as well. Lexi's heart rate sped up as if she'd run the hundred-meter dash without stretching. After years of not practicing.

"Come here, Lexi," he said softly, sitting up against the pillows he'd arranged against the headboard.

Lexi moved on her knees, their gazes fastened on each other like magnets powerless against the pull. He reached out a hand, settling it on her hip as she moved so one knee was on either side of his thighs. He put his other hand on her waist, lowered his gaze to his hands, then stroked them up, all the way, over her sides, brushing against her breasts before traveling up to her neck, her cheeks, and finally tunneling into her hair. They moved in tandem, her leaning down as he leaned up, their mouths meeting in the middle, her hands going to his broad, strong shoulders. She sighed into the kiss, happy to give up control of her emotions in favor of living in this moment. In this second.

Will crushed her against his chest and Lexi loved the closeness, the teetering-on-the-edge burst of need that emanated off both of them as he switched the angle of the kiss, as her hands went to his hair, his back, his arms, anywhere she could touch. She fumbled with the buttons on his shirt, eager to feel his skin against her own, against her lips. When she'd unfastened a few, she pressed her mouth to his neck, his collarbone, and let her hands spread the shirt, widening the opening so she could run her fingers over his muscles, the slight dusting of chest hair. When she began trailing her fingers down, his abs bunched and he grabbed her wrists, pulling her hands away from his body.

Will shifted, moved them so she was lying underneath him. "Let's slow down."

"No thank you," she said, yanking him back down for another kiss. He laughed against her mouth but her humor fled as he trailed his lips along her jaw, her collarbone, his hand sliding under her shirt, fingertips dancing over her heated skin.

The duality of what she felt overwhelmed her: passion and humor, happiness and an intense ache. Desire and tenderness. Protected and vulnerable. Both of their shirts were discarded and Lexi lost her ability to process. She knew reality would come crashing back in like a monster intent on destruction but right now, it was only them.

Sighs and kisses, smiles and touches that fired her up and soothed her all at once. Only them. Only this. They took their time, learning and lingering. Lexi wondered if she'd ever felt so appreciated or adored. The few instances she'd been with a man, there'd been one sole purpose, but with Will, everything had layers. Definitely an end goal but one that he was in no rush to reach. It was like he couldn't get enough of her and Lexi felt the same. She wanted everything and even if he gave it, she wondered if it would ever be enough.

Lexi had never wondered what it would be like to fall in love. For most of her teen years, she'd been too focused on track. In college, she'd worked hard, run hard, and only wanted fun on the side. Plus, she'd always had her parents as a compass for what love looked like. It was all-consuming, no room for anything else other than basic needs like working to put food on the table. Lexi had never wanted that kind of fixation on another person, that feeling of being so wrapped up in them you weren't sure of who you were without them.

But now, with little slivers of moonlight sneaking through his blinds, Will's hands cherishing her as he whispered her name with a reverent sigh, she could understand that kind of falling. She knew, after tonight, she'd have to do a better job securing her heart and protecting herself. Lexi had always considered herself immune to this sort of feeling, the sensation of getting lost in someone. But Will made it very real and that worried her. The engagement was a lie but the feelings weren't and if she wasn't careful, they'd multiply to a point she wouldn't be able to pull back. She wouldn't be able to save herself.

Twenty-four

Will had never bathed with a woman. Showered, sure. But he hadn't even had a bath by himself since he was a boy. There was definitely something to be said for sharing the tub with a gorgeous woman. Especially when that woman was Lexi. He might not know where she was at emotionally but he now knew exactly where he stood. The fall had happened. He'd landed. Now it was about managing the ground beneath his feet, hoping she'd catch up one day.

Will ran his finger along the nape of her neck. She'd tied her hair up on top of her head, much like the first day he'd met her just a couple of weeks ago. Only now, the steam from the water was making the little pieces sticking out curl. She shivered when his finger continued to glide up and down.

"I could live in this tub," she said, a contentment in her voice he wanted to take credit for.

"I'll just deliver your meals here, then?"

She laughed. "Perfect."

She was. He needed to put the brakes on his snowballing emotions. For one thing, they were still in the very early stages of dating. For another, they were tangled in a web of half-truths that had the potential to tie knots in a lot of relationships. He needed to tread care-fully but he also didn't want to deny the intoxicating feeling of falling. Whether this was why no other woman had seemed right, he didn't know. What he did know was that Alexandria made him *want* all of the things his mother nagged him about finding, that his sisters teased him about feeling.

Lexi used a cloth, ran it up and down his thigh. His knees were bent on either side of her and even though he'd never given much thought toward bathtubs, he was grateful to the designer of this one. They fit perfectly together.

"I was thinking, since you wanted Maisie to meet Ethan anyway, maybe we could meet up at Side Tap this week. Introduce them." Maybe if they spent more time with people who knew the truth, she'd realize how much of what was between them was real.

He wanted to show her that the only thing fake about them was the term *engagement* and the announcement in the paper.

She sighed and he loved the contented sound of it. "Sure. We'll have to see how the week goes, though. I said no to Brett for a shift and if he asks me to work, I need to say yes."

It took effort to push down the part of himself that wanted to smooth out her life. He knew better than to offer and needed to be okay with plans being a maybe rather than a for sure.

"I understand. I enjoyed meeting your mom today. You sure you feel okay about things?" He'd enjoyed witnessing Lexi's happiness over seeing her *mother's* happiness more than he anticipated. Regard-less of her self-deprecating personality, she definitely put others first.

Her body moved against his and he forgot his own question until she spoke. "I can't remember the last time I felt this good."

The near purr of the words had him gritting his teeth. She leaned her head back, angled it so she was looking up at him. *Beautiful* wasn't the right word. It wasn't enough to encapsulate how looking at her stole his breath.

"I wouldn't have predicted her happiness over my getting married."

Will stroked a finger along her jaw. "I'm glad it didn't make things worse. Our anniversary slash birthday celebration is next Saturday. It's fall-themed," he said.

"It's a special night for your family," she said with what sounded like a hint of uncertainty.

Leaning forward, he grabbed the body wash and squirted some in his hands, pushed her forward a bit to wash her back. He moved his hands over her, pressing into the tight muscles, wanting, more than was prudent, to take care of this woman.

He ignored her sigh of enjoyment and explained. "It is. I want you there. By my side. With me. I don't always love the flashy events but this one is being put on by my family to celebrate my grandfather. I want you to meet him. I want him to meet *you*."

"Fall-themed. Will it be ultra-fancy?" Her shoulders tensed even as she dropped her head down, exposing her neck.

He stroked his hands over her back, let his thumbs dig in. "I wouldn't say ultra. Something tells me you'll look amazing in a cocktail dress."

He felt the muscles tense under his hands. "Lexi. I'm going to ask you not to be stubborn about what I say next."

"No guarantees."

Will cupped his hands to hold water, let it wash over her back. "You're already on a limited budget. I'm not going to feel right about causing you financial stress."

"You're in a very vulnerable position to be offering to Pretty Woman me," she said, a warning in her tone.

It made him smile and recall Shakespeare's famous quote: *Though she be but little, she is fierce!*

"Pretty Woman you?" It'd been a while since he saw that one with Kyra.

"Yeah, you know, give me your credit card and send me shopping on Rodeo Drive."

He pulled her back against his chest, wrapping his arm around her middle, doing his best not to get distracted by her skin.

"Rodeo Drive is in Beverly Hills. The best I could do here is the Shops at the Bravern," he teased, referring to the luxury mall his sisters and mother often shopped at. He squeezed her closer when she started to turn, a low growl in her throat that absolutely delighted him. God, she was adorable and fun. "But I was actually hoping that you'd allow one of my sisters to lend you clothing for this and whatever future events we might have. There won't be many and they have more dresses and outfits than most of the shops they frequent."

She relaxed almost immediately. "Oh. Okay. I suppose that would be all right."

Will pressed a kiss to her neck, his fingers trailing up and down her arm. "Thank you."

"I have told you repeatedly, I'm not really a fancy-event kind of girl," she said, that hint of vulnerability nestling into his heart.

"I should tell *you*: I think you're so much more than you see yourself as."

She turned, water sloshing as she faced him. "I like the way you see me."

He couldn't stop his gaze from roaming her body or the hunger that lodged in his chest. She was stunning.

Needing to lighten the moment, for both of their sakes, he gave her a smirk. "Me too. Especially right this minute."

She laughed into their kiss and he was pretty sure they got water everywhere. At the moment, though, he couldn't have cared less. All that mattered was the woman in his arms. The one who was quickly becoming someone he cared about a great deal.

Seattle Times

LOCAL

- Art festival needs further funding. How can you help?
- William Grand's fiancée is a former all-star track athlete. What's got them *running* for the aisle so quickly?
- Restaurant pavilion to open in Queen Anne District

ENTERTAINMENT

- New brewery backed by hometown hero
- Grand family celebrates 50 years in business

Twenty-five

When Lexi got home Sunday afternoon, her mom was awake and working in her office. Leaning against the doorjamb, she watched as Gwen hunched over her worktable, a pair of glasses perched on the tip of her nose as she used tweezers to glue a tiny vase of pink flowers to a small table with a red-and-white-checkered cloth. If she took away the fact that this was how her mother buried her grief rather than facing or dealing with it, they were quite exquisite creations.

"I can feel you watching me," Gwen said without looking up.

"That whole *eyes in the back of the head* thing is no myth," Lexi said, walking into the room and taking some time to peruse the displays.

Scenes from so many books her mother loved. There were little place cards in front of each. She added new ones all the time: Lyssa Kay Adams, Helen Hoang, Melissa Foster. Lexi hadn't read most of the books her mom created scenes for. Not because she had anything against romance books—she loved reading—but she had more varied tastes. And didn't want to plant unattainable wishes in her own head. But maybe the books were actually helping her mother find herself.

Gwen put down the items and turned, a grin blooming on her

face. "Hello, my darling daughter. How was your night? And your morning?"

Lexi didn't blush but she did laugh and dart her gaze away for a quick second. "Pretty spectacular, actually."

Gwen walked close, pulling Lexi into her arms. "That makes me happy."

Wrapping her arms around her mother, she took a deep breath, closing her eyes and absorbing the moment. She just wanted her back all the way. But did a person every truly return to themselves when they'd lost someone who made them whole?

She didn't want to feel that for Will. For anyone. It scared her that she knew, in the depths of her brain and heart, that she could become Gwen. She could fall in love so hard she never recovered.

"You okay?"

"I am. I love you, Mom. I hope you know that."

Gwen squeezed, reminding Lexi how frail her body was. "I do. And I love you back."

Lexi pulled away, grinned. "I brought apples."

Gwen nodded. "I promised you pie. But I'm working on this." A little flush of guilt washed over her mother's cheeks.

"It's okay." Races weren't run without laying the groundwork. Her mother still planned to make a pie. That was a good sign.

Lexi turned back at the door. "I'll run out and get the stuff we need for piecrust. Should we do one of those already-made ones?" This conversation on the heels of an amazing night almost felt normal. The kind of normal she'd forgotten existed.

Her mom picked up the glue, maybe just to have something in her hands, because she didn't go back to work. "We could try a homemade one. It's been a while but I remember the recipe."

Push. "Come with me."

Her mother's expression shut down. "No thank you." Her fingers tightened on the closed bottle. *Well, that lasted all of thirty seconds.*

"Mom."

"Don't do this."

Irritation and possibly a little sleep deprivation that she wasn't at all sorry for spurred her on. "Don't do what? Ask my grown mother to come to the grocery store with me? Mom. I can't do everything."

The lines around Gwen's eyes deepened even as her gaze flashed with anger. "Order and have it delivered. Don't be a martyr."

"Jesus. A martyr? Really, Mom? I'm asking you to come run one errand with me. Spend some time with me outside of this godforsaken house."

Her mother smacked the glue bottle down on the table. "Don't you talk about this house in a negative way. It's not just an errand to me."

"Then what is it?" Lexi worked to soften her voice. "Tell me what it is so I can help."

"You can't help," Gwen said, fury and sadness in her tone.

"I can."

"Stop."

"No." Lexi didn't mean to shout but she couldn't keep pretending it was all okay.

"I can't go there. The grocery store I spent hours at every week? If I do and I see people I know, they'll want to know how I am and I'll say I'm fine when I won't ever be. They'll give me pitying glances and talk behind my back. I can't go anywhere we used to go because all I'll see is him and part of that sounds wonderful but it'll rip me apart because I'll have to talk about him. It'll remind people that I'm here and he's not." Her mom's shoulders shook even as her voice broke.

Lexi hurried forward, pulled her into a tight hug, stroking Gwen's hair like her mother had done for her when she was little. "Okay." She murmured the word over and over again.

Gwen's tears softened but her hold on Lexi didn't. "I'm sorry."

"Don't be," Lexi said, still stroking her hair. "I'm glad you told me. You should have told me."

Lexi pulled back, used her shirt cuff to dry her mom's eyes. Gwen sniffed, gave a little laugh of embarrassment.

"I guess we've both been keeping things to ourselves." She arched her brows and for a second, Lexi thought of telling her the truth. But she was happy with Will. She liked being with him and wanted to be with him more. She didn't want to ruin this moment, any hint at progress. It hurt no one to leave it as it was.

Squeezing her mom's arm once more, Lexi stepped away. "I'll go grab the stuff for pie. If you're not up to making it when I get back, we can save it for later this week."

Gwen let out a shaky breath. "Grab a couple of premade shells. That way we'll get pie no matter how I'm feeling."

Lexi laughed. "Okay. Text me if you need anything else."

———

Lexi's emotions felt like they'd taken the front-row seat on a roller coaster. She sat in the grocery store parking lot, head resting against the seat. Last night was the kind of thing her mother's books talked about: a connection that went beyond physical. One that shook her because if it was this powerful now, what would it be like two weeks from now? Five weeks? Could she see further than that?

Her phone buzzed. It was like being popular again, only this time she didn't need the adoration and attention of others. It wasn't something she'd ever craved until it went away and she'd felt a little lost without it. Pulling her phone from her pocket, she checked the message. Jackie had amusingly named their group chat We're Still Cool.

Jackie

> Guess what? We were invited to the Grands' birthday bash. No getting out of hanging out now. Becs, you going?

Becca

> I am. Lexi, you've been all over the socials.
> Also, where the hell are your socials? You
> need my help.

Lexi hadn't googled Will again because she didn't really want to know what was being said. Living inside this bubble was different than the one she'd been trapped in for the last few years. This one was fun.

She felt like a teenager again when she typed the words:

Lexi

> What are you guys wearing?

Jackie

> Something new. Shopping trip?

Becca

> I have a few dresses that were sent to
> me by local designers. You girls want
> to try one each?

Lexi's heart rate sped up. *It's okay to say yes.* Sure, Will said he'd talk to his sisters but guys forgot things and this way she didn't have to get to know them by borrowing something. Plus, her friends wanted to do this with her. She'd forgotten what it felt like to have a circle of friends. Of support. She leaned so heavily on Maisie for all of her emotional, mental, and friendship needs she found herself wondering if her bestie needed a break.

A new text popped up as she urged herself to respond affirmatively to Becca's kind offer.

Ethan

> Wondering if I can set up a Zoom call with you and Brady and I to talk things through. Easier for him right now to do it from home.

And another.

Brett

> Can you work today?

Lexi answered him first.

> **Lexi**
>
> I can be there in an hour?

Brett

> That'll work.

She switched over to Ethan's messages.

> **Lexi**
>
> I'm not at the dress shop tomorrow.

Bitsy had also decided to hire a few part-timers instead of having someone there full-time. That way, she didn't have to rely on one person so heavily. Lexi planned to work on her project, typing up her interview and finishing off this week's reading, but she could juggle it all. Better than having nothing to juggle.

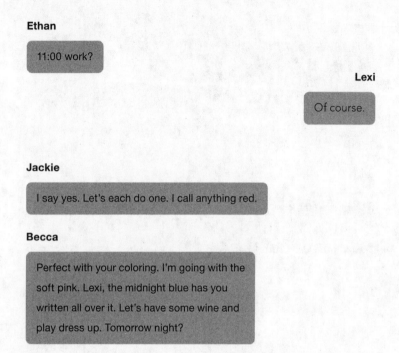

Ethan

11:00 work?

Lexi

Of course.

Jackie

I say yes. Let's each do one. I call anything red.

Becca

Perfect with your coloring. I'm going with the soft pink. Lexi, the midnight blue has you written all over it. Let's have some wine and play dress up. Tomorrow night?

Nerves bubbled, making her hands feel shaky. She'd gone from no plans to too many plans. One job to too many jobs. One friend to several. Being single to exclusively dating someone who seemed too good to be true.

When the phone rang, she actually jumped before she pressed ACCEPT on her Bluetooth.

"Hello." Her breath whooshed out. *Fucking breathe. Calm the hell down.*

"Hi." Will's voice came through the speaker like much-needed oxygen that soothed all her fraying edges.

"Hi."

"I want to see you."

She smiled, ignored the incoming texts.

"You just saw me. A lot of me."

"Mmm. Now I'm addicted. Come over."

"I have to work."

"After?"

She should say no. But she didn't want to.

"It could be late."

"I'll take whatever I can get."

Lexi felt like she was watching her heart from afar, watching it slip slowly from its rusty, vine-covered cage and from her grasp. "I'll see you tonight."

When they hung up, she went back to the group chat.

Jackie

> We should plan an engagement party for you, Lexi.

Becca

> Any excuse for a party. Also, check this out. You two are so hot I'm fanning myself with my phone.

Little fingers of guilt tapped on her shoulder, sending her nerves for one more loop the loop on that roller coaster. It didn't matter that they thought she was engaged. She wasn't really lying. Okay. She was lying but still. They were just excited to have reconnected but it would die off and by the time everyone learned the truth, they probably wouldn't even still have the group chat.

She clicked on the link and gasped. It was clearly a photo from Side Tap, and the credit said *Seattle Times*. Lexi recalled the photographer who'd been weaving in between people.

Seattle's own William Grand supporting his longtime friend Ethan Reynolds's "Fall Festacular" at Side Tap Brewing while getting cozy with his fiancée.

Becca sent another link. This time to her own Instagram where she'd shared the photo and captioned it:

Look at these hotties! My girl Alexandria the Great & her fiancé, William Grand of Grand Babies. Aren't they beautiful? SO many good wishes for them. Drop a congratulations below.

There were more hashtags than Lexi knew what to do with. There were also several thousand likes. Holy shit. The photo itself was beautiful. Not quite black and white, not color, it was that in-between style. In profile, it captured them with their gazes locked on each other, Will's index finger stroking down her cheek.

They might not be engaged but there was absolutely nothing fake about the feelings between them.

In that moment, Lexi understood her mom's desire to hide in the house and push the outside world away. Unfortunately, she didn't have that option.

Lexi

I have to go; bunch of errands.
Tomorrow works for dresses.

Lexi whipped through the store, grabbing the items they needed for pie and a few other necessities. She ignored her phone buzzing in her pocket and focused on what needed to be done. On the drive home, she got caught up thinking about how Gwen had opened up. She hadn't gotten her mom out of the house but the fact that now she knew *why* meant maybe she could approach things differently.

The Seattle traffic conspired against her and Lexi ran, literally, into Fairway Bistro about four minutes after the time she'd promised. The place was packed. With a quick glance at Brett, she set herself up and asked one of the waitresses where she was needed.

Three hours into one of her busiest shifts ever, she was actually feeling pretty good. Sure, she'd messed up a little here and there, but the good thing about the hectic pace was she couldn't dwell on it.

But like all of the things that threw a kink in her step, the next moment happened without warning. When she came around the wall that separated the pass-through bar from the dining area, she saw Carolyn and Will's mom walk in. When she turned to go back the way she'd come, panic zipping through her veins, she smacked into Brett, not only knocking him back a step but causing him to drop the salad he was carrying.

She heard the muttered curse words under his breath as she bent to help clean up the mess.

"Leave it," he said, his irritation barely masked. "Just go greet the two women who came in. Seat them in Reese's section."

"I can't," she whispered, picking up lettuce and putting it back on the plate. "I'll go get someone to remake this. I'm sorry."

She couldn't go out there. God. She could just imagine Carolyn's face if she greeted her as a waitress. Will's mom's disdain. Carolyn's triumph? No thank you. She tried to take the plate from Brett.

He yanked it, sending more salad flying. "Just *go*. Help them."

Okay. Time to appeal to her already cranky boss. "Brett, please. I can't help those two women."

She watched his jaw tighten. "Why?"

Oh, because I'm fake engaged to the older woman's son and the younger woman would love a reason to get further into his mother's good graces. Because it would be humiliating and I can't handle that right now.

"I just can't." *Please let it be good enough.*

"Lexi. I've exhausted my patience where you're concerned."

She frowned at that. "Hey. I'm here covering a shift because you asked."

He shook his head. "Greet the women or go home. And don't come back."

Her mouth dropped. Her fingers were sticky with the salad dressing and her heart felt like it might leap out of her chest.

"You can't fire me over this," she whisper-hissed.

"I didn't say you were fired. I said do your job or leave. And don't come back."

Lexi undid her apron and tossed it on the plate he was still gripping like a ledge he was about to fall off.

"I'll pick up my last check next week. Make sure my tips are added to the envelope."

Lexi walked past him, grabbed her stuff from her locker, and hurried to her car. It felt like she held her breath the whole way there and when it came out in the safety of her car, tears came with it.

Twenty-six

Will frowned at his phone, only half listening to his father run through the pros and cons of walking away from Home Needs versus staying the course. Lexi had canceled on him last night and wasn't returning his texts.

Their night together had been incredible and he knew, without a doubt, he was falling in love with her. Of course, he couldn't tell her that. She was a runner. A fast one. With a fear of falling. Those two things were not a good combination.

"William," his father snapped, slapping his hand down on the table. "If it's not too much, do you think we could have your input?"

"I swear, William, ever since meeting *that* woman, you've been a different person." His mother had her hands folded on the table, looking at him like he was an abstract painting she couldn't understand.

She was right, though. Lexi was changing him. "*That* woman's name is Lexi. My input is we walk away. They wanted to ride our reputation because Nolan is wrecking theirs. I'm not sure why we feel the need to expand so dramatically. We're spread thin as it is. I've been talking to Holden Wright of Comfort Plus. He's agreed to a meeting."

"With what goal?" Maddie asked, leaning back in the black leather chair.

A quick glance at Kyra, who nodded in support, gave him the push he needed.

"A possible collaboration on some new products—a line of products, actually. Ones that will allow us further reach without selling our soul. I also spoke to Kyra. She's been researching ethically sustainable products for a while now. She thinks they're a great partnership for what she hopes to do when she's finished her degree, and it would let her be part of something big now."

His grandfather had his fingers steepled under his chin, listening and watching. Will hated the feeling that there was something not being said.

"Set up the meeting," his granddad said. When Will's father started to argue, his own father silenced him with a look. "I know you want Grand Babies to be an empire but Will is right. What we've done has worked. What I wanted was a family-run business in a city I love. That's what we have. That's what I want to leave behind."

Will's gaze snapped to his granddad. "Are you okay?"

His grandpa chuckled. "I'm just fine, William. But I do have some news. I was waiting for the birthday party to share but maybe this is better with just us. Just family."

Will gripped the pen in his hand to the point that his knuckles turned white. "What news?"

The rest of his family leaned in as though Jeremy Grand didn't have a booming voice that could captivate an entire ballroom.

"I'm retiring. Stepping down."

"What? Dad. Why?" Will's dad pushed back from the table. "What's going on?"

"Are you ill, Jeremy?" his mother asked.

"No, Emily. I'm old," Jeremy said with a laugh. "I want to travel with my wife. I want to sleep in and go to bed late. I want to pass the torch. It's time. Fifty years. I don't know where they went. I can tell you, though, they've been incredible. Watching all of you come aboard and help me make my dream soar is more than any man could ask for. Now that there's a chance for a clear direction for Kyra to come aboard as well? That's all I've ever wanted."

"You don't think that if you were going to cast me in the role of CEO, you should have given me a heads-up?" Will's dad put his hands on his hips, his suit jacket stretching with the movement.

Will didn't understand how that was his dad's takeaway from all of this. He looked at Maddie, who was oddly silent, before turning toward his grandfather. "I'm happy for you. You deserve this next chapter."

Jeremy reached out, patted Will's hand. "Thank you, William. So do you." He looked at his own son, the cool expression of a man who'd made many powerful decisions. "To answer your question, no, Jackson. I didn't think that, because I'm not naming you as CEO." He looked over at Maddie. "Madeline is stepping into my shoes."

The look his sister gave their grandfather suggested that she'd known. Will shook his head, a smile gracing his lips. "You knew."

Maddie grinned. "You're not the only one with secrets."

Kyra clapped and hugged their sister even while their parents were frozen in shock. "I'm so happy for you."

"This is outrageous. And an insult," Will's dad finally said.

"This is how you thank us for giving you our whole lives? Our children? Our time and energy? Really, Jeremy, I thought more of you."

His grandfather waved away the words with a hand through the air. "Oh, stop. This is what's best for all of you. You can be mad but you'll see, staying in the positions you currently hold will give you time to be together. To figure out what your own next steps are. I love this place with my whole heart and soul but I love my wife too, and it's time to make our lives together the priority. Don't wait as long as I did to realize time is fleeting. There's more to it than work."

The words churned in Will's gut. "You're really okay, though?"

"I'm excellent, William. I'm following my gut and my heart like I

194 | Sophie Sullivan

did when I started this company. If you're smart, you'll do the same. I look forward to meeting Lexi."

"Would have been nice to meet her before you invited her to join the family," his mother said, huffing out a breath.

Will stood. "I apologized for springing that on you. You need to let it go. She's an incredible person who cares for everyone around her. You'll respect her or you won't see either of us." He put a hand on his grandfather's shoulder. "I'm happy for you, Granddad." Looking over at Maddie, he smiled, his chest tight. "I'm happy for you, too, Sis."

The grin she gave him reminded him of when they were younger. "I'm your boss now. You have to say that."

Will laughed, his emotions feeling like dice in a Yahtzee cup. "I have a meeting."

He hadn't reached his office yet by the time his sisters were on his heels, following after him, Kyra overtaking him and reaching his office first.

When they were all inside, Maddie shut the door. Kyra pounced. "It's not pretend anymore."

He knew what she was talking about. "The only part that was ever pretend was the engagement."

"You're in love with her," Maddie said, leaning against the door.

"I don't know what I am," he said honestly. Was this what love felt like? The worry that someone wouldn't want him back the same way? The fear that Alexandria could walk away at any moment and leave him with an emptiness he'd never be able to get over? A lightness at the thought of her? Images of what it would be like to wake up next to her every single day? For good?

Before either of them could push, he looked at Kyra. "She needs a dress for the party. I told her you might have something she could borrow and that I'd give you her number."

Kyra walked over and wrapped her arms around him, hugging

him hard. He squeezed her back, his thoughts whirling like a tornado. When Kyra stepped away, he looked at Maddie.

"You didn't tell us."

Maddie left her spot at the door and moved to the leather couch, sat down. "I was shocked. He only told me a couple of weeks ago. He's been thinking about it for a lot longer, though."

"Dad is pissed." Kyra shook her head as she walked to the mini fridge beside the couch and pulled out a water. "So is Mom. But Grandpa made the right decision. You're going to be awesome at this, Mads."

"You absolutely are. And Dad will get over it. So will Mom. Your vision for the future aligns more with Gramps's. We tried Dad's way. It wasn't going to end well."

They sat there, the three of them, all a little lost in the events of the morning. Things were changing. Will knew change was inevitable. That didn't make it less frightening. His fingers itched to text Lexi, to call her and hear her voice. But clearly, she needed some space. He just hoped it was temporary.

Twenty-seven

Technically, she hadn't been fired. She'd quit. Sort of. She'd simply made a choice. *You chose your fake fiancé over a job. Not cool, Lex. Not cool.* But the thought of serving Carolyn and Emily had been just one more punch Lexi couldn't brace for.

She'd had her Zoom call with Ethan and Brady this morning, ironing out a few details like wages, expectations, and scheduling. She'd texted Jackie and Becca to tell them tonight wouldn't work and then turned her phone off. Because even though she hadn't been fired and she actually had something to celebrate with this new opportunity at Side Tap, Lexi couldn't shake the feeling that everything was about to come tumbling down around her. Which was saying something since she hadn't risen up from the rubble of three years ago yet.

"I made some eggs," Gwen said from the doorway.

Lexi continued staring at the ceiling of her childhood bedroom. It no longer had posters of Taylor Lautner or Nick Jonas, but the little pieces of popcorn ceiling that had ripped when she took them off were a reminder of her former self. Her hopeful *anything can happen* self.

"I spoke to the counselor while you were on the computer today," Gwen said.

Lexi sat up in her bed, looked at her mom. "That was hours ago. Why didn't you tell me?"

Gwen shrugged one shoulder. "You were mopey and I didn't know what to say."

Lexi laughed but there was no energy behind it. "It would be a good time to point out the irony. Also, I'm not mopey." *Lies.* She *was* mopey and it was pissing her off.

"What happened?"

Lexi threw her legs over the side of the bed, contemplated getting up, having some eggs. It wasn't often Gwen made them anything to eat.

"Nothing."

"You were never a very good liar," Gwen said.

Lexi stared after her when she walked away. *A lot you know. You think I'm engaged. That a man like Will would marry me. A woman who can't even hold a job as a fucking waitress.* She might not have quit but it definitely wasn't something she'd been good at. Lexi got up and found her mom in the kitchen. The eggs were in a bowl on the counter, dishes in the sink. A bag with the logo AURORA NURSERY caught her gaze.

"What's this?" She was already opening the bag before her mom could respond. She looked back over her shoulder when she saw what was inside. "Tulip bulbs?"

Gwen scooped a small forkful of eggs off her plate, nodding. "Maisie dropped them off for me. She was in a rush; she's doing an engagement shoot and wanted to beat the traffic."

"Okay. Why?"

"Why what?"

Lexi's laugh felt rough. "I feel like you're being deliberately obtuse. Why the tulips, Mom?"

She finished chewing before setting her plate down. "I used to like gardening. Do you remember?"

Lexi nodded. She used to like gardening; Lexi used to like run-ning. They used to be and do a lot of things.

"The therapist asked me to think about something I used to enjoy. Something from the past that really had nothing to do with your fa-ther. And I remembered I liked gardening. So I asked Maisie to pick me up some tulips. I'm going to plant them."

"When?" Lexi's heart was beating too fast. This was progress. This was reclaiming something and moving forward. Holy shit. This was hope.

"Now. Want to help?"

Lexi nodded, her throat uncomfortably tight.

"Do you want to eat first?" Gwen gestured to the eggs.

Lexi shook her head. "I got fired. From waitressing." That was all she could say. How could she tell her mom, right now when Gwen was fully engaging in the moment, the reason why? That she'd been embar-rassed to greet her pretend future mother-in-law who'd shown up with a woman who suited Will better than Lexi did? No.

"I'm sorry, honey. But you got the other job. You paid your tuition, right?"

They headed for the stairs. "Yes. To both. But it still sucks to be fired from a job I didn't even like. One I couldn't seem to get better at. It makes me feel like a failure." Or like she didn't deserve the things unfolding in her path. Side Tap. Will. Fuck. She really liked Will. And that was unexpected. Because she'd always promised herself she wouldn't become her mother.

At the bottom of the stairs, Gwen touched Lexi's arm, turned her so they were facing each other. "You're the most resilient person I know, Alexandria. You're not a failure."

Lexi hugged her mom, smiled into her hair. "You say that now but I haven't wrecked your flower beds yet."

When Gwen laughed, the vise on Lexi's heart loosened.

By the time the sun was setting in the sky, the cool air turning cold, Lexi and her mom had dirty hands and a front garden bed full of tulip bulbs.

"It's going to look like a rainbow," Lexi said.

Gwen sat back on her heels, surveying their work. It didn't look like much, just a box of dark dirt, freshly watered. But they'd pulled all of the weeds, turned the dirt, smoothed it out, and planted in a literal rainbow shape. It was going to be amazing.

"It is. I can't wait until spring."

Lexi stared at Gwen, who'd started gathering up the tools and discarded bulb bags. It was the first time in a very, very long time she'd heard her mom say something about the future. That her mom had been anticipating something.

Before she could respond, a sleek and unfamiliar Mercedes pulled into their driveway. Will's sisters exited the vehicle, Kyra opening the back passenger-side door.

Maddie smiled sheepishly. She was dressed in a pair of linen slacks and a dark-green cable-knit sweater. Her hair, the same color as Will's, was pulled back from her elegant face in a twist.

"Hi. Sorry to just drop by," Maddie said as Kyra rounded the back of the car, her arms full of plastic garment bags.

"We're not, really. Will said he couldn't reach you but you needed dresses so we raided our closets and brought them to you. Is this a bad time?"

Gwen, a trowel in one hand, dirt on her cheek, all but beamed at them. "It absolutely is not. I'm Gwen Danby, Lexi's mom."

"Oh, it's wonderful to meet you," Kyra said, both sisters walking down the little path beside the driveway.

"Yes, so nice to meet you. You were gardening. What did you plant?"

"Tulips," Gwen replied.

"Love tulips. Perfect timing to get them in," Maddie said.

Kyra tilted her head toward Maddie. "She loves gardening but never has the time. Me, I like fake flowers because it seems cruel to buy or plant something I'm bound to kill."

Lexi couldn't process the moment. Will's sisters were standing in her driveway with what were likely designer dresses, chatting about tulips and gardening.

"You should start with a succulent," Gwen said, gathering up the rest of their things. "They're easy to care for."

Maddie laughed and picked up one of the shovels, pitching in like she wasn't dressed for an elegant dinner party. "Don't encourage her. She's really bad at it. Good at other things but really, painfully bad at gardening."

The three of them laughed and Lexi stared on, feeling like an observer.

"You girls are going to try on dresses?" Gwen asked as they walked toward the open garage to put the stuff away.

Lexi forced herself to follow behind. It was one thing to let Will in. But his family? It was easy to ignore his mother and father because, really, they didn't like her all that much. But Kyra and Maddie? They were lovely. Funny, smart, driven, and successful. The kind of women Jackie and Becca would hang out with. *And you.*

"If Lexi is up for it," Kyra said, looking at her over the armload of dresses.

Gwen's smile pulled Lexi out of her low-grade panic over forming extra attachments. "How fun. You should text Maisie. That's her best friend. She should be here, too. If she's done working."

Maddie took some of the dresses from her sister. "My wife, Rachel, wanted to come but she's a bit under the weather."

Lexi looked her way. "I'm sorry. Is she okay?"

She didn't understand the soft smile that ghosted Maddie's lips. "She is. She'll be fine. How'd you enjoy the treat basket the other night?"

Warmth immediately flooded Lexi's face and a whole bunch of

other areas, too. The other three women laughed and she couldn't help but join in.

They moved and talked around her and within half an hour, Lexi was cleaned up and standing in her bedroom with Will's sisters treating her like she'd always been around, sharing their thoughts on dresses and tidbits about their day. They told her about their grandfather's announcement while her mom served them wine Maisie had left the other night.

Kyra glanced at her phone. "Will wanted assurance that you're okay."

Little fingers of guilt gripped her heart. He cared about her. He'd been clear about that and the truth was, she cared about him. She could do that and still not fall all the way, right? Weren't there varying degrees of falling? She picked up her phone, turned it back on, and checked her messages.

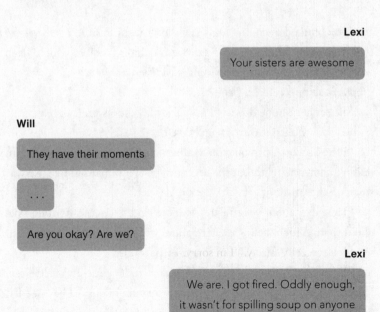

Lexi

Your sisters are awesome

Will

They have their moments

. . .

Are you okay? Are we?

Lexi

We are. I got fired. Oddly enough, it wasn't for spilling soup on anyone

Will

> I'm sorry. What can I do?

Lexi

> I'm surrounded by women who are making me laugh, my mom is happy, and I'm about to try on some of the most beautiful dresses I've ever seen. I'm okay.

Will

> Okay. Text me later?

Lexi

> I will

Lexi blinked away the tears she didn't want to fall. *Throw yourself into the moment.* Maddie and Kyra were debating colors while Gwen went to answer the door. Apparently, Maisie was there.

Kyra stepped closer. "You okay?"

She set her phone down. "I am. Your brother is pretty great."

Maddie moved toward them. "We think so."

"He was worried about you. Is this too much? We know your mom doesn't know the truth but the rest of it . . ." Kyra paused like she was stuck on the words.

"He cares about you, Lexi," Maddie said. "There's nothing fake about that. Which means we care about you too." Maddie spoke with so much sincerity Lexi's heart squeezed painfully.

"I'm a fired waitress, a part-time, *mature* student just shy of a degree. I live with my mother and we're barely staying afloat." They needed to see her as she really was. Will was seeing her through rose-colored glasses. They needed to see the truth so they could have the whole picture.

"You're a woman who makes my brother laugh and smile," Maddie said as Maisie's and Gwen's voices came from the hallway.

"When he talks about you, his eyes actually light up."

Her heart ballooned to near bursting.

"What someone does isn't nearly as important as who they are," Maddie said quietly as Maisie and Gwen joined them.

"Oh my God. Those dresses are amazing. I'm Maisie, Lexi's bestie, but I'll totally trade her in for whichever one of you is willing to give me one of those dresses."

All of them laughed. As Maisie and Kyra took point, deciding which ones would look best on Lexi, Maddie chatted with Gwen, even going down the hall to see her miniatures. Lexi took it all in. The moment, the women, the feelings. Things had changed in a heartbeat. And not just in a bad way. Hours ago, she'd felt alone and unsure. Defeated. And now?

Now she felt like anything was possible.

Twenty-eight

Maisie stood behind Lexi, making her feel like she *was* back in high school again, getting ready for a party or a night out. Of course, then she'd have been with Jackie and Becca. And she would be again tonight.

Nerves assaulted her in a way they never would have as a teen. She'd been too young and full of herself. How did someone who knew so little of the world feel so incredibly confident? Graduating made her feel like she was ready to take on the world. But even before her dad's death, it'd been harder than she expected. Maisie peered around her so she too could look in the full-length mirror on the back of Lexi's bedroom door.

"You look smoking hot. Will's sisters know how to shop. Every dress is gorgeous but I think this is the one." Maisie walked over to the closet where they'd hung the gowns. All of them, Gwen included, had fun trying on the real-deal name-brand designers. Prada, Chanel, Ralph Lauren. The collective cost of the couture garments in her room would probably buy a new car. Kyra had said she didn't wear any of the dresses anymore. On one hand, Will's younger sister reminded her of Maisie with her enthusiasm and openness, which made it easy to connect. On the other, the woman handed her thousands of dollars' worth of dresses and said she could donate what she didn't want to keep. Which, while sweet, flashed a light on their differences.

"I really thought the burgundy would be the one with your hair and eyes. I had no idea you looked so amazing in green." Maisie lifted a pale-pink dress from the hanger and held it up against her body.

The emerald-green Calvin Klein she'd chosen had a V-neck bodice that was both sexy and discreet. *Perfect for polite society.* Lexi smirked at her reflection, loving the way the light bounced off the sparkling bodice. The waist cinched before flaring out into a flowing, tulle skirt that would swish beautifully while dancing or walking. Plus, it'd be easier to sit down in.

A knock sounded on her door right before her mother called out, "Honey? Will's here."

Pressing a hand to her stomach, she told herself that everything would be okay. The scales were starting to balance.

"You got this," Maisie said, putting a hand to her back.

Air whooshed out of her lungs. "I do. And even if I don't, Will always has it together enough for both of us."

Lexi pulled the door open, watched as her mom's eyes filled with tears.

Gwen clasped her hands together and tucked them under her chin, just staring. "It's like prom, only better."

Stepping into her mom, she gave her a hard hug.

"You are stunning. Your dad would be so happy to see you happy. So proud of the woman you've become."

Tears threatened so she moved back, gave her mom a cheeky grin. "Or he would have mocked me for going to a snooty, upper-crust party."

Her mother laughed, putting an arm around her waist as they walked toward the living room.

"I heard that," Will said as they walked in. "Some of us snooty upper crust are pretty fun."

Speaking of stunning. The man was gorgeous. His dark hair was newly cut. His strong jaw was clean-shaven and those deep-brown eyes sparkled with happiness. She enjoyed him so much she didn't let herself think about what-ifs and what-happened-whens. Dressed in an actual tuxedo, he could have been the next Bond.

Their gazes locked but he spoke first. "You are the most beautiful woman I've ever met."

Lexi laughed, a little too loud, almost on the verge of squeaky. "Stop. It's not even my dress."

Will came forward as Gwen dropped her arm. "Don't do that. Don't diminish how amazing you are. Not just in looks either."

Maisie took Lexi's spot, pulling Gwen into a side hug. "Our girl is growing up," Maisie said with a sigh.

Everyone laughed, but Will kept his gaze laser-focused on Lexi. She pulled her lip between her teeth as he mouthed, *Stunning.*

"Let me take a couple pictures," Maisie said, extricating herself from Gwen.

"It's not actually prom," Lexi moaned.

Still, they posed for photos and Lexi couldn't help but think her mother looked happier than she had in a long, long while. Every day was still hard but there were little moments of progress. Things that might look like nothing to anyone else but meant something to Lexi. Two nights this week, when Lexi had needed to go to the second Side Tap location, Gwen had gone to bed instead of falling asleep in her chair. Yesterday, she'd offered to make Lexi a sandwich and jotted down a few items for Lexi to pick up at the store. She was taking an interest. She was coming back. She'd even pitched in with the pie. They'd made the filling together and used the premade crusts. It was delicious.

Maisie and her mother said goodbye at the door. It wasn't until it was closed behind them that Lexi noticed the limo on the street.

"Seriously?" She looked up at Will.

He lowered his gaze and shrugged in such an adorable way Lexi's heart expanded, grew bigger, right there in her driveway with the October moon shining down on them.

"It's a company thing. Usually, we book one or two for the family for special events, but I wanted to be alone with you, so we have it all to ourselves."

Lexi turned into Will's front, grateful she'd splurged—*thank you, Ethan, for the starting bonus*—on a long, black wool dress jacket.

Putting her hands on his face, she held his gaze. "You are the sweetest man I've met. I feel like you're not real and any minute now, I'm going to wake up back in my old life that was falling apart."

His gripped her wrists, leaned in so their noses almost touched. "Not falling apart, just temporarily disrupted. But I promise you, you're not sleeping."

No, she wasn't. She was very much awake and aware and she planned on taking advantage of every moment she had with Will. For once, she needed to take her own advice and stop waiting for the other shoe to smack her upside the head like a sledgehammer.

In the heels she wore, she didn't need to go on her tiptoes, so she wrapped her arms around his neck. "I've never made out in a limo."

Will bounced his eyebrows playfully. "Me neither. I'll tell the driver to take the long way."

———

It was like a fairy tale as she and Will entered The Grace, a historic and elegantly restored hotel in the heart of Seattle, overlooking the water. The lobby floor gleamed, light from the multiple chandeliers hanging on the regal tiled ceiling creating little bursts of light. High marble countertops lined the reception area. A sign to the right of the tall, gold-enameled doors pointed them in the direction of the ballroom where the gala was being held.

They checked their coats before entering the room. With every step, Lexi's stomach swirled with a combination of excitement and nerves.

"Breathe," Will whispered, patting her hand. It was gripping his biceps.

Loosening her fingers, she laughed. "Sorry. This is pretty swanky."

"It is. But there's an open bar and it's a celebration, so it'll be fun."

The archway to the ballroom was decked out in gorgeous garlands of leaves in all the fall colors. Each of the round tables was dressed with a burnt-gold tablecloth. The centerpieces consisted of multicolored mini pumpkins, fat cream-colored candles, and beautifully dried flowers resting on dark-wood, cutting-board-style planks.

Will said hello and nodded to several people as they wove their way between the tables, heading for the front of the room near the stage, where they found Will's family.

Kyra jumped up when she saw them and came around to give Lexi a hard, unexpected hug. "You look amazing! I'm so glad you found one that you liked."

Still holding Lexi's shoulders, she leaned back, looking down the length of her. "It suits you perfectly."

Lexi smiled. "You're too generous. I think Maisie and my mom will be trying them all on again while we're out."

"You look pretty good yourself, kid," Will said, leaning down to kiss Kyra's cheek. In a two-tone yellow dress with sparkly, Cinderella-like heels, Kyra was stunning.

The others stood. Lexi said hello to his sisters before Will introduced her to his sister-in-law Rachel, whose skin shimmered in her gold gown. She gave Lexi a quick, welcoming hug, easing the knots inside Lexi's gut.

"I'm so happy to meet you. Try and breathe. Their parents aren't as scary as they seem," she whispered, squeezing Lexi's shoulders.

Will's father was a tall man who shared features with his son but in a more imposing sort of way. He gave her a tight smile that contra-dicted his words. "Nice to meet you."

"We really need to have a proper family meal, dear," Emily Grand said to Will. "It's preposterous that this is the first time we're all sitting down together."

When she stepped back, Will whispered in Lexi's ear, "Preposter-ous," making Lexi laugh.

His grandparents were both elegant and adorable. His grand-mother was a tiny woman, barely up to Lexi's shoulders, dressed in a Katharine Hepburn–style dress while his grandfather looked like an older version of Will's dad, distinguished in his tuxedo.

He charmed her immediately, giving her a hug instead of a hand-shake. "I told William, you'll know when you know. When she's the one, it'll just hit you differently."

A little kernel of longing lodged in her heart at the mention of her being Will's one. *Stop. It's a fairy-tale night, not a real-life fairy tale.*

Once the introductions were made, they'd only just sat when a waiter appeared by their sides to take drink orders. Champagne flowed as the Grand family shared memories of the store and its his-tory all while saying hellos and chatting with people who stopped by their table. It'd been just her and her mom for so long Lexi had sort of forgotten what it was like to have a bigger tribe.

When her father was alive, her parents had multiple friends. They enjoyed hosting dinners and game nights. When people came over, their house was filled with food and laughter and love. The love was still around, but there was definitely less of the other two.

Which, Lexi realized as she sat here now, was an absolute shame. They hadn't just lost her dad. They'd lost so much more.

"You okay?" Will leaned in, his fingers dancing along the line of skin between her shoulder and neck, sending shivers over her body.

"I am. This is wonderful."

"In small doses," he whispered.

She laughed. "Be grateful. You're a lucky man, Will."

Using his index finger, he turned her chin toward him. "I am grateful. For them and for you. I agree. I'm a very lucky man."

The heat in his gaze warmed her from her toes to her head.

"Quit making googly eyes at each other," Kyra said, leaning over into their space. "You're making me jealous."

Will pretended to push Kyra's face back with his hand, making her and Lexi laugh.

"You're a lucky woman, Alexandria. No annoying siblings."

"Until now. Now she has us," Maddie said from across the table.

"I apologize in advance," Will said and the others laughed.

Lexi laughed along with them but inside, she reminded herself that as real as this was, it was also pretend. She wasn't marrying this man. She wasn't going to join his family even if she got to know them. Their limo wouldn't turn back into a pumpkin at the stroke of midnight but William Grand wasn't her prince. This was a fairy tale Lexi had inserted herself into and when Will's infatuation ended or the truth came out, she'd be alone again. He'd brought so much into her life. It would be so easy to let herself believe it could always be this good or better. What would have happened if Cinderella hadn't married the prince?

Lexi listened to the Grand siblings, Rachel, and Will's grandparents laugh and joke as more people filled the room. His parents sat rather stiffly, joining the conversation when spoken to but they didn't seem to be in a very celebratory mood, whispering back and forth to each other. She liked that the others didn't let it dampen their night and that they pulled her into the fold so easily. Like she belonged there. Lexi chose to believe that even if Cinderella hadn't ended up with the prince, she would have found her happiness on her own terms. When all of this was over, she'd do the same.

Twenty-nine

Will chatted with an acquaintance he'd known for some time but his gaze kept wandering to Lexi, who was listening intently to whatever Kyra was telling her as they browsed the silent auction table. The money would go to charities. As much as his mother got under his skin at times, she was doing wonderful work in the community. The tension at their table hadn't been easy to ignore but the food was excellent and his grandparents already seemed enamored with Lexi. Maddie fidgeted with her linen napkin, her shoulders ramrod straight, her expression guarded even though he could see Rachel was doing her best to make her laugh. The plan was for Will's dad to give a speech wishing the company a happy birthday, Will to honor his grandfather and grandmother and their success, and his grandfather to announce Maddie taking over as CEO, followed by a few words from his sister.

He and Kyra had tried to soothe her nerves but their father's snide comments since Granddad told them hadn't made it easy. Will was just happy to enjoy one of these things without feeling like his mother had him on some sort of eligible bachelor display. But he didn't like seeing either of his sisters worked up over something that should be a celebration.

Excusing himself from the conversation, which he was doing a lousy job listening to, he headed Lexi's way. She captivated him. The way her hair was swept up off her neck, exposing delicate skin he'd explored with his mouth. The way she played with the snap on her clutch, opening it and closing it, a tiny tell no one else would notice but one reminding Will that no matter what she showed to the world, she wasn't entirely comfortable in this setting.

He'd just about reached Lexi, locked eyes with her, felt that spark of lust and something much deeper that happened every time they were together, when someone said his name.

He turned to see Nigel, the fiancé of Lexi's friend, striding toward him. From the corner of his eye, he saw Lexi's look of recognition morph into nerves only to be immediately smoothed out again into a welcoming expression.

"How's it going?" Nigel said, a bright smile on his face. The guy was polished and friendly. Will had enjoyed talking with him at the party and he knew Lexi enjoyed reconnecting with Jackie even though there was hesitancy in her tone the times she'd brought up her old friend.

Will shook his hand. "Great. Thank you for coming."

Lexi headed toward them.

Nigel dropped his hand, looking around. "Thanks for inviting us."

Will laughed. "Trust me, if I were in charge of the guest list, it'd be more like the party you guys threw. That was a lot of fun."

"Speaking of, we should go for dinner or something; the four of us or six, I guess. Becs and Jackie are pretty inseparable and now that they've got Lexi back in the mix, we might be in for a lot of get-togethers."

The idea of planning couples get-togethers and having more of Lexi in his future appealed to him in a way he'd never expected.

"There she is," Nigel said as Lexi came the rest of the way to where they stood. "Hey. Great to see you and be part of the celebration." Nigel leaned in to kiss Lexi's cheek.

After greeting him, she moved back, closer to Will. "Good to see you too. It's quite the party, isn't it?"

Will put an arm around her waist, smiling as she nestled into his side like it was the most natural thing in the world. "My parents know how to host an event."

Nigel chuckled, nodding. "I've been to my share of these things, whatever the celebration. They don't always feel so welcoming so I'd say you're right."

As a former pro athlete, he'd likely attended far bigger events than this. And maybe if Grand Babies had gone the route Will's father had wanted, they would've opened up more doors, but in this moment Will was perfectly content with exactly what he had. And he didn't see that changing anytime soon.

In a flurry of glitter and satin, Jackie joined them, a little squeal leaving her mouth as she hugged Lexi.

"I was sad we didn't do the whole dress-up thing earlier this week but it worked out for the best because this dress is gorgeous. Your future sisters-in-law have amazing taste."

Lexi pulled back from Jackie, her smile a little more forced than it'd been. "They absolutely do. I'm so glad you guys are here. Where's Becca?"

Jackie hooked a manicured thumb over her shoulder. "On the dance floor. What have you been up to? Your texts are so quick and we haven't been able to nail you down to a girls' night."

Will smoothed a hand over the soft skin of Lexi's back, hoping his touch lessened the tension coiling in her.

"Actually, I started a new job and I've been busier than I expected."

"Congratulations," Jackie said. "What are you doing?"

Lexi stood a little taller next to him. "Technically, my title is operations manager for a soon-to-be-opened second Side Tap location." She leaned toward her friend just a little. "But really, it feels like I'm just on a huge shopping spree and it's amazing."

They all laughed. "I would love that job. But seriously, carve out some time because we want to hang out and talk wedding stuff. I'm pretty sure Becca will be wearing her own ring by Christmas."

"I was just saying to Will that we should all go for dinner. We've been to Side Tap a couple of times. Maybe we should go there," Nigel said, wrapping an arm around Jackie's waist.

Jackie nodded. "Yes. That's a great idea."

Lexi tensed beside him before blowing out a breath. "Actually, we're having a Halloween party there. You should come. You'll love it. Costumes mandatory, great food. I'll email you the information."

"We absolutely will, but I still want some solo time," Jackie said.

The emcee for the evening tapped the microphone, letting them know speeches would start soon.

As they walked back to their table, Will noticed his mother gesturing somewhat dramatically as she spoke into his father's ear. His dad's posture was rigid, like he was a cement version of himself. *Just do the right thing, Dad. Don't let ego get in the way.* Will looked at Lexi, saw her glancing around the room, and stopped.

"You okay?"

She met his gaze, her own vulnerable and sweet, unleashing a protective streak in him that he didn't know he had. She nodded. "I am. I hate lying. I mean, at least we're actually together but Jackie sees me as who I used to be and that's not who I am now. She put me on some sort of pedestal and thinks I'm a better version of who I was. It makes me feel awful for lying, but also like a complete fraud. She wants to get together and pick up where we left off but I feel like if she knew who I am now, she'd want nothing to do with the real me."

People milled around, jostling past them to get to their seats. Will ignored them, turned Lexi into him, bending his knees so he could see her eyes.

"Who you are is a woman who has worked her ass off, fighting back against some hard knocks to land on her gorgeous feet. You've knocked me off mine and I couldn't be prouder to have you here with me tonight, celebrating and spending time with my family. Sometimes our own self-doubt colors how we think others see us. She may have put you on a pedestal, Lexi, but so what? You deserve to be there. You're an incredible woman. You guys were teenagers the last time you were close. You weren't rich or powerful then. Just a great track star. Whatever she liked about you then is still inside of you. Only better."

Desire slid over his skin when she pushed her hands up into his hair, likely making it stand up at odd angles. He absolutely did not care and he tugged her closer, despite the crowd around him.

"I think that as soon as speeches are over, my fake fiancé should take me back to his place so my boyfriend can get *really* lucky."

Will laughed as he closed the distance between them, kissing her with as much restraint as he could, given the audience. "That sounds absolutely perfect."

Will was glad he'd written his speech down because now, the only thing he could think about was Lexi. He pulled her seat out for her to sit down, meeting his dad's unhappy gaze. The lines around his eyes were more deep-set than usual, his frown more pronounced. Granddad was chatting with Rachel and seemed oblivious to the tension. Will moved around the table, squeezed Maddie's shoulder as he leaned down.

"You've got this."

She turned her head slightly. "Let's hope so."

The emcee welcomed Jackson Grand to the stage. The crowd immediately quieted when his dad tapped the mic. "Thank you all for coming and celebrating with us tonight." He lifted the champagne flute he'd brought with him. "Happy birthday, Grand Babies." The crowd interrupted with applause. His father cut off the response. "This company has always been a part of my life, my makeup. I've given it my heart, my time, my energy. Everything."

Will's jaw tightened. Like she felt his nerves, Lexi covered his hand on his thigh and squeezed.

"I had a big speech planned out," his father continued. "All about how proud I am of being part of this company and this family."

Will's stomach tensed.

"Family is an important thing, and those connections and bonds matter even more when you're in business together. Trusting and relying on any co-workers matters to a company's success. You would think that working with family would ensure a built-in trust. That there wouldn't be secrets and behind-the-scenes conversations and decisions you have no part in. The kind of decisions that change a man's course. And yet, tonight as I wish my father a congratulations on fifty years of running a company, I'm also, regrettably, acknowledging I didn't hold the place in it I thought I did. The future of Grand Babies is not in my hands. And it won't be in my father's either. My daughter Madeline Grand-West will be stepping into his very large shoes. And I, after twenty years of working there, am stepping down."

Will's heart plummeted into his gut even before he saw the shocked and saddened faces of his grandparents.

He wasn't a pessimist but even he should have thought, with everything that had been going so well, something was bound to go wrong.

Thirty

Lexi stood on her back porch, wrapped in an old gray robe, her mom's slippers on her feet. The Pacific Northwest sunrise was worth not being able to sleep the night before. The mug of coffee was warming her hands even as the caffeine brought her senses slowly awake.

Last night had been . . . surreal. And hard. When she snuck out of bed this morning, she'd stared at Will, his face relaxed in sleep even though he'd had a hard time finding it. A little piece of her had giggled over the fact that she had a boy—a *man*—in her childhood bed. The more mature part of her had urged her to make coffee.

As she sipped, she thought about how the party had taken a deep dive off an awkward-as-hell cliff after Jackson Grand made his declaration. He and his father had argued, Will's grandpa walking out. Maddie, proving herself without prompting, followed her dad's speech with an apology, made a couple of jokes, and asked people to focus on celebrating and enjoying the eight-tiered birthday cake, before she promptly left. Will and Lexi had followed suit, dropping Kyra off on their way to Lexi's.

"Hey," Gwen said, joining her on the porch with her own cup of coffee. She sank into one of the weathered Adirondack chairs.

Lexi turned against the porch post, smiling at her mom, who curled her feet under her in the chair. "Good morning."

"How was last night?"

"Amazing. Incredible. Fun. Awkward."

Her mom paused, cup almost to her lips. "The first three sound good."

Lexi quickly filled her in on the events of the evening. Her mom's quiet eyes widened. "Wow. That must have been hard on everyone."

Lexi nodded, thinking about how hard it was on *Will*. She hated that discord within his family for him. She knew how draining it could be to not see eye-to-eye on something with a parent. To feel responsible. To fail at finding a way to fix things.

"Am I interrupting?" Will stood in the open doorway between the porch and the kitchen. His hair was mussed, his expression sleepy, his smile soft, and Lexi's heart lurched painfully against the wall of her chest like it was trying to claim him, saying *mine*.

"Not at all," Gwen said, looking up with a kind smile. "There's coffee."

"You're wonderful," Will said, his voice full of gratitude as he turned back toward the kitchen.

"I made it," Lexi called after him, making her mom laugh.

"You're wonderful too, honey," Will called.

Laughing into her coffee, Lexi caught her mother's gaze, more astute than it should be for this early in the morning.

"He's good for you, sweetheart."

"He's pretty great." And it was okay to enjoy that without over-thinking things.

"Were you thinking about a big wedding? I'm sure, with his family, there'll be quite the guest list."

The happiness inside of her deflated like a popped balloon. "We're just focusing on now." Truth.

"Weddings don't plan themselves," her mother said, setting the mug down on the wide arm of the chair.

A breeze washed over them, sending a chill through her. "No. But there's lots going on right now. Bitsy asked me to interview a couple of part-timers for the store. I'm cutting my hours down there to be more available at Side Tap." The fact that she could do that and it was actually better financially was something to really celebrate.

"You should at least pick a date," her mother said somewhat sharply.

"Date for what?" Will asked, joining them on the porch.

Lexi met his gaze, her stomach dancing nervously. "The wedding."

His brows lifted. "Ahh. Yes. We'll figure all that out. For now, how about I take you two out to breakfast?"

Will might have missed the way her mother's shoulders stiffened, her invisible shields powering up, but Lexi saw it immediately. She sent a look, subtly shook her head. Will stepped closer to her, his scent and warmth both unnerving and welcome. It was strange, and somehow wonderful, to have him in her space.

He leaned in, kissed her temple, put one arm around her shoulder.

When Lexi looked at her mom, she saw Gwen watching them. Will gave her arm a quick, reassuring squeeze.

She saw the excuses spinning around in Gwen's expression.

"How about, if you're up for it, we do something a little different?" Will said, watching her mother closely.

Gwen's hands closed around her cup tightly. "Different?"

"Yeah. Instead of some noisy diner, I'd love for you to see my gardens. My sisters and Lexi told me about you starting your own again. My house isn't far from here. My sister-in-law's family owns Bean There, the coffee and baked goods chain. Her family drops off fresh treats every Sunday morning to all of us. It's really awesome but always way too much for just me. We could have breakfast there, you could maybe give me some ideas for an area in my backyard where I was thinking of adding some flowers?"

Like he could sense the intensity of her heartbeat, Will tightened his hold on Lexi, both of them watching her mother.

"Your sister is a gardener. Doesn't she give you advice?" Gwen's fingers flexed on the cup.

"Maddie loves gardening but doesn't have a ton of time for it. She's pretty busy. I'd really love your thoughts on it."

As well as she knew her mother, Lexi had absolutely no idea what she'd say. But hope swelled like a wave inside of her.

"I need a ride home anyway and I know Lexi has to check in with Side Tap today so we can make it quick. We have to eat regardless, right?"

Gwen stood up and Lexi feared she'd just walk away, ignore the invite and request. She looked at Lexi, her gaze flashing with an uncertainty that made her look younger.

"I don't want to be gone long."

Lexi had to bite the inside of her cheek so she didn't cry. She forced a nod, watched Gwen walk inside.

Before Will could speak, she set her mug down on the railing and curled herself into him, around him, her arms at his waist, holding him close, burying her face against the softness of his T-shirt, the solidness of his chest. She heard his cup set down next to hers as his arms wrapped her up, his chin resting on her head.

"Hey," he whispered, bending his knees so he could speak into her ear. "You okay?"

Tears burned the backs of her eyelids. Lexi held him tighter, her fingers twisting in his shirt. "Magic. You're magic, Will Grand."

—————

Her mom sat shotgun beside her, twisting her hands as the radio played what the station labeled its "Halloween Playlist." So far, they'd played some Meat Loaf, Michael Jackson, and the theme song from *Ghostbusters*. Will had folded himself into the back of her car without complaint. Lexi turned down his driveway. Gwen's breathing hitched, her knuckles going white.

Lexi reached over, set her hand on her mom's. "After breakfast, when we drive home, maybe you could make a list of stuff we need? I'll go to the store."

Gwen's hands relaxed under Lexi's. "Sure. Could you stop at Michael's for me?"

Usually, her mom ordered her craft stuff online, but if it distracted her from her nerves, Lexi would stop anywhere.

"Of course." She parked the car in front of the double garage.

If not for Will needing to get out on that side, she wondered if Gwen would have just stayed in the front seat. But she got out, and Will got out. He smiled at her, put a hand on her arm.

"Welcome. Do you want to eat or take a walk first?"

Let's just get her inside away from the car. Away from the idea of leaving.

"I'm so hungry," Lexi blurted.

Will laughed and Gwen's shoulders relaxed.

"You should have seen her in her track days," Gwen said with a smile, following Will to his front door. "I had to buy bulk snacks just to keep her going with all the energy she burned."

"I was the same and I didn't even run." Will unlocked the front door and opened it but gestured for them to go ahead.

Even though she liked that they were chatting, that her mom seemed more at ease, she didn't like being the focus. "It *is* breakfast time. Not so strange that I'd be hungry."

Will closed the door behind them.

"Oh, Will. Your home is beautiful."

Lexi held back a little, taking joy in her mother's obvious delight as Will showed them through the house. The rooms were large and open with several floor-to-ceiling windows that let in copious amounts of natural light. They moved through the kitchen where a generous basket of goodies was waiting, headed to a study off that and then up a small set of stairs that led to the second floor—almost a hidden staircase.

"Why don't we eat and then we can tour the backyard before it rains?" Will said after they'd toured the upstairs and come back to the kitchen.

"Absolutely," Gwen said. "I'm just going to use the restroom."

"You doing okay?" Will asked, taking Lexi's hand and using it to pull her close. He leaned down, brushed his lips over hers, sweet, soft, and familiar. Dangerously familiar.

"I'm good. Thank you for taking the time to do this. The fact that she's here is bigger than you know."

He pressed a kiss to her forehead. "I know you and I can see how big it is. I'm glad I could offer something. Help in some way. At least with your mom."

Moving to the fridge, he grabbed some juice. Lexi checked a couple of cupboards and found some plates, then some cutlery.

"Has anyone in your family contacted you since last night?" Lexi opened the goldish-brown cloth tying the baked goods into the basket.

As he got glasses out, his mood seemed to shift, get heavier. "No. Or maybe. I turned my phone off last night. I'll go over to see my grandparents this morning, touch base with my sisters. I'm not ready to speak to either of my parents."

Lexi hated the anger laced with pain. "Your dad is probably lashing out because his pride was hurt." Useless words that may or may not have been true, but sometimes it felt good to believe there was an underlying reason.

Gwen joined them as they set muffins, croissants, fruit pastries, and scones on a large serving platter.

"Oh my. You get this delivered every Sunday?" Gwen asked.

Will poured each of them orange juice after asking if that was their preference. "I do. I freeze some, share with the neighbors, and bring some into work on Mondays and put it in the staff room."

Lexi was glad that instead of heading into the formal dining room to sit at the beautiful live-edge table with seating for twelve, they each took stools at the rounded kitchen island. It felt more comfortable. Less intimidating.

As each of them nibbled on their choice of goodies, Lexi watched her mom for signs of nerves, tension, or sadness.

Gwen wiped her mouth with a linen napkin, set it in her lap. "You know," she said, looking toward Will, who sat to her left. "Parents never intend to let their children down. I think because kids rely on us from their first breath until they fight for independence—because for all those developmental years we seem to have the answers and cures for everything—kids come to think of their parents as powerful. Capable. Their job is to fix things, make them right, see to their child's needs. Solve problems that seem much larger than a child can handle."

Lexi set her piece of muffin down, wondering where her mom was going with this.

Gwen didn't look at her, only Will, when she continued. "What you start to learn as you get older is that your parents are *people*. Regardless of their role in your life, they've only ever been flawed human beings. You start to see that more as you age, as you come to recognize and acknowledge your own flaws. It's hard to see someone you put up on a pedestal, even if you didn't mean to or don't think you did, slip off it."

Gripping her own napkin, Lexi's throat felt tight. Scratchy.

"I know my parents aren't perfect, Gwen. I've probably known since I was a young child. I get what you're saying. I appreciate your insight. But my dad is a selfish man."

Gwen reached out, set a hand on Will's forearm. "That may be true. And some people aren't as good at parenting as they should be. But if you take out the dad part, he's also a man who has worked for years toward something he thought was a guarantee. He was blind-sided. Likely hurt. And maybe even a little vulnerable when he realized that life doesn't always go the way you plan it. When you have no plan B, you can make some pretty poor choices while you're scrambling."

Pursing his lips as her mom removed her hand, Will met her gaze, his full of confusion and uncertainty. Her mom took a deep breath, letting it out slowly before picking off a piece of her chocolate croissant.

"Tell me about Side Tap, Alexandria."

With Gwen's words floating around in her brain, trying to find a place to land, Lexi caught her mom up on what she'd been doing for the second location.

"I met Ethan's brother and his wife. All three of them are technically my bosses but I work mostly with Ethan. He set up a little corner of his office for me. This week I'm ordering furniture, checking in on building permits. I'll be setting up everything from our napkin supplier to our entertainment schedule until we get people hired for each of those roles. But when we do, I want to be able to hand over information on suppliers and retailers, best costs."

Will, who'd started setting the baked goods in a container, stopped and smiled at her. "You really love it."

Lexi laughed, sat up straighter on the stool. "I do. The title *manager of operations* seemed so abstract, but it's incredible. There's so many moving parts, things that have to happen, schedules that have to line up and work in tandem."

"I'm so glad you've found this, sweetie," Gwen said, now reaching out to squeeze Lexi's arm. "All of this. Will, this job. Happiness."

There was an undertone of sadness despite her mom's smile that concerned her.

"We deserve good things, Mom. Isn't that what you tell me?" She pulled her arm away, got up to put her plate in the sink. "Speaking of, Maisie says the piece you're making for the wedding couple is absolutely extraordinary. When do I get to see it?"

"Your miniatures are such a unique hobby. I absolutely love them. I hope it's okay that Lexi showed them to me last night."

"Of course."

Will put the juice away, loaded the dishwasher. "Would you consider another commission piece?"

Lexi's chin snapped up. What was he doing? *Oh God, please don't commission our cake topper in an attempt to make my mother happy. Don't dig us any deeper.*

"For you, absolutely. What were you thinking?"

Will leaned on the counter close to Gwen, his forearms resting on the marble slab. "I'd love to do something special for my grandfather. I have a photo of him standing in front of the store fifty years ago when he opened it. Think you'd be able to create a miniature version?"

Gwen's eyes lit up. "I don't see why not. Do you have the picture?"

"I do." He stood up, rounded the counter, planted a kiss on Lexi's mouth for absolutely no reason, letting his hand slide along her shoulder as he headed for the study. "I'll grab it."

Gwen stood up, walked to Lexi, and took both of her hands. "You've found forever, sweet girl. He's perfect for you."

"Mom." Lexi tried to swallow around the thickness in her throat. The things that weren't true were feeling dangerously possible. Terrifyingly real. And now, from the look on her mom's face, it wasn't just Lexi falling. It was her mom, too.

Gwen was just rising from the ashes of her husband's death, taking almost full breaths again. What if she found out the truth and it destroyed her, made things worse? What if it undid the progress and damaged their relationship at the same time?

Worry formed knots in her stomach as Gwen hugged her, held her tight.

Lexi didn't know how to tell her the truth at this point. Especially since her feelings were becoming more real every single minute.

When Lexi brought her mom home shortly after a walk of Will's beautifully landscaped grounds, they'd both puttered around, getting little things on their own lists done. A few hours later, Gwen asked her to come into her workroom.

Lexi came into the room to see Gwen standing by the table, a glossy white box with a decorative lid set on top of it. "Maisie's coming to pick this up."

Lexi stared at her a moment, the smile creeping up on her. "You finished it?"

Gwen's gaze brightened. "I did. Just now."

With great care, Gwen opened the box and pulled out her creation.

On a rounded, porcelain white base, the bride, in a gorgeous white gown, intricately patterned with little swirls that looked like flowers, lay across a bench, her head resting on the groom's leg. Her dark curls seemed to actually flow down. The groom, in a tuxedo, complete with a red bow tie that was beyond adorable, read from a miniature book. Lexi leaned in to see that it said *Pride & Prejudice* on the cover.

It was exquisite, personal, and so amazing Lexi's eyes filled with tears. She swiped at the first few that fell.

"Mom. It's stunning. This is unbelievable."

When she looked up at Gwen, still bent at the waist, she noticed her mom grasping her hands the way she did when she was nervous.

"You really like it?"

Lexi stood up. "Mom, this is one of the most beautiful things I've ever seen. My favorite thing that you've made. It's wonderful." She didn't stop the tears that continued to fall, instead, pulling her mother into a tight hug.

"I'm so happy you love it. I hope Maisie and the couple will."

Giving her another squeeze, Lexi stepped back. "Everyone is going to love it. I don't want to push too much but you could really make a business out of this, Mom. It's so unique and special. It could be cake toppers, your scenes, anything you want."

"Oh, honey. I'm too old to start a business."

Lexi looked around the room. "You're not, Mom." She looked back at her mom. "You're still young." She wanted to say more but didn't want Gwen to shut down.

She'd met with the therapist a couple of times now and Lexi noticed she was keeping a journal, making an effort to be a little more present. Pushing harder didn't always equal progress.

"You can start slow. Or just think about it. But Mom, this is remarkable. I'm so proud of you."

Gwen beamed, throwing her arms around Lexi. "You're the best daughter, sweetheart. I know it's not always easy."

Maybe not. But what was? Lexi breathed more easily than she had in a long time. Aside from her runaway feelings that she needed to rein in, she felt like maybe, just maybe, she and her mom would be okay.

She pulled back. "I have to go out to the second location of Side Tap. I want to time the commute, but I want to get a better feel for the space. The contractor is supposed to be stopping in. I'll bring back dinner? We could watch a romcom?"

Gwen laughed, set the lid on the box. "Either you've been hiding your romantic streak or Will brought it out in you."

"Or I'm just indulging your sappiness," Lexi joked, heading for the door.

"Lexi?"

She turned at the doorway.

Gwen shoved her hands in the pockets of her jeans. "Could I . . . come for the drive? To see where you'll be spending time?"

Breathing very slowly, like reacting fast would erase the moment, Lexi nodded. "Of course," she said, surprised her voice came out steady.

"Okay." Gwen pushed past her, saying she'd be ready in a few minutes. Lexi leaned back against the doorframe, put her hands over her face. She fought the urge to happy-dance as hard as she did the sob wanting to break free. Even good things could make a person feel like their insides were being gripped in a giant's fist.

One step at a time. One little victory. She dropped her hands, sucked in a breath. *Keep moving forward. When it gets hard, dig deeper.* It was good advice in college and apparently, it worked for adulthood too.

Thirty-one

Usually Sundays flew by like a blink but this one had the endurance of a marathon runner. After checking his emails and making a to-do list for the next day, Will tossed his phone on the coffee table and settled back against the soft couch cushions. They were heading into a busy season. He needed to touch base with marketing and advertising, and at this time of year he enjoyed being part of the conversations around store displays. He'd left messages with Comfort Plus and had a lunch meeting scheduled with Holden on Thursday. They'd officially squashed the deal with Home Needs, which had pissed Fredrick off to no end. Will had plenty to keep him busy. Keep his mind off Lexi and the way she'd hugged him, held him when her mom agreed to come to his place.

Relief at a distraction from his own thoughts coursed through him when a knock came at his door. He'd seen both of his sisters when he dropped by his grandparents' place for lunch so it wouldn't be them. He paused. He wasn't ready to see his parents. Will was certain he'd never been this mad at either of them. He took a fortifying breath and squared his shoulders, just in case. When he got to the door and saw through the peephole that it was Ethan, everything inside him relaxed.

He opened the door to find his best friend dressed for the crisp weather in a leather bomber jacket and gloves, a light-gray Side Tap beanie tugged over his slightly-too-long hair.

"Hey. Thought I'd check in. Last night was quite the show and you're not answering your phone."

"I turned it off. Come on in."

Ethan shook his head. "Actually, I was headed out to the new site just to go over a few things with my dad. Thought maybe you'd come for a drive."

"Let me grab my coat."

Ethan backed his Ford Bronco out of Will's drive and didn't hesitate to dive into the previous evening's events. "What the hell, man?"

Will shook his head, leaning back in the passenger seat. "I don't know. I really don't know. I mean, I knew he was pissed about Granddad's announcement, about Maddie taking over, but when you break it all down, it makes sense. My dad is good at his job in the position he's in now. Maddie is ready for this step and it causes the least amount of disruption. Plus, even though my dad would never admit it, Maddie's vision is a lot more in line with what my grandfather wants."

"How's Mads doing? Has to be a punch to the gut to have her father act like that."

That was Will's exact concern. Maddie deserved this position. And it was his grandfather's decision to make. "She seemed okay. I had lunch with her, my grandparents, and Kyra. My phone is off because I'm avoiding my parents but I wanted to check in on all of them. Everyone is a mix of hurt, shocked, and frustrated."

"Took the spotlight off you and your fiancée for a night," Ethan pointed out, merging onto the freeway.

Giving a humorless laugh, Will stared out the window. "It'll give the *Times* something better to write than who is Alexandria Danby and does she deserve William Grand." He hated the bitterness in his tone but he also hated that other people felt they had the right to decide what was best for anyone other than themselves. Like a person didn't know their own damn mind.

"And who is Alexandria Danby?"

Will looked over at his friend. "What does that mean?"

Ethan sent him a quick glance. "She was a waitress you helped out in an awkward moment who became your fake fiancée before she became your real girlfriend. I've seen you with her. I've seen her talk about you. Which part is fake?"

His friend knew him too well. "Right now? Only the engagement. And honestly? A huge part of me wishes it were real. That I had a very real hold on this woman."

"She's wearing your ring."

Will smiled. "For show."

"Could you see yourself actually marrying her? How does she feel? She's one hell of an employee, I'll say that. She works her ass off and we're not only on schedule for most things, we're ahead for some of them. Brady actually smiled the other day. Not seeing him weighted down with stress is a huge relief."

Will had no doubt about her work ethic. It was one more thing that drew him to her.

"I never expected any of this. I couldn't have predicted it. I only met her less than a month ago but I swear, E, every minute I spend with her makes me want the next and the next and the next."

Ethan whistled, the sound loud in the enclosed space. "Maybe planning a real wedding will shift your parents' focus away from your dad's wounded pride."

Will laughed, scrubbed his hands over his face. "Jesus, man. Don't say that. This all started because the idea of my parents staying out of my love life was so appealing."

"Love, huh?" Ethan looked over at him, then turned on the wipers. Will ignored his friend's not-so-subtle question. There were too many other things to deal with. He could do a deep dive on his feelings some other time.

They drove for the next twenty minutes chatting about beer, football, life, and work. It was nice. A little break from all the rest.

"You okay, man? You got quiet. You miss your fiancée?"

"You're a jackass," Will said even though he kind of did.

Ethan's chuckle cut off abruptly when he turned into the mostly empty lot of Side Tap South. Lexi and her mother were standing outside of Lexi's vehicle talking to Ethan's dad.

"I'm not sure if it's romantic or creepy that you mooning over your girl conjured her up."

"I'll repeat—you're a jackass," Will said, getting out of the SUV. He ignored the way his heartbeats quickened as he locked eyes with Lexi. Her smile spread slowly, a shadow of uncertainty crossing her features.

"Hey," she said with a wave.

"Be cool, Ponyboy," Ethan said, smacking him on the back then walking ahead of Will.

That was becoming more and more difficult every day.

Thirty-two

"Hey, yourself. This is a nice surprise. When you said you were going to Side Tap, I thought you meant the other one. Great to see you, Gwen. Twice in one day. I'm a lucky man." Will leaned in to kiss Lexi's cheek and immediately inhaled the scent of sweet vanilla with a hint of citrus that he was coming to associate with her. "Hey, Mr. Reynolds."

"Boys," Mr. Reynolds said, wearing a slightly amused expression. They'd always be boys to Ethan's dad.

"Oh, this is a happy surprise." Gwen leaned closer to Will. "Alexandria wanted to show me where she's working but this man said he couldn't let us inside without permission." She was bundled in a long, thick black coat, a red scarf bunching at the neck.

It was nice to see her out again, the cold adding color to her cheeks.

Lexi sighed, looking cozy and chic in a shorter, dark-gray, puffer-style coat. "Mom. It's fine." She sent Ethan a glance and Will stepped closer to her, without even meaning to, when he saw the flash of embarrassment. "I should have called you, told you I was swinging by. I actually wanted to ask about a key to get a look at the place. I didn't know this was your dad."

"Will, this is your fiancée? There was no picture with the

announcement. I didn't know." Mr. Reynolds clapped Will on the back, smiling at the others.

Ethan smiled while his dad took it all in. He and Ethan's mom had divorced while Ethan was in high school. The few times Will had hung out with them, watching a game at Mr. Reynolds's house or at the bar for a beer, he'd enjoyed himself very much.

"Congratulations. Ma'am," Mr. Reynolds said to Gwen. "I apologize for not knowing who you all were. It's a pleasure to meet you. And you."

It was as if Gwen just realized Mr. Reynolds was someone other than the annoying contractor who wouldn't let them in. Will slipped his hand in Lexi's, amused by the furrowed arch of her brows, the gentle squeeze of her hand.

"Let's make some introductions. Mr. Reynolds, this is my fiancée, Alexandria Danby, and her mother, Gwen Danby. This is Gregory Reynolds, Ethan's dad. Ethan's my good friend, Gwen."

"And my boss," Lexi murmured to her mother, like a reminder that she might be evaluated by any and all interactions.

Hands were shaken, hellos exchanged. The rain picked up and Ethan jutted his chin toward the door. "Let's get out of this rain."

"There's something that gets said a lot in Washington," Mr. Reynolds said.

Gwen laughed, light and airy. Lexi's brows rose again. Will squeezed her hand. *Interesting.*

When they entered the building, the others started forward, heading for the large square bar that broke up the otherwise open space. Will tugged Lexi to a stop and pulled her close.

"I promise I wasn't following you," he said, bending his head for a kiss.

She returned it with a pleased sigh that Will loved the sound of. "So you say," she teased, then gestured toward her mom with a tilt of her head. "It was her idea to come with me."

"That's excellent." He ran a hand down her slightly damp hair. "I'm really happy for both of you. Family matters."

She squeezed his hand. "It does. Even when they drive you nuts."

She tilted her head to the side, gave him a wry look. "What do you think of my mom's reaction to Ethan's dad?"

The others were chatting behind the bar, Gwen listening with rapt attention to Gregory as he explained how they'd chosen the wood and the stain.

"I wondered if I was the only one who noticed. Interesting. That's my only comment on that. But I am glad you got her out of the house." He figured he might as well go with his gut. It had served him well so far. "I came with Ethan to get my mind off you."

She ducked her head, traced a pattern on his jacket. "That didn't work out so well, did it?"

"I'd have to disagree," he said, lifting her chin with his finger.

Her gaze steadied his heartbeat and made his lungs feel tight at the same time. "Lucky for both of us, then."

"You two just going to stand over there making out or are you going to join us?" Ethan called.

Gwen laughed again and Gregory told his son to watch his manners. Something Will had never heard him say before.

Lexi backed away but kept her fingers linked with his as she started toward the others. On the right side, floor-to-ceiling windows would let in the light. Even now, with the sometimes oppressive gloom of the Pacific Northwest, it was a beautiful view of mountains and clouds.

To the left, the windows were more standard but still added to the open feeling of the room. The venue didn't have the raised levels of the original Side Tap, but it definitely had the appeal. High ceilings with gorgeous, thick wood beams added more character. Their shoes tapped against the long wooden floor planks. The contrasting stains of wood were comfortable, classic, and uniquely Side Tap. The bar was wide and perfectly square but for an opening where the staff could come and go.

"It looks great in here, E," Will said. Industrial-style wrought-iron lighting hung from the beams.

"That's what happens when you hire a good contractor," Mr. Reynolds teased, nudging his son.

"That and a large bill," Ethan said with a grin.

"Worth it when I find you nothing but the best," his dad returned.

"My husband has a construction business," Gwen said quietly.

All heads turned her way. Will felt Lexi's intake of breath, sensed her holding it in.

Gwen straightened and Will could all but see the courage glowing around her frame. "Had. He passed away."

"I'm so sorry for your loss," Gregory said.

Gwen met Gregory's gaze. "It was a long time ago now. This place is lovely. I can imagine it filled with people having a wonderful time."

Lexi put a hand on her mom's shoulder. "The original Side Tap isn't far from our place, Mom. Maybe we could go sometime. I think you'd really like it. Maisie's coming to the Halloween celebration." She turned to Ethan. "She'll be our official photographer for the event."

"Can't tell you what it means to me, Lexi," Gregory said, "to have you step in the way you have. Helping out even in areas that you're not in charge of has taken a lot of weight off both my boys' shoulders. Doesn't matter how old your kids get, you're still their parent. Still worry about them."

"That's absolutely true," Gwen said with a side glance to Lexi.

Will squeezed Lexi's hand again, happy for something that might seem small to others but he knew was significant. Just her being here was big but to talk about her husband with strength, to participate actively in Lexi's life—it mattered. Baby steps.

"As you can see, Lexi, the furniture you ordered is going to fit perfectly. I loved your idea of long benches for some of the farm-style tables instead of chairs," Ethan said.

"I'm glad you like it. It'll work perfectly with the relaxed vibe you guys have going."

Will liked watching her transition into a woman with more confidence, like she pulled on an *I can do this* cloak.

"This is actually going to happen. We've been waiting for the final permits but all the paperwork is done now." Ethan looked at his dad. "She's even set up interviews."

A warm smile graced Mr. Reynolds's face. "I know, son. We're all grateful." He looked at Lexi. "My daughter-in-law says you're an angel."

Lexi laughed. "That's sweet of her. She's so lovely. And your grandkids are adorable."

Ethan smiled, crossing his arms over his chest. "Having you step in is a big help but you're not running yourself thin, are you? You're still at the Dress Hut full-time, right?"

"Practically. She works so hard," Gwen said, staring at Lexi with pride.

"I'm helping Bitsy replace me. She's changing her hours so that's helping me transition away from there. I think she's looking forward to spending more hours there herself. I just hope she'll keep it open. Business isn't what it used to be for her. And I'm no longer waitressing. Just taking one course at school. My schedule is actually less hectic than it was."

Will wondered if she'd even realized that she'd accepted the compliments from both men. He wanted her to value herself and how hard she worked.

She looked at her mom, her expression softening. "But I do have a paper to finish, so we should get going."

Will didn't want to say goodbye. "How's the cake topper going?"

Both Gwen's and Lexi's expressions went radiant, filling him with warmth and something more than just affection.

"She finished it. It's so beautiful it made me cry. Maisie and I have both told her she should open an Etsy shop to sell custom miniatures," Lexi said.

Gwen's cheeks turned pink. "I sold one to your fiancé."

Will laughed. "I have no doubt you'll be able to sell more." The Danby women were fierce even if they didn't recognize it in themselves.

"Miniatures? Like that reality show?"

Before any of them could say anything else, Gwen and Gregory began discussing her miniatures. Ethan, Lexi, and Will moved toward the back of the room where a stone fireplace took up a large chunk of the wall.

Ethan looked at Lexi, and Will hoped like hell his friend wouldn't say something stupid.

"If our parents get together, we could be stepsiblings. Then when you two get married, we'll be real brothers, Will." He winked at Lexi.

Hopes dashed. "Shut up, man."

Lexi laughed. "Slow down. Not only is there no real wedding, I'm not sure if my mom is built to try for forever again."

Ethan grimaced. "Sorry."

She shook her head. "It's okay. It's nice to see her smile, engage with someone who doesn't know her as the woman she used to be. Someone's wife. She's figuring her new self out, so who knows where that will lead?" She looked at Will with such intensity his heart squeezed in response. "Sometimes the strangest things happen and you could never predict them."

"I should get going, Ethan," Mr. Reynolds said, walking over with Gwen. "It was a real pleasure to meet you ladies. You've got my card, Gwen. You call me anytime and I'll take a look at your basement."

"What's wrong with the basement, Mom?"

"You've been talking about ideas for the house. I'm not ready to sell but Gregory said he could give us an estimate on some renovations that would turn the basement into a suite."

"He'll give you a discount," Ethan said, clapping his dad on the shoulder.

"Mom, we don't have to make any decisions right now."

Gwen held up the card then slipped it into her pocket. "It's just an idea. You've been tossing them around for a long while. Be happy."

She should be happy if her mom was thinking about moving forward and making some changes, but Will sensed that she was more worried than thrilled.

For a minute, he wondered what it would be like to whisk her away, no family, no drama, no business deals or takeovers. Just him and Lexi and no fucking worry on her face. Just happiness. At some point along this strange detour, her happiness had become incredibly important to him. He needed to spend some time thinking about what to do with that. About how to make the fake parts of their relationship real because despite the discord in his life right now, Alexandria Danby was his life raft. Looking at her, he knew, the way he knew a good business move in the depths of his soul, she was it for him.

Thirty-three

Gwen fell asleep on the way home so by the time they got into the house, Lexi didn't want to press her about anything. She'd done that enough. And now that her mom was entertaining the idea of remodeling, new worries surfaced. Had she pushed too hard? Would this ultimately set her mom back? Was she being selfish?

The week ahead was going to be a busy one. It included helping Bitsy interview a middle-aged woman who wanted something close to home with good hours. The Dress Hut could definitely accommodate that.

She had a list of suppliers she was cross-referencing to make sure that the ones Ethan currently used were still the best option. Tuesday morning, she woke early to go for a run.

Her phone buzzed as she scrolled through her playlists trying to settle on one.

We're Still Cool

Jackie

How is it only Tuesday?

Becca

> I thought it was Wednesday. Thanks for that dream crusher.

Lexi smiled.

Lexi

> You could pretend it's Saturday
> and go back to bed.

Jackie

> If only. I'm so excited about the Halloween party. I
> know it's couple themed but next year we should
> totally go as track stars. Your old uniform fit, Lexi?

Becca

> Hey. I don't have a track outfit. I hate
> running. You two were weirdos.

Lexi

> About to go running right now so
> I'm still weird. My college one might
> but probably not high school.

Becca

> You two could be track stars and your
> men can be your cheerleaders.

The conversation made her stomach twist. Who knew if Will or either of them would be in her life next year?

Lexi

She selected a playlist and started her run, pushing next year, old friends, new friends, her mother, and everything that wasn't the road in front of her to the back of her mind.

Instead of heading to the high school to use the track, she wove through her neighborhood, letting her muscles warm and loosen. Jogging had never been her thing. She'd trained to run races quickly and win them. This was different. It gave her time with her own thoughts, the cool, slightly dewy morning air slapping her awake. Like her feet only knew familiar paths, she found herself running toward the Dress Hut before it even registered. It wasn't until she saw Bitsy that it did. Her soon-to-be-former boss was dragging a large object that looked suspiciously tree-like, trying to hold the door with her hip while maneuvering whatever it was. Lexi quickened her pace.

"What are you doing? Let me get that," Lexi said, her breath a bit choppy as she wrapped her arms around what was indeed a fake tree.

"Baking a cake. What does it look like I'm doing?" Bitsy asked, doing a little heavy breathing of her own.

"The door stopper is right there. Grab that so we can prop it open."

The door swung against the tree when Bitsy moved to grab the little wedge. Once she'd propped the door open, they worked together to wrangle the poky plastic pine inside. Bitsy sat down on one of the waiting area chairs while Lexi shut and locked the door.

"I repeat, what are you doing?" Lexi laughed, thinking she wouldn't miss the work here as much as the quirkiness of this woman who'd given her a job when she was just a teenager and again when she was a slightly broken adult.

"Exactly what it looks like." Bitsy gave her a cheeky smile. Her silver hair curled around her face, her funky, blue-framed glasses making her eyes look bigger. "I'm dragging a fake tree into my store."

Lexi put her hands on her hips. "Any particular reason?"

Sucking in a deep breath, Bitsy stood up, moved to the top of the tree, and started dragging it toward the window. "I'm going to do a Christmas display."

Lexi picked up the bottom of the tree. Now that they weren't trying to shove it through a doorway, it was easier to move. "You just randomly decided to come in super-early and do this? We're a week away from Halloween. It might be a bit early."

Together they propped the tree upright in the little staging area in front of the window. Currently, it had a few mannequins dressed in fall sweaters and accessories like scarves and hats.

She held out a hand to help Bitsy step down off the platform. Bitsy waved her away.

"I was up anyway. At my age, you might as well sleep by the bathroom, you gotta pee so much. Plus, I move slow. You'll see as you get older. Things that used to take no time take an eternity. Trust me, it'll be Christmas by the time I get it all worked out."

Guilt stabbed her in the chest. "I can come back and help with this stuff."

Bitsy patted her arm on the way past, moving behind the counter. "You don't need to take care of me, Lexi. My store, my responsibility."

Lexi leaned her forearms on the counter as Bitsy puttered around behind it. "I left you in the lurch."

Bitsy's glasses slipped down her nose, so she peered at Lexi over them. "Honey. You found a replacement, you're interviewing more, and you're still here three mornings a week. It's not like business is booming. I don't think you know what *left you in the lurch* means, college girl."

Lexi laughed but uncertainty rolled around in her gut. "I'll come help with stuff if you need anything. You know that, right? You're like family to me."

Thinking about how nice it had been to have a big noisy dinner with Will's family before the night had gone sideways, Lexi wondered why she'd let herself believe it was just her and her mom. It wasn't. There was Bitsy, her card-sharp friends, Maisie, who included her and Gwen in everything.

Bitsy stopped going through receipts, pushed her glasses up her nose. "Oh yeah? Then how come it was Lenora who told me you're engaged to some big-shot Seattle hottie?"

Lexi's heart dropped like a boulder into the ocean. "First, please don't say *hottie* ever again."

"Hunk?" Bitsy smiled but Lexi saw the hurt under it. Felt it.

Swallowing past the lump in her throat, she shook her head.

"Arm candy?"

"Bitsy." Her voice cracked. She hadn't thought about the people around her, *in* her life, the ones who'd been there forever, who would be impacted by a tiny fib that had snowballed into something so much bigger.

"Just invite me to the wedding."

"Obviously." Because how could she tell her the truth now?

Moving around the counter, she gave a hug to Bitsy, who returned it, holding Lexi tight. "I'm proud of you, honey. You deserve every bit of happiness this world has to offer you."

"I love you," Lexi whispered.

"I know. Back at you. Now get out of here. You're sweaty and not working. I have a business to run."

Lexi laughed, sniffled, and turned away. She was at the door when Bitsy called her name.

"It's okay to live your life. You don't have to feel guilty about letting things go and moving forward. Sometimes the next step means leaving a few things behind. That doesn't mean they're gone.

Everything you go through is part of you. Makes you who you are. But you can't become who you're meant to be if you stand still. I'm glad you're not standing still anymore."

Lexi could only nod because she really didn't want to cry. Bitsy smiled like she understood. "See you tomorrow. You're training the new girl."

She left laughing but as she increased her pace, pushing herself, making her muscles burn, she felt the tears sliding down, cold and sharp, as she raced into the wind.

Thirty-four

Will stepped out of the shower Wednesday morning to see his phone almost vibrating off the countertop with incoming texts. He'd tried to talk Lexi into the shower with him but she'd left saying she had to work at both jobs today and had a paper due. Wrapping a towel around his waist, he dried his feet on the bath mat, not letting himself think about how Lexi's guard seemed to be slipping back into place.

He picked up his phone and walked to the bedroom, scrolling to see his sister had called an emergency meeting with everyone's presence expected.

"Settling right into boss mode, aren't you, sis?" he said with a smile. It looked good on her and gave them something to focus on other than their parents being jerks this week.

When he'd finally turned his phone back on Sunday, he'd received countless messages from both parents, group texts started by them, voicemails, and a link to an article in the Sunday *Times* casting doubt on the strength of their familial bonds given what had gone down Saturday.

It was a lot of unnecessary drama and he hoped like hell Maddie had an idea on how to end it. He hoped his parents would show up. After he dressed, he texted his sister that, wondering if she had a backup plan in place should they act like spoiled children.

Maddie

We'll give them twenty minutes' grace and then go to their house. Gramps and Gran are on board but I think they'll show.

Will

I'm sorry it's turned like this. No wonder pride is seen as a downfall.

Maddie

LOL. I have news. It's important.

Will

Are you okay?

His brow furrowed. Maddie was one of the strongest women he knew but she didn't always share things, preferring to keep her worries and concerns between herself and Rachel. Which he understood now more than ever. When something good or bad happened, he wanted to talk to Lexi.

Maddie

I am. But we can't move forward like this. See you soon.

They didn't need to go to his parents' house. Everyone was waiting in the boardroom when he arrived, including Rachel. There was coffee and a selection of treats from Rachel's shop on the table and tension thick enough to choke on in the air.

"Good morning," Will said.

It was the first time they'd all been in a room together since the party. Rachel squeezed Maddie's hand before the two of them took a seat. His grandfather held a chair for his grandmother and Kyra took a chair next to him. His parents looked like they might stay standing, another attempt at the upper hand, but his mother gave his dad a look that had him pulling out her chair first.

"I trust everyone read the link I sent," his father started. Despite his hard tone, he looked tired, as if the days had worn on him just as much as the rest of them. "I'm finding it rather ironic that we decided not to go with the very lucrative Home Needs deal to protect our shiny reputation only to tarnish it ourselves."

His grandfather flexed his fingers, the lines on his hands showing age but not weakness. "Yes. And is there any irony in the fact that you were the one to damage that reputation when you didn't get what you wanted with that deal?"

"I'm not sure that's the right definition of *irony*, Grandpa," Kyra said.

Will covered his mouth to hide his twitching lips and saw Maddie shoot Kyra some *knock it off* daggers with her eyes.

"The best word to describe all of this is *shameful*," his grandmother said. Small of stature but big of heart, she rarely attended meetings even though they were all equal shareholders. "How you behaved was unforgivable, Jackson. If you had a problem with your father's decision, you should have spoken to him, not the *Seattle Times*. That's hardly the place to share family news. There or in the middle of a celebration. Which you all but ruined."

His grandfather reached out a hand, covered his grandma's when her voice shook. "Your mother is right. But I shouldn't have just sprung it on you. I'd talked to Madeline and I have reasons for my decision. I should have been more open about that, and for my part in it, I apologize."

His mother leaned into his father, said something only he could hear. To his credit, his father straightened and looked his own father in the eye, his frown softening.

"I'm not a big fan of being blindsided by important information," he said, his gaze moving to Will. "It feels like Emily and I are the last to know about important family milestones. Like engagements." He looked at Maddie. "And promotions." Then back to his father. "And retirements."

Will's stomach clenched. "It was never my intention for you to find out that way, Dad."

His dad's gaze burned into his. "But it was always your intention to marry a woman your mother and I knew nothing about?"

"Is that what bothers you most? Not that he's getting married but that you didn't have a hand in choosing her?" Kyra said, her thumb furiously clicking the end of her pen.

"Kyra. Don't speak to your father like that. How dare you," his mother put in before his dad could respond.

"She's not a child, Mom. You can't reprimand her," Maddie said.

Several of them started to speak at once and things were already elevating when Rachel stood up.

"Stop. All of you. Stop."

Everyone's gaze turned her way. Maddie reached out, took her hand, and pressed her lips to the top of it. Rachel sat back down, folding her hands on the table.

"I love all of you. I've been part of this family for more of my life than I haven't. I've watched all of you grow and change and adjust. Sometimes gracefully, sometimes painfully. You're all angry and hurt and I get that but you're also so lucky and I think you forget that."

No one said anything. Rachel was here for one reason: Maddie wanted her here for whatever she needed to share. It seemed prudent to listen to a woman who truly knew what she was talking about. Not only did Rachel work with her own large family, but they ran a small empire successfully.

"Everything that happens with my family's company goes through lawyers, board members, and accountants. I understand, Jackson, that you wanted to expand but your father and Will were right. The financial possibilities aren't as important as this core group of people. You have something very special in this room. You don't always show it the right way but you all love one another so much. I've seen that. I've felt it. Grandpa," Rachel said, looking at him with respect and love. "You should have foreseen the dent to Jackson's pride. I think, if I'm understanding you correctly, you were trying to save your own son from waiting too long to extricate himself from a very consuming business. Because what matters isn't what we do or sell. It's who we surround ourselves with."

Grandpa looked at Will's dad. "Your mother and I wanted to ask you and Emily to join us on a cruise. Our treat. I've been thinking about this for a while. It's time and Rachel's right—I didn't want you to wait twenty years too long to enjoy time with your wife, outside of this building, or with your family. I'm sorry for the way I went about it."

His father said nothing but his expression softened and he reached for his mom's hand.

"Mads will serve this company well and I think all of you can agree on that," Rachel said. "She's been Jeremy's right hand for years now while you've done what you do best, Jackson. And you, Emily, have created such an amazing social network. I'm so in awe of the connections you've made in the community, the impact you've helped this company have on so many charities."

"Thanks, honey," Maddie said, sucking in a somewhat shaky breath. "Rachel's right. We've always had our strengths and we've played to them. But I don't want this position if it comes with tearing us apart. These last several months have felt like we're chasing down different dreams. Will and I just want to build on what Grandpa has created. But Mom, Dad, you both seem so driven to expand. Mom, you're on more committee boards than I can name. Dad, you work sixty-five hours a week and think you can do more. I don't want to. If that's the direction you want to take this company, then I won't take part. I'll step back."

His father's hands curled into fists. "I want to work with my family. That has always come first for us."

"If that holds true, then we can't go forward like this." Maddie looked at Rachel, who gave her a slight nod, then faced all of them again. "Grand Babies is a household name, particularly in the Pacific Northwest. I think Will's idea to partner with Comfort Plus is a good one. I also think we can expand our online reach to a more global level, and Dad, I'd like you and Kyra to work together on that. You have the company and business knowledge that will pair perfectly with her social media and marketing knowledge. It's a compromise."

"I'll agree, communication hasn't been our strength," Will added. He hated his part in that but he would never be sorry life had led him to Lexi. And thinking of her and communication, he decided to make it clear to his family where he was headed with his own future. "I'm sorry all of you were blindsided with the news of my engagement. To be honest, I didn't mean for it to get printed in the paper." Still half-truths, but they'd turn out well in the end. "But I'm in love with this woman and I very much want to bring her into our family. I know you had a vision for my future, Mom, but I think you and Dad need to figure your own out and let us take care of ours."

Maddie laughed. "On that note and the idea of bringing people into this family and starting fresh with open communication, Rachel is pregnant. We're going to be moms."

Everything else fell away, ceased to exist. His parents and grandparents rushed to them first while Will looked at Kyra and mouthed, *Did you know?*

She shook her head and then they went to join in on the hugging.

The conversation bounced around like a Ping-Pong ball stuck in between those bouncing rubber stoppers but the mood shifted and Will felt, for the first time in a long time, that even if they weren't perfect or didn't see eye-to-eye, maybe they'd all be okay. With one another, their roles in the company, and themselves. The direction of their own, individual futures. And the verbal acknowledgment of his feelings for Lexi in a room full of people he loved made him 100 percent sure of what he wanted down the road. He wanted Alexandria Danby, his fake fiancée, to be his real wife.

Thirty-five

She would *not* freak out. It was a costume party. She could wear anything. But then Kyra suggested Will and Lexi go to the Halloween party as a bride and groom.

"It'll be funny," she said. "Adorable." And since the engagement wasn't real, what harm would it cause?

Not so funny since she couldn't find a goddamn wedding dress at any secondhand shops. Why had she left it to the last minute?

She threw her car into park, grabbed her things, and made a dash through the rain into the house.

When she got inside, she leaned against the door and let out a long sigh. She'd left everything to the last minute because she was running out of minutes in a day to get everything done. She didn't even want to go to this party tonight. She'd suggested to Will that since she'd helped Ethan's event planner pull everything together and it was expected to be a big bash, maybe they could quietly bow out and dress up, or down, as a couple on their honeymoon at his place.

But people had been invited. People from her past, their present. His sisters. He'd told her that family tempers and feelings had been tentatively smoothed out and that Maddie and Rachel were having a baby. She wanted to congratulate them in person. She sighed heavily, making little droplets of water from the hair hanging in her face scatter. This was why her mother liked to hide away in the house.

After hanging her jacket and purse, she went upstairs, wondering if she could make something work with one of the dresses Kyra had lent her.

Gwen, who had been having more good days than bad lately, was curled in her chair reading, a cup of tea at her side. She looked up as Lexi hit the top step.

"Hi. Looks like it's pretty wet out there."

"Seattle in the fall. I'm not a fan today."

Gwen put down her book. "Your party is tonight, right?"

Lexi walked over to the fireplace and stood in front of it, hoping to rid herself of the chill.

"Yeah. I'm not really in the mood to go."

"Me neither," Gwen said, smiling.

Lexi shot her a narrow-eyed look. "Were you ever going to?"

Gwen shrugged, still smiling.

"I have to," Lexi said. "I want to see how it all turns out, if I'm honest. Plus, it might look strange if I don't show."

"You worry too much about what other people think."

Since Will was excited and she was falling into some pretty serious feelings about a man she was only supposed to have pretend feelings about—or a pretend engagement with—everything was getting muddled.

"It's not that. Never mind, it doesn't matter. I have to go figure out what I'm wearing."

Lexi started for her room.

"Aren't you going as a bride?" Gwen got up from her chair.

Lexi whirled, her emotions fraying at the edge. "I was. But finding a dress at the last minute is apparently impossible. I'll see if one of Kyra's dresses will work. Will and I can go as a prom couple. This is stupid. I hate Halloween. I'm going to shower first."

She didn't mean to snap. At the bathroom door, she turned to apologize but Gwen had already walked away. Lexi yelled at herself in her head. *Way to take it out on your mom.*

She texted Maisie before putting on her shower playlist, which would hopefully pull her out of her mood.

Lexi

I cannot find a wedding dress.
This is too much and, I think, a sign.

Maisie

You don't believe in signs.

Lexi

I believe in this one. I have no dress for tonight.

Maisie

Let me see if I can find someone who has something. Give me twenty. Breathe. You should have copied me. We could have been zombie cheerleader twins.

Lexi

There's still a chance I might have to.

Doing her best to wash off a long, overwhelming day under the hot spray, Lexi knew something had to change. She couldn't keep lying to everyone about her and Will. *And you can't keep lying to yourself. You're falling. You've fallen, Lexi. You've slipped off a ledge you swore you never would.* At least things were good with work and school. She'd aced her midterm thanks to a woman Will had put her in touch with. She'd been easy to interview and very informative. Side Tap might not be a forever job because it was a family business at its core but the work energized her, reminded her that she had bigger aspirations.

By the time she'd dried off, pulled on a robe, and taken a towel to her hair, she was feeling slightly more human. While going over menu layouts today, Ethan had teased her about the party tonight saying he hoped she had some fun couples games planned for the evening. Will was picking her up in about an hour, which meant time was running out. She texted him quickly that there was a change of plans and she'd be going as a prom queen. Close enough. She'd never been one but hell, she'd never been a bride either. That was the whole point of pretend. That line was blurring a lot lately. She'd woken up in Will's bed a few days ago with a cozy, blissed-out feeling like she belonged there.

She startled when she walked into her room and saw her mom sitting on her bed.

Gripping the towel between her breasts, she let out a heavy laughing breath. "You scared me. You okay? You sure you won't come tonight?"

Gwen shook her head, looked around the room like she was seeing it for the first time. Lexi walked to the edge of the bed and sat down facing her mom.

Putting a hand on her arm, she waited for Gwen to look at her. "Mom? Are you okay?"

Gwen put her hand on top of Lexi's. "I am. This room hasn't changed much but you certainly have. Part of me felt like if the house stayed the same, if I didn't change, you didn't change, maybe it would feel less like my entire life is different."

"It is different, though, Mom. I don't mean just because Dad is gone. That part will always hurt, but there's good stuff too."

Gwen shook her head, her smile not lighting her eyes. "You're the good stuff. I've held you back, held you in the past with me for too long."

Unease trickled through Lexi's bloodstream. "I don't have to go tonight. I really don't want to." She especially didn't want to leave her alone like this.

"Don't even think about skipping it. This is exactly what you should be doing. Having fun, going out. Living your life. With friends. You'll go and you'll celebrate and you'll keep moving forward because you're right—that's what he'd want us to do. Now, let's get you ready." Her mom squeezed her hand.

"I'm going to wear that red dress of Kyra's. I always wished I'd worn red to prom instead of that blue dress."

Gwen stood, pulled Lexi up. "You looked beautiful then and you'll look beautiful tonight. The only thing is, this means you can't wear this for your actual wedding but I think that's okay. You should have your own, one you've chosen to wear on the day you marry the love of your life."

Lexi's brow creased, her heart thudding heavily in her chest. "What are you talking about, Mom?"

Gently, Gwen put her hands on Lexi's shoulders, started to turn her while saying, "It's bad luck for the groom to see the bride in her wedding dress before the ceremony, so you won't be able to wear this again."

Words and air got trapped in Lexi's throat. A strange sound left it as she stared at her mother's wedding dress, out of its protective garment bag, hanging on a cloth hanger from the top of her closet. She'd seen pictures and once, when she was little, she'd seen the real thing. For months and months after her father died, Gwen had looked through all the photos. Lexi hadn't realized Gwen even had the dress accessible. As much as she clung to the past, Gwen didn't pull out the pieces of it very often.

Her parents hadn't had a lot of money when they'd married. They'd had a simple ceremony, choosing to use their savings on the house instead of an elaborate event. She knew her mother was proud of finding her dream dress at a discount price.

Lexi walked forward slowly, looking at the timeless white gown. A tight silk halter top bodice was unadorned but elegant in its simplicity and the way it narrowed at the waist. The full skirt flared out just a little at the hips, and the bottom of the dress had a thick ribbon of pale-pink silk. Her mother had worn a dollar-store tiara and a pair of pink Converse shoes.

"Mom. It's so gorgeous." When she turned back, her mother was right there, tears in her eyes.

Lexi shook her head. "I can't. I can't wear this, Mom." It felt wrong yet somehow so tempting. It was so beautiful she almost ached to slip into it.

Gwen smiled, her lips quivering even as her eyes swam with the unshed emotion. "You can, you should, and you will. Consider it your something borrowed."

Lexi gave a watery laugh of her own. "That's for the actual wedding. This is just . . ." She stopped, cleared her throat, and looked down at the floor. *Just a ruse, a misunderstanding. A lie.*

Gwen dipped down a little, bending her knees. "Hey. Don't cry. Why are you crying?"

"I can't wear your dress."

Gwen wiped her tears just like she had when Lexi was a little girl and a sob threatened to escape her lungs.

"I want you to, honey. It'll be like I'm there with you tonight. I love you. I see you. I want you to embrace your future. I'm going to be okay. We can't stay stuck forever."

All words Lexi had been saying, things she'd been thinking. Gwen pulled her into a hard hug, smoothed a hand down her still-damp hair.

When she pulled back, she put both hands to Lexi's cheeks. "I'm still the mom. My house, my rules."

Lexi laughed again at Gwen's lousy attempt at a stern tone.

"Get dressed, Lexi. Your prince will be here soon. And I expect you to be out long after the clock strikes midnight."

Thirty-six

Will nearly swallowed his tongue when Lexi opened the door in a wedding gown. Not *just* a wedding gown but one so beautiful he thought maybe he was imagining it. Maybe everything he'd begun to want more than he'd ever wanted anything was happening. There was no word strong enough for the emotions coursing through him. The top of the dress let her showcase the delicate sexiness of her collarbone, her toned shoulders and arms. The cinched waist made her seem curvier, and the skirt billowed out romantically like she was a princess in a movie.

Words rumbled around like rocks in his head, trying to force their way out of his mouth. He stepped closer even as they continued to hold each other's gazes, something much stronger and deeper than simple passion or care flickering between them. An all-consuming need thrummed inside him like a heavy pulsebeat.

"You look fucking amazing," he whispered. He cleared his throat, tried again. "Let's skip the party and get married tonight."

Some of the tension in her gaze—which he hoped was from wanting him as much as he wanted her—lessened and she tipped her head back in a laugh. Her dark tresses were pulled up away from her face and he had the overwhelming need to press his mouth to the long column of her neck, right in the hollow of her softest skin.

When he did, she gasped, igniting the need inside of him to something he'd never felt before. He swallowed her surprise with a kiss that he wasn't sure could convey how much he felt. But he was willing to try.

Taking her face between his hands, he memorized the feel of her lips against his own, the taste of her with a hint of something fruity she must have put on her lips. He groaned at the touch of her hands on his shoulders, the way her body pressed into his as she gave him back everything she had with the same urgency he felt.

Will moved his hands down, circling her waist and drawing her closer, lifting her right off the ground. He couldn't get close enough. He wondered if he'd ever get enough of this woman. He knew it might have started as a pretense, but this was it. She was it. She owned his heart whether she knew it or not and he had no intention of letting her go. As soon as this party was done, he was going to talk to his fake fiancée about making the commitment between them very, very real.

———

Side Tap was decked out for Halloween in the strangest way Will had ever seen. While the day's colors were typically black and orange, Ethan had used white and cream pumpkins, gorgeous yellow and white flowers, hundreds of extra twinkle lights—the kind with bigger, round bulbs and white light—ribbons of silk and organza (he'd been an active participant in Rachel and Maddie's wedding conversations) as streamers, and so many candles it might have been a fire hazard.

"Oh my God," Lexi whispered when they walked in the double doors. "It was supposed to be gaudy. Skeletons and cobwebs. It's Halloween. I helped plan everything out."

"Guess he made some last-minute changes. It's incredible. Look," Will said, holding her hand tightly with his own while using the other one to point to the banner that read: CONGRATULATIONS ALEXANDRIA & WILLIAM.

Son of a bitch. His joke about making this an engagement party must not have been a joke. And he'd kept it as a surprise.

"The guests of honor are in the house! Everyone welcome the bride and groom."

Will turned to see his friend behind the bar dressed like Rip Wheeler from *Yellowstone*, a microphone in hand. He even had a fake beard to go with the dark glasses and the black Stetson. One of the waitresses stood beside him dressed as Beth Dutton, clapping and whistling over the music and other shouts of congratulations.

He'd known the theme was couples, but it was pretty incredible to see it in action. They walked farther into the bar, where the longest farmhouse-style table was dressed like a head table. Ethan had even tacked a sign to the wall that said BRIDE AND GROOM SIT HERE.

Maisie bounded over to them dressed as . . . he had no idea who she was dressed as. It looked almost like a one-piece bathing suit, the top half red with a yellow *i* in a black circle across her chest. The bottom was black, she wore a mask, and her hair was flat and straight. She wore red tights and knee-high black boots.

"Holy shit, you are the prettiest bride I've ever seen. And I've seen a lot of brides. When you didn't get back to me, I figured you were doing the prom thing." Maisie threw her arms around Lexi's neck.

"I thought you were coming as a zombie cheerleader," Lexi said over the roar of music and people milling about, waiting for a chance to say hello.

Maisie pulled back. "As if. Ethan looped me in on this a while back. The theme is couples."

"Okay, I have to know, then—who are you supposed to be?" Will pulled her into a hug as well.

When she stepped back, she pointed to her chest. "I'm Elastigirl! From *The Incredibles*. I figured this was a surefire way of manifesting a better half with huge muscles."

Lexi laughed with her friend. Will vaguely recalled the Pixar movie about the superhero family. Maisie stayed by their side as several people hugged them, shook their hands, congratulated them, and asked where they'd be registering. He felt Lexi's tension notching up like a clock ticking.

Maddie and Rachel, dressed as David Bowie and Iman, gave them hard hugs.

"I'm so excited for you guys," Lexi said to the two of them.

Rachel winked at her and rubbed a hand over her flat stomach. "You'll be an auntie."

He felt rather than saw Lexi's flinch. She smiled brightly and turned to Kyra, who joined them and was dressed as Barbie. Will glanced around, wondering whom she might have brought as Ken. His protective brotherly instincts surged thinking about his little sister and a guy he might not know. For one brief second, he understood why his mother might find comfort in choosing one of their partners. What guy was good enough for his baby sister?

"Why are you frowning? Your bride is standing beside you, this party is in your honor, and Ethan has a new beer on tap," Kyra said, giving him a playful shove.

"I'm wondering where your *Ken* is," Will said.

Lexi laughed, squeezed his hand. "Leave her alone."

In her bright-pink, short spaghetti-strap dress, his sister did an awkward curtsy. "Thank you, Lexi. You are now my favorite."

After Will helped Lexi navigate her way through the crowd with her dress, they sat at the head table. So many people stopped by while they sampled a finger-food menu Ethan had created for tonight. Lexi's grin was genuine when Jackie and Nigel came by, her dressed as a cheerleader to complement Nigel's quarterback outfit.

"You said it was a Halloween party, not an engagement party. Thank you for inviting us," Jackie said.

"We didn't know," Lexi said over the increasing volume of music and people.

"We didn't but we're so glad you could come," Will said, slipping his hand onto Lexi's knee, giving it a gentle squeeze.

"You guys look amazing," Lexi said, her hand coming to the top of Will's.

Will sensed Lexi's restlessness as the conversation carried on. He pushed back in his seat as the music changed to a slower tempo.

Putting a hand on Lexi's bare shoulder, loving the feel of her skin beneath his palm, he said, "If you'll excuse us, I'd like to dance with my bride."

Lexi tipped her head back, looked up at him. Will leaned down, kissed her, running his finger along her jaw.

"That sounds wonderful." Her reply was just a little breathy.

"Oh, you two. We should dance too, honey," Jackie said.

They parted ways on the makeshift dance floor that Ethan had set up in the raised area of the pub where Will and Lexi had once shared appetizers. That seemed like a lifetime ago. He pulled Lexi into his arms, gripping one of her hands while keeping his other hand pressed low on her back. She smelled like honey and Lexi and he wanted more nights like this: dancing, being with friends, laughing. He wanted it to be real. Forever.

Lexi seemed as lost in the moment and the subtle synchronized sway of their bodies as he was. Twinkle lights danced overhead, and though it was crowded, it was easy to pretend it was just the two of them when he leaned back to gaze into her eyes.

Because she was all he could see.

He bent his head to hers, pressed their foreheads together like it would help her *feel* what he was thinking.

The hand he wasn't holding slipped up around his neck like she too craved a closeness that couldn't be quenched.

The words floated around in his heart and his head, adrift, bouncing off one another, looking for a place to land.

"I don't want this to be pretend," he whispered, staring into her eyes.

"What?"

"Us. I want it all to be real. The engagement. A life together. It's not pretend for me. Any of it. It's not a misunderstanding. It's the most real thing I've ever known. I love you, Lexi. I want you. Always."

He couldn't read her expression as he watched it change. Her eyes widened, her lips parting before forming a small *o*. Her hand loosened on the back of his neck like it'd been covered in grease and slipped right down to her side.

"What are you doing?" she whispered.

He smiled. His sweet, cautious Lexi. "I'm telling you I love you. For real." He felt like a helium balloon someone had let go of: free, soaring. The words were energizing and powerful. Not just because he'd said them to her but because he felt them in every molecule of his being.

"I love you." He grinned, liking the way the words felt in his mouth, how they sounded out loud. "I love you."

And just like that, like an unexpected branch popping a balloon and stealing all of the life out of it, making it shrink until it disappeared, Lexi pulled away. She picked up her skirt, shaking her head, and looked at him with sadness swamping her eyes.

"I can't do this. I have to go."

Will stood on the dance floor, staring after her as she wove through the crowd, ignoring people and pushing past. Stunned, he didn't even go after her because despite the fact that he knew what he said was true, he very much loved her, what had just happened didn't feel real. More than that, he didn't want it to be.

Thirty-seven

Like an actual runaway bride from some stupid romcom her mom would read or watch, Lexi hurried out of Side Tap to the parking lot. The drivers were laughing and chatting, leaning against their vehicles. The October moon hung low in the sky, creating an eerie glow.

Will's driver pushed off the back of the limo. "You okay, Ms. Danby?"

She nodded, biting back tears with sheer willpower. "I need to go home."

He didn't ask any questions, just opened the door for her, let her slide into the cool leather seat. She heard Will shout her name as the door closed. In a romcom, she would have escaped. The camera would pan to her gorgeous, tear-streaked profile looking out the back of the tinted limo window at Will, standing in the moonlight. It'd do a close-up on him, standing devastated because she was absolutely awful, and in the movie version, everyone would hate her for just a minute, but it would be nothing compared to how she felt about herself right now.

But this wasn't a movie and the other door opened, Will sliding in beside her just before the driver took his spot and started the vehicle.

How was she supposed to hold her tears back if she had to talk to him?

His face was etched with concern. "Lexi. What's going on?"

She ran the silky organza of the dress through her fingers, unable to look at him. "This was a mistake. All of it."

"Coming here?" He sounded genuinely perplexed.

Lexi looked up, blinking rapidly in the hope of staying dry-eyed. "Being together. I'm not built for the fairy-tale ending, Will. It's too much. And who really gets the happy ending, anyway? Look at my mom. Her ending was ripped away and it changed her forever. I can't handle that. I can't do this." She gestured to the dress. "This isn't me. I can't be with you knowing that one day, somehow, it'll fall apart. My mom is a shell of who she used to be and I feel like I'm just figuring out who I am again. But all of the lies on top of the real is making my head spin."

He scooted closer, taking her hand between both of his. "No more lies. Tell me how you feel, Lexi. How do you really feel about me?"

Therein lay the problem. "I don't want this. I don't want to fall so hard I won't ever be able to get back up. I've got my mom, finishing school. I never should have sat down with you that day. It was so unfair of me. All because I couldn't face the fact that I'd amounted to nothing."

Anger flashed in his gaze. "Stop. I fucking hate when you do that. *You* are not *nothing*. You're *everything*."

She shook her head, pulled her hand back. "No. I can't be and you can't be for me. You're amazing, Will. You deserve someone who matches you in every single way, and that isn't me. I've been letting myself go along with all this, letting myself believe it could maybe become real."

"It *is* real. I love you. That's as real as it gets."

Her heart cracked like a windshield, right in the center, sending little cracks in every direction.

"We just got caught up in everything. We need to go back to our own lives." She needed to finish helping her mom get better, finish school, tell her old friends the truth. If she couldn't face who she'd become, the real version of herself, how could Will possibly love her? The person she'd been in the last several weeks wasn't the real her. She didn't even know who that was anymore.

"Tell me you don't love me," he said, his voice harsh and low.

She looked into his eyes, her heart pressing against her ribs painfully, and told one more lie. The one that would set him free. The one she needed to tell because he needed more, deserved more.

"I don't love you," she whispered.

_____

Lexi didn't bother coming into the house quietly when the car dropped her off. The last thing she did before turning away from Will was give him back the ring. It was never really hers. And she shouldn't have believed he could be either.

She'd seen Maisie's Jeep in the driveway. Clearly, her friend had seen her leave and beaten her home. So much for crawling into her bed and blocking out the world. Locking the door behind her, she slipped off her shoes, eager to get out of her mother's wedding dress.

"Lex?" Maisie's voice came from the top of the stairs.

"It's me," she said.

Her body felt like a pumpkin, carved out and cut up. How could doing the right thing make her ache this much? Maisie came down the steps, stopped when she saw Lexi. She'd thrown some joggers and a sweater on.

"What happened? Where have you been? Where did you go?" She kept coming forward, looking at her like she knew that Lexi was crumbling from the inside out because _Maisie_ knew her, knew who she was, who she'd been. Will only had a small window of knowing her as a frame of reference. He liked her spirit and drive but she wasn't the kind of woman he needed.

"Lexi." Maisie put her arms around her, pulled her into a hug. "What happened?"

Tears fell but words didn't come. She'd done this to herself. She'd let herself believe she could be part of a world she didn't belong in. Will thought he knew her, thought he *loved* her, but he'd only had a little snapshot of her life, of *her*.

Things had been going so well in the last few weeks it was easy to believe they'd just carry on that way, but Lexi knew better. When things fell apart again, he'd see that she wasn't a woman on an upward trajectory. Her mother wouldn't sell this house, she'd always be missing part of herself, which meant Lexi would always have to care for her in some way.

"Come on. Let's get you out of this dress."

Gwen was asleep in her bed, a small victory. Lexi changed into sweats and a sweater, then curled up on the couch while Maisie made her some tea.

"What the hell happened?" Maisie handed her the mug. Lexi wrapped both of her hands around it, letting the warmth seep into her skin.

"He said he loved me. He wanted it to be real. Us, the engagement. Forever."

Maisie groaned. "Lexi."

"What?" she snapped, sipping the tea, letting the burn sting her tongue.

"You love him back."

Setting the tea down, Lexi looked toward the hallway then back at her friend. "It doesn't matter how I feel. I don't want to be her, barely able to make it from one day to the next because I tied everything I was, *who* I am, into one person to the point that I literally cannot exist without them. I'm never going to be a socialite or a high-society, country-clubbing Page Six woman. I couldn't even be a waitress, for

God's sake. I lied to people who used to be my best friends. To my mom. I took the easy way. Didn't push her. Didn't leave the Dress Hut. Didn't finish my degree. I took the path of least resistance because I'm too much of a coward to face hard truths. Jesus Christ. I already am her." She flopped her head back against the cushion. "And Will deserves better."

"Better than what, Alexandria?" Her mother's quiet words came from the hallway. She stood there in a pair of flannel pajamas, wringing her hands together. "Better than a woman who was lucky enough to know, accept, and give love? One who got to have over twenty years beside the person who knew her best?"

Lexi swore under her breath. "Mom." She started to get up but Gwen came farther into the room, stood at the end of the couch.

"I lost him but I wouldn't trade having him for anything. I'm sorry you think I'm broken and I'm sorry you think being broken is a bad thing. Everything we do, choose, and feel shapes us, Lexi. You've been so worried about me for years because I don't want to leave the house, socialize, go to places where he and I used to go. But I'm okay with all of those choices. I don't *need* you to take care of me or put your life on hold for me. You do it and I let you so yeah, I guess we've both taken the easy route. But I didn't when it came to your dad. Loving him wasn't the easy route. Marrying him wasn't *the path of least resistance*. The things that are worth it in life rarely are. You can blame me for not wanting to move forward with Will and let him accept you for who you are but the truth is, you're scared."

Lexi stood up. "Yes! I'm scared. I don't want to lose a chunk of my soul or my heart. There's not that much left to lose! Don't forget that you lost *Dad*. But I lost him and *you*. The best parts of you died with him and I've been standing here all alone."

Gwen's hand flew to her mouth as she sucked in a breath. Tears filled her eyes. Maisie stood up, pulled Gwen into her side.

Her friend's voice was calm when she spoke. "It's late. Let's not say anything else that is going to be hard to take back."

"Mom." Lexi had no idea what to follow that up with.

Before Gwen could say anything, Maisie turned her by the shoulders and led her back to her room. Lexi sank into the couch, pulled her knees up, and rested her head on them.

She felt the couch dip with Maisie's weight, felt her hand on her shoulder. "You're not alone, you idiot."

Lexi snorted, lifted her head. "Comforting."

"The only person who isn't okay with who you are, who you've become, is you. I don't know how you can look at yourself and think you're not good enough for Will. That he's better than you or that Jackie and Becca are. No one's life is perfect, Lex. We don't fit into neat little boxes with no overlap. Instead of comparing yourself with the eighteen-year-old version of you, look for the pieces of her that are still in you, fighting every single day in every area of your life. You're not a track star anymore but you are still *her*. You keep thinking because you don't have awards or accolades, and your career hasn't taken off the way you planned by this age, you should hide that."

"Everyone else has their shit together, Maisie."

Maisie laughed. "According to *who*? I mean, Will asked you to pretend because he couldn't have a firm conversation with his mother about staying out of his dating life. I'm working out of a closet in my apartment that I turned into an office. So you couldn't waitress. So what? You took longer to get your degree. Life wasn't a straight path. So fucking what? Look at you. You're stronger than ever. The eighteen-year-old you couldn't have faced the shit you've gone through in the last three years. You've held yourself and your mother together. You don't give yourself any credit. You didn't lose the house when your father would have. You made sure every one of his employees were paid out properly, taking the debt on yourself and working out a payment plan with the bank. Will isn't blind. He sees *you*. Better than you see yourself. You don't like country clubs but neither does he and he grew up in them. He sees the fierce determination and loyalty you apply to every area of your life. Maybe you're the one who doesn't see him. You're not just selling yourself short; you've done the same to him."

Lexi had no words. She felt like all of the dishes she'd ever dropped, smashed, and shattered on the ground, needing to be swept up. Maisie leaned her head on Lexi's shoulder. Lexi let her head fall against Maisie's.

She'd lost her dad and pieces of her mother. She'd lost her scholarship, her chance at the future the eighteen-year-old Lexi had planned. Those things were beyond her control. But this loss? *Will*. She might have no one to blame for that loss other than herself.

Thirty-eight

Will looked out the window at the November sky, dark and gray. That's how he felt inside. Lexi wouldn't return his calls or his texts. It'd been three days. Ethan said she was working, doing all of the things she'd promised, but wouldn't discuss anything personal. Said she was being polite and professional in an almost robotic fashion.

"Hey," Kyra said. She walked into his office with a bit of hesitation, not her usual bouncy self.

"Hey." He turned from the window as she came in.

"Not to add insult to injury but Lexi asked that we do a press release saying the engagement is off. She figured it would be the easiest way to spread the word."

Will stood abruptly, knocking his chair back. "She's talking to you? She called?"

Kyra shook her head, and he saw the sadness in his sister's gaze. "No. She texted. I asked if I could see her, if we could talk. She told me how much she likes me, how wonderful all of us are. Said to take care of you."

Slapping his palms on his desk, he gritted out, "Fuck that. I don't need anyone to take care of me. She's so goddamn worried about everyone else she's willing to walk away from a chance at being truly happy."

"I'm sorry." Kyra's voice cracked and Will's head snapped up.

"What are you sorry about?"

"I wanted it to be real for you because I see the way you two look at each other and I pushed. I'm just like Mom."

Will let out a harsh laugh, coming around the desk to pull his sister into a hug. "Maybe in the *wanting me happy* part. None of this is your fault."

"I picked the ring."

He laughed again. "Is that thing real?"

Kyra leaned back, insult laced in her tone, expression, and body language. It almost made him laugh. "Of course it is. Why would I let you give her a fake ring?"

His brows drew together. "Because it was never supposed to be real?"

Kyra patted his chest. "But that's not true, is it? I think it's been real for you since the minute you saw her. Your mistake was pretending it wasn't."

"When did you get so smart?"

Kyra squeezed and let him go. "I had good teachers. You should talk to Mom and Dad."

He nodded. "I know."

When she left, he pushed down the ache that had taken up residence in his chest, like a rock sitting in a hollow cave, and went to set a few things straight. Things had become less tense since the family meeting they'd had. Like they were all walking on thin tiles and no one wanted to be the reason for the break. Will had a feeling from the way both of his parents talked to him the last couple of days that his sisters had filled them in on Lexi leaving.

His mother was on the phone when he went into his father's office.

His dad was sitting, one ankle crossed over his knee, reading a report on the couch.

"William," his dad said.

His mother hung up the phone. "Hi, honey. How are you? We haven't seen much of you this week."

"Lexi and I were never engaged." Shit. He hadn't meant to blurt it out.

His mother's face went pale. His father stood up. "I knew it. That girl doesn't suit you at all. I knew something was off. What does she want? Is she blackmailing you for something?"

His mother stood up, coming around the large walnut desk that was once his grandfather's.

"No. She's not blackmailing me and she suits me better than anyone I've ever met."

While they stood there, staring at him, he told them everything: how they'd met, how they'd gotten closer, and the misunderstanding about the engagement.

"I don't understand," his mother said. "You said you loved her. Why would you let me believe that?"

He did love her. But that wasn't the reason he'd been okay with a fake engagement. Will ran a hand through his hair. "Because you're on my case constantly about being with the right woman, about getting married, tradition, and legacy."

"What the hell is wrong with that?" his father said, pacing as he always did when he was irritated.

"What's wrong with that is it's one thing to guide me in business and groom me to take over. But my personal life is *mine*. I don't want or need your help. I'd love your approval but I don't *need* it. Lexi and I weren't really engaged but I fell in love with her for real and I plan on winning her back."

"William." His father stopped in front of him. "I didn't say anything because the damage was done but I did some digging. This girl's credit is abysmal. She lives at home with her mother. They'll likely lose their house in the next two years based on what I learned about her income and their expenses. For God's sake. She was a *waitress*."

His father shook his head in disgust, like he could shake the word off his being.

Will stared at the people who'd raised him, people he loved and respected. People who didn't understand him at all and the feeling was mutual.

"Waitress, CEO, what the fuck is the difference?"

"Watch your mouth," his father said at the same time his mother gasped his name.

"I really thought what Rachel said last week got through to you two. Let me restate it in my own words. It doesn't matter *what* we do, Dad. Our company is successful because of *who* we are. Our customers come back because we stand by our products, because we believe in them. Because we make a commitment and stick with it. They know they can count on us and put stock in what they purchase from us. We've never been a bottom-line company. We're about family and that's what sets us apart."

"Damn right it is," his grandfather said from the doorway where he was leaning, hands tucked in the pockets of his suit pants. His gray hair was a little long, sweeping across his forehead. "The boy is right. You do what you love and everything else follows. You find someone you love and it doesn't matter if they're a waitress or a queen. You live life with your heart. It's got nothing to do with other people's perceptions. The reason Grand Babies and this family have succeeded is because we're a real family, providing something other real families need."

"I thought you were retiring. This has nothing to do with you, Dad," Will's father said.

His grandfather laughed, pushed off the doorframe. "It has everything to do with me. It's my company, son. I'm not retiring until the new year and that doesn't mean I won't be around or that it's not still mine. One day it'll be yours and William's and the girls'. And if you remember correctly, Jackson, I let you find your own way in this company, in your life. I didn't make you follow some imaginary set of rules on how to exist in the social circle I deemed worthy of you." His grandfather stepped closer to Will. "I was supposed to pair up with a completely different woman when I met your grandmother. It was a charity event, orchestrated by my mother and one of her friends. They had grand plans to set up their children. I didn't care one way or another. I was there for the open bar, the dancing, and the flirting."

"Dad," Will's father groaned, some of the energy draining out of his rigid posture.

His grandfather grinned. "But I took one look at your grandmother and that was it. My bachelor days were over. I didn't even have a choice. Something about the way she looked at me hooked my soul for good. You know when you feel that. Don't let yourself doubt it and for God's sake, don't be stupid enough to lose it trying to please any of us."

Will laughed despite the fact that his parents looked shell-shocked. "Thanks, Gramps."

"You've got good instincts, Will. Trust them."

Will looked at his mom and dad. "She might not be who you would have chosen for me. But she's who I choose for myself and I hope you'll accept that. Accept her. Because I'm in love with her and my world won't be right without her in it. I need to go."

"This is ridiculous," his father spat out.

His mother took her husband's hand. "Not really. I was crazy about you for months before you finally asked me out. I'd like to think that even if I hadn't come from money, you'd have fallen for me anyway."

His father's expression morphed. Softened. "What? Emily. Of course I would have. I've loved you for more than half of my life. All

I want is for all of you to be happy. To make you proud. To give you everything."

She smiled up at him, putting her hand on his chest. "Love isn't a business plan, sweetheart." She looked at Will. "I want you happy. I tried to hurry it along."

"There's a whole song about that, isn't there? About not hurrying love?" His grandfather grinned and started humming.

"She makes me happy, Mom."

His mother came to him, wrapped her arms around his waist. "Then that's all that matters. I'm sorry about how I behaved. How I pushed."

"It's okay. You're right. Being happy, in the end, is all that really matters," he agreed.

How could he get Lexi to realize that? That love didn't care what you did for a living or who your parents were. That there were some things that couldn't be faked. And when they were as real as what was between him and Lexi, a person ought to grab on tight and never let go.

He had a feeling that was the part she was most worried about. Having to let go. She was scared. So was he. But they'd have each other for the journey and that would make the fear bearable.

Thirty-nine

On a Saturday, six weeks earlier, Lexi had sat in this very spot and lied her ass off. As she waited for her guests to join her now, she kept her gaze down, not wanting to chat with Brett, who was clearing tables for one of the new waitresses. A petty part of Lexi enjoyed that she wasn't very good. Because some things were harder than others and no one really knew what they'd be good at until they tried.

She missed Will with an intensity that terrified her. But until she could face herself in the mirror, she couldn't be who he needed. Jackie and Becca came through the patio doors, joining her at the table she'd sat at with Will. She'd asked Brett if it was okay to pull a second table so there was room for the three of them.

"Finally," Jackie said, leaning down to hug Lexi. "I thought you were going to put us off forever. Where did you go at the party? Did something happen?"

"I didn't even get to see you. I'm sorry." Becca removed her jacket, hung it on the chair. She too leaned down to hug Lexi.

"Don't worry about it." Lexi was just grateful no one had seen her dramatic exit.

The waitress, a young girl, probably barely old enough to serve liquor, came to the table.

"Hi. Can I get you ladies something to drink?" Her smile was sweet and Lexi had a vivid flashback to a time when everything seemed wide open and attainable.

"The service is definitely better this time," Jackie said with a laugh. "I'll take an iced tea."

"Oh, that sounds good. Me too," Becca said.

The girl looked at Lexi. This girl would go through her share of up and downs too. She wouldn't be in control of some of them but it was up to her how she faced them. It took Lexi too long to realize that.

"I'll have the same. Thank you."

The girl smiled, walked into the restaurant.

"Okay," Jackie said, putting her perfectly manicured hands on the table. "I say we do a girls' night. We'll make it themed. Besties old and new. I met your friend Maisie and we were talking about it. She's on board. Becs, a bunch of people follow you from high school, right? We'll invite some of them. Lena and her wife, your friend Jamie."

Becca nodded enthusiastically, making notes in her phone.

"I can't," Lexi said.

Both women stopped and looked at her. She took a deep breath, wishing she had her iced tea just to have something to do with her hands. "Actually, that's not true. I don't want to."

Jackie's face crumpled. She looked so sad that Lexi reached out and put a hand on hers.

"I *want* to reconnect with you two. I just don't want to have high school parties or hang out with a bunch of people I wasn't close to ten years ago."

"Oh," Jackie said, pulling her hand away.

"Let's do something smaller. Us. Your friend Maisie. We won't worry about a bunch of people we used to know. Hell, we didn't worry about them back in the day, why would we now?" Becca laughed. "Though I'm always curious what people are up to. Where their lives led them."

Tucking her hands in her lap, Lexi took one more fortifying breath. "Probably not where they planned. I know that's true for me."

The waitress brought their drinks, setting them down with a slightly shaky hand. "Would you like something to eat?"

"Hmm, should we just share a veggie platter? Maybe some hummus and pita?" Jackie asked Becca.

Becca looked at Lexi. "That okay with you?"

Since her stomach rolled like an angry ocean, eating wasn't on her agenda. "Sure."

The waitress wrote it down and left.

"Lexi, are you okay?" Jackie asked after taking a sip of her tea.

"I lied to you guys. Right here on this patio," Lexi said. The relief of telling them made her shoulders feel ten pounds lighter. She sat up straighter.

"What are you talking about?" Becca asked, her gaze narrowing.

Lexi told them everything. The truth about living at home, her mom, the Dress Hut, Will. Waitressing. They sat, listening intently, their expressions unreadable. Even Jackie, who could usually broadcast her feelings with a look, gave nothing away.

"Why would you lie?" Becca asked softly.

"You guys came in looking like you'd barely aged. I was having a bad day. Everything was going wrong and there you both were like a visual reminder of where my life was supposed to go." She pointed at Becca. "You with your million followers and book deals." She looked at Jackie. "You with your big rock of an engagement ring, Lena with her partnership. I couldn't even carry soup." She showed them the little spot on her left thumb pad. "Look, I have a scar from spilling it."

Becca covered her mouth, and her eyes suggested she was covering a laugh. Jackie leaned in like she was really concerned, then leaned back.

"Nigel's mother hates me. I mean, can't stand to be in the same room as me. She only comes to our house when I'm working late and when I get home, I notice all of these little things she's changed. A vase in a different spot, my towels folded differently. One time, she rearranged my silverware drawer because the small and large spoons should go next to each other. Nigel says I'm just being paranoid, that she's just trying to help. Hates. Me."

Becca gave Jackie's shoulder an encouraging squeeze, then looked at Lexi. "I bought my first one hundred thousand followers. You can do that. I was feeling lonely and bored and tired of like three people responding to my posts. At that time, even bad engagement was good for me."

Lexi's gaze widened. "I had no idea."

Jackie smiled. "Why would you? What we present in public or online is very rarely the whole story."

"I'm sorry. I feel like an awful person," Lexi admitted.

"You avoided us because you were lying and didn't want us to know the whole truth?" Becca asked.

Lexi nodded, feeling like a child who knew she was about to get scolded.

"Because you cared what we thought. Because you remembered who we used to be, individually and together. We were happy to see you, Lexi. We were high on some successes *that* day. But that doesn't mean every day up to that point was perfect."

Jackie murmured an agreement. "A month before he proposed, I showed up at Becs's with a bottle of cheap wine—the exact one you brought to our house." She winked at Lexi. "I drank the whole thing and told her Nigel was never going to ask me. That we were going nowhere."

"You guys seem so happy together," Lexi said.

"We are. But it takes work. Life takes work. And patience, friends who can pull you out of the pit of despair and remind you to shake it off. That you can do this. I'm sorry you thought we'd judge you poorly for doing your best to deal with things that were out of your control."

Tears burned. "I'm sorry I put my own insecurities on you. I was really happy to see you guys too. I've missed you and thought about you. I just wasn't happy with who *I* was and didn't want you to see that version of me."

Becca reached across the table but pulled back when the waitress brought their food. She set it in the center of the table with some side plates and napkins. They thanked her, took a minute to add some snacks to their plates. Lexi's stomach had calmed a bit so she added some carrots and dip to hers.

"I think who we are can change more times than we can count. You have to take the moments that make you happy and hang on to them. Have you talked to Will?" Jackie asked. She bit into a piece of celery.

"No. I want to. I miss him more than I thought possible but every time I think about phoning or texting, I think, if it hurts this much to be away from him after only six weeks, I understand why my mother fell apart. Twenty-five years of loving someone so much it becomes a piece of you. Now I feel like I misjudged her as well. We were only ever dating and I haven't wanted to do anything since I walked away. Not get dressed, shower, do my hair, go out. I kept thinking my mom should just get better, move on, but now I don't know how she's come as far as she has."

"She won't ever forget him, Lex. Neither will you. He'll always be part of her and you. But she'll move on, become a different version of herself. Not better, not worse, just *changed*," Becca said, dipping a piece of broccoli in the hummus.

"See," Lexi said with a watery laugh, "you *have* grown up. You're so smart. How the hell do you know so much?"

"It's easier to pick apart someone else's life and spot the ways to fix it than it is your own." Jackie grabbed some pita chips, put a few on Becca's plate.

"She's right. Plus, writing books is hella hard. Like, way harder than I thought, so I've been doing all of this research and reading all of these books, trying to figure out how I can say something different. Something that matters."

"What you guys have said to me matters."

"We judge ourselves through pretty harsh lenses," Jackie said.

"Hmm," Becca said, swirling a pita chip in the dip. "You're giving me book ideas. The book is tentatively titled *Finding Your Own Happy*. Maybe I need to explore the idea of accepting the different versions of yourself, past and present, as the road to getting there."

"Careful how you word things or you'll end up in a whole different section of the bookstore with finding your happy and getting yourself there," Jackie said, stabbing the air with a chip for emphasis.

The three women dissolved into laughter and for the first time since she was twenty-two, Lexi felt like maybe everything would work out okay. More than that, maybe she wasn't doing so bad after all.

Forty

Lexi nearly ran into her mom as she opened the door to leave, in a rush to get to Side Tap. It was after hours but Ethan had sent a cryptic text saying there were things they needed to discuss. She was feeling better since meeting with the girls yesterday but still hadn't figured out what to do about Will. Should she call him? Text? Ask him on a date with the real her? As soon as she found out what Ethan needed, she was taking the first step. If he didn't want her, she'd deal. But she wasn't walking away. They weren't over.

"Hey," Lexi said, stepping aside so Gwen could get through the door. She'd started taking short walks around the neighborhood.

"Hi. You're heading out?" Gwen took off her oversized plaid flannel. The beanie on her head made her look younger. So did the hope in her eyes.

"I'm heading to Side Tap. Ethan wants to go over some things." She shut the door, giving her mom the attention she deserved. She hadn't yet apologized to her and she felt like she should but she didn't know what to say. *Sorry I misjudged who you are, how hard it is to rebuild yourself after losing your husband, and for pushing you on my agenda instead of understanding your need to do it your way? Hmm. Yeah. That will all work. Say that.*

"You worked at Dress Hut all day," Gwen said, disapproval wrinkling her forehead.

"Yes, just helping to get a few things settled. Bitsy knows I'm done after Christmas. It's okay, Mom. I can do it. The money is really helping and I'm happy with Side Tap but it won't last forever."

"Speaking of money," Gwen said, playing with one of her buttons. "I spoke to Gregory."

Lexi zipped up her jacket. "Who?"

"Ethan's dad. Mr. Reynolds."

Lexi froze. "Oh."

"Don't look at me like that, Alexandria. He's a contractor. I asked him for his opinion. I told you I might. He's coming over this weekend."

"I shouldn't have pushed."

Like she hadn't spoken, her mother continued, as if she was saying it as much for herself as for Lexi. "I love this house. I always have. I know I need to put the past behind me to some extent but I'm not ready to get rid of it."

"Mom." Lexi stepped closer. "I never should have said that. We'll figure it out. I promise." Somehow. She understood not wanting to lose the connection to her past. They'd shared so many memories in this house.

"*I'll* figure it out, honey. You're not *my* mom. I'm yours. He's going to tell me his thoughts on renovating the basement into a suite. We don't use it much and I don't need more space than we have upstairs."

"That's a great idea," Lexi said, her voice catching.

"I agree. Now, I'm moving forward. Are you?"

She didn't have time for this. She was worried Ethan was going to say Brady could handle things from now on. "Mom."

"Don't mom me, Alexandria. I told you all along I wasn't broken, just sad."

"I know. I'm sorry. I'm sorry for the things I said and how I pushed."

Gwen took her shoulders, squeezed. "Stop being sorry. But know this: I *wasn't* broken. Losing your dad gutted me but we've done okay, you and me, haven't we? I know I could have done more. But we've survived, right?"

Lexi nodded.

"I'm coming back, sweetie. But what would actually break me, tear me right in two, is if my beautiful daughter gave up on love because I scared her into thinking it's not worth the bumps and bruises."

"Mom." She didn't know what she wanted to say—which was good, since her throat had gone impossibly tight.

"You can't predict the future. It'd be boring if you could. You take the moment you're in and make the most of it, honey. If it doesn't work out or something happens, you fall down, let yourself hurt, and then get back up. Will loves you. And you love him. That won't stop because you're too scared or stubborn to be with him. You'll just come to your senses years from now and realize you wasted all that time. You can't change the past but you can regret it. I hate that your father is gone but I don't regret one minute of loving him."

Lexi pulled her mom into a tight hug, breathing her in and out and letting the pieces of her mending heart settle into place. They didn't all go back where they started but they were there. Ready to stop running.

———

Lexi hurried into Side Tap, so many emotions rolling around inside her it was a wonder the momentum of them didn't bowl her over.

Ethan stood at the doorway when she stepped inside. Strange. Cue nerves. She was losing this job. She loved this job.

"Hey," he said, locking the door behind her.

"Hi," Lexi said, drawing out the word.

"I'll be in my office. Put him out of his misery, Lexi. He's a fucking grump without you. I know part of it was a misunderstanding but know this—he loves you. I adore you. His family, most of them, adore you.

One piece of it might not have been true, but the rest of it, the friendships, the job, you and Will? That's as real as it gets. You're doing a great job for me because you're smart as hell. Don't be stupid about this."

With that, he leaned down, kissed her cheek, and gave her a little nudge toward the back of the space. The area she'd first had appetizers with Will was lit with more candles than she could count. She didn't see Will but it was as if she could sense him.

Still, even knowing in her heart that he was there, when he stood from one of the high-back chairs, then turned and met her gaze, Lexi couldn't move. It was as if the brick of ice in her chest melted just from the sight of him. The pieces of her jumbled heart rearranged as he came closer, finding their proper spots. She felt like she could finally breathe.

He came down the stairs. Dressed in jeans and a sweater, his hair styled messily, which she loved, his gaze steady. Sure.

"I wore braces until I was sixteen. The first time I kissed a girl, her lip got caught in them and cut her bad enough she bled for what seemed like hours but was probably only minutes."

Lexi stared. Of all the things she'd thought of them saying to each other over the last week, that statement wasn't even in the running. She didn't know how to respond.

He walked closer. "I used to have nightmares as a kid. The only thing that made me feel better was this little weird-looking stuffed animal. I don't even know if it was an animal. It was more like an oddly shaped pillow with a face."

Lexi's brows bunched. Will came closer.

"My high school girlfriend dumped me because I couldn't do a chin-up."

Lexi felt like she had to say something. "Okay."

He stopped in front of her. "I still can't. I still have that stuffed animal thing. I still get nervous when I have to speak in front of others. I hate the country club but really like their Monte Cristo sandwiches so I go when my mother asks because at least I can have that. I failed my first math class in college and fell in love with a girl in my second year who only wanted to date me for my money. I give Kyra a hard time for beating me at word games and making me watch cheesy romance movies but the truth is, I love watching them and I suck at word games."

A nervous laugh bubbled out of her. "What are you doing?"

He was so close their fronts brushed when she took a deep breath. "I'm telling you about all the versions of me. They aren't perfect. I'm not perfect. I know you're not either but you're perfect for me and no matter what happens between us, I need you to know I really do love you. I didn't get caught up in something and run with it. I saw you on that patio and it was like the sun came out after years of hiding."

She sucked in a breath and they moved at the same time. He kissed her or she kissed him, she wasn't sure, but they wrapped themselves around each other like they'd been apart for months. Lexi didn't know how long they stood there, his lips moving over her face, down her neck, her hands running through his hair, over his solid shoulders and chest, but it felt like not long enough when he pulled back.

"I fucking miss you." He dropped his forehead to hers.

"I miss you too. So much. I'm sorry. I'm sorry I ran away. Sorry I got scared. I'm terrified of losing you and I promised myself I'd never let myself feel that way."

"I didn't realize it was a choice," he said, his voice husky.

"Turns out, it's not. The choice is love you and be scared or love you and be alone and miserable."

"You love me?"

She nodded, her heart getting too big for her chest again, like it was reaching out to connect with its other half.

"You said you didn't," he whispered, and the hurt in his gaze undid her.

"I lied."

He laughed. "Say it."

"I love you. I love you so much even though I'm scared one day you'll leave me, either because I'm exhausting or because of something you can't control, and then I'll never be okay again."

"If something happens, you won't be the same. But eventually, you'll be okay."

She nodded. "I'm figuring that out. But I'm not okay walking away from this just to protect myself from possibly getting hurt. I love you. I'm sorry I said I didn't. It's all been real for me, too. Everything except the engagement and then I was standing there in my mother's dress, a symbol of her past, and you offered me this future and I just couldn't wrap my head around it. I couldn't wrap my head around having it or losing it. So I ran."

"I don't know where this will go but I can tell you I've never wanted anyone the way I want you. I want a life with you. I want to be your husband. I've never wanted that before. To be tied to someone in just that way, with that label. I want to live my life loving you, picking you up when the unexpected knocks you down, leaning on you when life does the same to me. I want to stand by your side whether you're a waitress, a roulette dealer, or an operations manager."

She laughed, swiping at her tears. "A roulette dealer?"

"I don't care. It doesn't matter what you do. It just matters that I get to be with you when you do it. Tell me you want the same."

"I do." She'd already admitted it to herself.

"It's good you're practicing those words," he said with a sexy smirk. He stepped away, put his hand in his pocket, and pulled out the ring she'd given back.

"I'd already fallen for you by the time I slipped this on your finger. We didn't intend to really get married at that time but I was almost positive I was in love with you then. Now I'm one hundred percent sure. This is what love is. It isn't perfect but it's exactly what I want and need. You. You're everything I want and need exactly as you are, whoever you become along the way. I love you, Alexandria Danby." He sank to one knee. "Will you be my wife? For real? Will you marry me in a real ceremony in front of our friends and family? Will you be mine forever or as much of forever as we can get?"

She couldn't stop the tears as she sank down to the floor with him, nodding as he slipped the ring on her finger.

"Yes," she whispered. "I'll marry you. I love you, Will. So much."

"For real?"

She laughed, pushed his shoulder, and threw her arms around him.

"I can get you a different ring."

"Not a chance. I love this one."

"Don't you even want to know if it's real?" He squeezed her tighter and stood up, taking her with him.

Lexi pulled back just enough to see him. "You're real. What we have is real."

"It is," he whispered, his hands framing her face. He kissed her slowly, like he was relearning every piece of her and had all the time in the world.

No one really knew how much time they'd get. Lexi used that as a reason to run. What she should have done was use it as a reason to dig her heels in, grab on tight, and never let go. She couldn't change the past but she could learn from it.

"Have you two made up yet?" Ethan yelled from somewhere in the bar.

Lexi and Will laughed. He picked her up and swung her around. "We're all good, man. Come on out."

Ethan came out of the office grinning. "How good we talking?"

Lexi held out her hand. "We're engaged. For real."

Clapping his friend on the back, Ethan kissed Lexi's cheek. "Congratulations. For the record, I already threw your engagement party."

"We don't need another," Will said, holding Lexi tightly to his front.

She rested her head on his chest. "Next time I wear a wedding dress, it'll be to marry you."

Will pressed a kiss to her head. "I can't wait."

Epilogue

There was a lot to be thankful for, Lexi thought as she put on the earrings Will had given her. Beautiful square diamonds that he said were every bit as real as her ring and his love for her. She'd told him she only actually needed one of those three things to be happy. Romantic, cheesy things were getting easier to say because she had so much emotion just idling inside of her all the time.

He came into his bedroom, met her gaze in the full-length mirror as his arms circled her waist from behind. That jolt of recognition and something deeper than just desire zipped through her body. She was getting used to that too.

"You look beautiful," he said, kissing her neck.

She tilted her head, giving him room as she leaned back into him. "You look good too. Everyone should be here soon."

He murmured something against her neck, then turned her into his arms and kissed her, pulling her body into his. They could get lost in this. It wouldn't be the first time but today was their first time hosting a special occasion as a real couple.

She pulled back. "I don't want to look like I have sex hair when our families show up."

Will laughed, put his hands up, and stepped back. "I didn't touch your hair."

She smirked at him. "You would have. Let's go make sure everything is ready."

He'd already asked her to move in but Lexi wasn't quite ready. Gregory had started construction on the basement, curiously deciding not to contract the work out. He said it was to keep costs to a minimum because he could do the work himself but Lexi and Will suspected it had more to do with him liking that Gwen kept him company while he worked.

It was nice to see her mother's smile, and Lexi was learning not to push or overstep. She hadn't been entirely fair to her mom and realized that part of her had relied on her mother's neediness to feel like she had a purpose.

When Gwen told her she'd be arriving with Ethan and Gregory today, she'd just nodded happily, not saying a word. Gwen gave her a mom-glare anyway, like she could read her thoughts.

Things had been a little harder to smooth over with Will's parents but with everyone else on board and eager to welcome Lexi to the family, she figured it was only a matter of time before his father softened toward her.

And if he didn't, it wouldn't matter, because there was nothing she wouldn't go through to be with Will.

"We could have had this catered, you know," Will said as she checked the turkey. She'd never made one before but her mother had many times. Gwen had walked her through the whole thing via Face-Time this morning.

"That would be cheating," she said, inhaling the delicious scent.

"Okay, but know that my mother will definitely be bringing a store-bought dessert," he said.

She closed the oven and turned to face him across the island. He picked up a bottle of wine, raised his eyebrows. She nodded. "That's fine. I don't care if she makes it herself but I wanted to be responsible for our first Thanksgiving meal as a couple. Unless the turkey is gross. Then I'm blaming you."

He laughed as he poured two glasses. "That's fair. Did you give Maisie the dates for engagement photos?"

Lexi took the wine, touched her glass to his, loving the way he looked at her. "I did. She's going to give us a few options when she gets here for dinner."

Will's mother had asked if they could make a proper and formal announcement, including a photo. Will had grumbled but Lexi, wanting to get on her good side, agreed for both of them.

Will pursed his lips. "Will she be able to be a maid of honor and a photographer?" He trailed a finger over the back of her hand.

It was hard to say who loved the act of him touching her more.

She was distracted when she murmured, "If anyone can."

It was like he craved the touch to make sure she was right there, and Lexi had absolutely no issues with that. She liked to reassure herself of his presence as often as possible too. Preferably with his lips on hers.

They leaned into each other just as the doorbell rang. Will frowned. "Bet that's my parents. With their store-bought dessert."

Lexi laughed, setting her wine down and following him to the door. The table was set beautifully thanks to Maisie and Pinterest. She'd sent Lexi about three hundred "pins" on how to lay everything out. Will teased her about her homemaker side, but she just wanted everything to be perfect. Or look pretty so that if the meal wasn't great, she could at least say she'd set a good table.

It was his parents, followed by his sisters, Rachel, Ethan, Gregory, and Gwen. They chatted as Will and Lexi got people drinks, Will taking Gwen out to see the area he'd marked off for a garden she said she'd help him with.

Rachel and Maddie, who clearly knew their way around a kitchen better than Lexi, helped with the final preparations.

Emily brought Lexi a beautiful bouquet of flowers and a gorgeous strawberry flan for dessert. Will's father gave her a side hug, said things smelled good.

Baby steps. These things took time. Will's grandparents would be joining them for dinner on Christmas but had gone to their daughter's house for today. Jackson's sister didn't work at Grand Babies. Over the last few weeks, Lexi had learned so much about his family, which included aunts, uncles, and several cousins. Lexi had never had a large family even when her dad was alive. Now it felt like she had the best of both worlds.

When the doorbell rang again, Lexi hurried toward the door to open it for her bestie. Before she got there, her friend came bounding through it, huge bunches of flowers weighing down her arms.

"I'm sorry. I hate being late. It's awful. But I brought flowers."

Lexi laughed because she couldn't actually see Maisie through the bundles.

"You're fine. Everyone just arrived."

Will joined them in the foyer. "Did you rob a florist?" he teased as he took three of the five bundles.

Maisie's cheeks and nose were red from the cold. Lexi took the remaining bundles while Maisie unwound her scarf from around her neck. Having been there a few times, her friend hung her coat and scarf, removed her shoes, then took a deep breath and let it out.

"What's with all the flowers?"

Maisie shrugged. "I wanted to bring some for you for hosting and then I realized Gwen would be here. And Will's mom and on and on. Plus, I couldn't choose." She laughed, shrugged her shoulders. "Happy Thanksgiving. I'm so grateful you both got your heads out of your asses."

Will erupted in laughter, leaned in to kiss Maisie's cheek. "You should give the toast tonight."

Lexi gave her friend a side hug and after they took care of the flowers and said hellos, made necessary introductions, they found their seats. Lexi's chest filled with warmth and happiness. The food graced the table in a long row of mouthwatering platters. Everyone was chatting and laughing, making the room feel full.

Will stood up at the end of the table. Lexi, to his right, stared up at her fiancé, happiness washing over her.

"Thank you for joining us tonight. Lexi and I are so happy that so many of the people we love could be here. It's been a bumpy ride but my hope is there are many more nights and occasions just like this one." He looked down at her, kissed her softly, then lifted his glass.

The others lifted their glasses as well, saying cheers. Lexi beamed, looking around the table, feeling very much like she was exactly where she was meant to be. Which was strange, given she hadn't expected the path she'd been traveling to lead her here. She looked at Will, then leaned in to whisper that she loved him.

"I love you too," he whispered. "You okay?"

She nodded. "Just happy."

"So am I."

She kissed him, pulled back, and gestured to the table. "Should I serve?"

Will leaned back with a mock frown. "Good God, no." He looked around the table. "Come on, everyone. Dig in. Help yourselves before my beautiful fiancée reminds us all what a horrible server she is."

Lexi laughed, delighted in this moment, in these people, and even in acknowledging the truth. She might not be cut out to be a waitress but she would always be happy she'd given it a shot. Without it, the future she envisioned would be very different.

And she wouldn't change where she was now, or who was beside her, for anything.

Acknowledgments

Wow. This was a hard one. I'm not sure why since I had the opening scene in my head for a very long time before I put it on paper. It could have been a combination of things that made this story more difficult for me to get the words out, but that's not the part that really matters. What does matter is that people believed in me enough to think I could do this and when it wasn't quite right, so many people helped me shape it and make it what it is.

Which, I hope, is a story about learning to see new versions of yourself, accepting the parts of yourself you'd rather forget, and facing the fear of change. That's a big one for me. Life can be all too scary sometimes, and writing usually provides me nothing but solace. With this one, though, writing about something I personally fear (losing people, change, etc.) made it trickier to navigate. I can only hope I did it justice and that you all fall in love with Lexi and Will the way I intended.

Thank you to Cassidy for working through this story with me and pushing me to see it in different ways. Thank you, Alex, for being there, for saying yes, for everything you've added to my life just by falling in love with *Ten Rules*. Thank you, Fran, for your constant encouragement and faith. Thank you to Matt, Kalie, and Amy. There's been a lot of change these last few years and I don't always handle it so gracefully, but one thing will never change: I love you all more than I could write even in three hundred pages. To my mom. For being my mom, for teaching me to love reading and encouraging me to write. To Bren for reading every idea via text first.

To so many people who support and encourage me. I'm incredibly lucky to have a circle of talented and kind people who don't block my DMs. Elle Cosimano, Alexa Martin, Lisa Felipe, Sarah Fox, Cole, Stacey, Kristyn, Falon, Courtney, Tarrah, Petra, Tara, Emily, and Austin—seriously, SO many people.

That doesn't even begin to address the people who deal with my inability to understand or appropriately use grammar and punctuation. To all of you, I am sorry and grateful.

This is one of my favorite covers of all time. I'm incredibly thankful for that as well. St. Martin's Griffin has been the most amazing publisher for me and my stories. And readers? Don't get me started. I have so much gratitude and love and appreciation for the fact that of all the books in all the stores, you choose any of mine. Thank you.

About the Author

Shelley Bell

Sophie Sullivan (she/her) is a Canadian author as well as a cookie-eating, Diet Pepsi–drinking Disney enthusiast who loves reading and writing romance in almost equal measure. She writes around her day job as a teacher and spends her spare time with her sweet family watching reruns of *Friends*. She has written *Ten Rules for Faking It, How to Love Your Neighbor, A Guide to Being Just Friends,* and *Love, Naturally,* and has had plenty of practice writing happily ever after as her alter ego, Jody Holford.